THE LIGHTHOUSE MURDERS

DORSET CRIME
BOOK 8

RACHEL MCLEAN

Ackroyd Publishing

ackroyd-publishing.com

 Created with Vellum

DORSET MURDER MAP

From the Dorset Crime series by Rachel McLean

Lyme Regis

Winfrith Police HQ

Wareham
Lesley's cottage

Blue Pool

Tyneham

Portland Bill

Bournemouth
Elsa's flat

Sandbanks

Brownsea Island

Old Harry Rocks

Corfe Castle

The Obelisk

The Globe

N

Illustration by Maria Burns

rachelmclean.com

THE LIGHTHOUSE MURDERS

CHAPTER ONE

"JUST GIVE ME FIVE MINUTES, love. I want to watch the news."

Gina O'Toole didn't wait for her husband to reply before making her way from the kitchen into the living room. The TV was already on in the corner; she'd turned it on as soon as she'd got the text from Hattie.

There's been an escape.

Gina had almost choked when she'd read that.

An escape.

There were hundreds of prisoners in His Majesty's Prison Service. Thousands.

It wouldn't be him.

But it might be.

Clutching her hand to her chest and still holding a tea towel, Gina lowered herself to the sofa.

The images of the prison were designed so as not to show anything you might want to see. HMP Portland was one of the UK's highest security jails, after all. Containing the most dangerous prisoners.

"Who is it?" she muttered. "Just give us a name." She chewed her bottom lip, ignoring Danny's calls from upstairs.

Poor Danny. He'd been neglected the last three years, after what had happened to his sister.

Gina crossed herself. She glanced at the crucifix above the mantelpiece and said a quick prayer. She kept one in each room of the house, so she could do this every time she thought of her daughter.

Of him.

And what he'd done to her.

She swallowed – bile, making her gag – and blinked.

Focus, woman. She needed to know.

A name. Just give us a name, for the love of God.

More images of the prison. She'd gone straight to the BBC News website when Hattie had texted. She knew better than to look at the tabloid websites.

Bastards, all of them. They'd plastered Susie's face all over their front pages, along with those other girls. And boys.

Once again, Gina crossed herself. A quick flick to the crucifix and she was back, focusing on the TV.

"We had reports about an hour ago of an escape during a prisoner transfer on the Isle of Portland."

Gina knew little of the Isle of Portland. Had never been there, certainly never intended to. She rarely ventured outside Weoley Castle these days. It wasn't Birmingham's most salubrious area, but it was home. Anywhere else...

Well, anywhere else might be unsafe for Danny. Look at what had happened to Susie when she'd got that job in the city centre.

Gina should never have allowed it.

She put her hand to her chest, about to cross herself again, when the image changed on the screen.

A photo.

A photo of the escaped prisoner.

It was him.

"Police have launched a manhunt on the peninsula and across Dorset. With so little time having passed since the escape, they're confident the escapee will be found."

Gina shook her head. He was cleverer than that. He'd be halfway across the country by now.

Maybe in Birmingham.

Her eyes went to the door just as it opened. Rick, scratching his chin. "What's going on? Danny's hungry."

Gina nodded at the TV. "It's him."

The photo of the man was still onscreen.

Rick turned pale. He put a hand on the wall. "Jesus, Mary and Joseph."

"Don't."

He ignored her. "It's him."

Gina turned to him. "That's what I said, didn't I?"

"He's escaped?" Rick slid onto the sofa and sat next to her, their thighs not quite touching. Rick's gaze was fixed on the screen, his face pale and his mouth open.

"Where is he?" he breathed.

"I don't know, do I? He could be anywhere."

"How long ago... how long ago did he escape? And how? That place is supposed to be fuckin' Fort Knox."

Gina nodded. Her mouth was dry. "I don't know. But he did."

She reached out a shaky hand. Rick grabbed it and put it on his thigh.

"We're going to get doorstepped again," he said.

She nodded.

"They'll send us one of those bloody liaison officers," he continued.

"Unless they find him."

Rick squeezed her hand. "They won't find him."

Gina took a shaky breath. He was right. Men like Trevor Hamm didn't just break out of prison on the spur of the moment.

They planned. They had associates. They disappeared, never to be found again.

She looked at her husband. "I don't think I can go through all this again, love."

CHAPTER TWO

"I can't believe I didn't pick up Stanley's calls while we were away," DCI Lesley Clarke said as she dropped her suitcase onto the bedroom floor.

"You were busy." Elsa had already opened her suitcase and was pulling out dirty washing. "It *was* our honeymoon."

Lesley gave her a smile. "I'm sorry about the... you know."

Elsa put a hand on her hip and gave Lesley a look. "I should have known that any hope you wouldn't get yourself embroiled in a murder investigation would turn out futile."

Lesley reached across the bed and grabbed Elsa's hand. "It won't happen again."

Elsa laughed. "Don't make promises you can't keep, sweetie." She blew Lesley a kiss. "Anyway, you have more important things to worry about now we're back. What are you going to do about Dennis?"

Lesley surveyed the pile of washing on the bed. There was no way she'd have time to do this.

She rubbed her forehead. "First thing is to go and see him. Find out what happened from the horse's mouth."

"How much does he know? How much do *you* know?"

Lesley frowned at her wife. "He's not guilty, if that's what you're suggesting."

"I'm not."

"Good. Because—"

"DS Dennis Frampton is someone you trust. I know that. And I also know you're a good judge of character."

Lesley winked. "I married you, didn't I?"

"Case closed, your honour."

Lesley laughed, then thought of Dennis. He'd been released from police custody the day before, and was due to appear in front of the magistrates on Monday.

She shouldn't be laughing. Not when her DS had been charged with murder.

"What evidence do they have?" Elsa asked.

"I've no idea." Lesley thought back to the messages she'd seen on DCI Mackie's phone. Messages to Dennis, on the day Mackie had died.

But the two of them had been working on an investigation. Dennis had gone to meet Mackie, and the man hadn't turned up.

And it was Dennis. Dennis was not a killer.

"They must have something," Elsa said. "In my experience—"

Lesley put up a hand. "Please. Just let me talk to him. I'll need to speak to his solicitor, too."

"Who's representing him?"

"I don't know. Someone good, I hope."

"Do you think Dennis might be corrupt?"

Dennis had annoyed the hell out of Lesley when she'd arrived in Dorset, with his old-fashioned ways and his unwillingness to change. He still kept a swear jar in a filing cabinet, although he knew better than to get it out now she was in charge.

But Dennis? Corrupt?

"No," she said. "That's impossible."

"But Mackie was investigating the Kelvins when he died," said Elsa. "And the Kelvins had no end of people in their pocket."

Lesley squared her shoulders. "Elsa, believe me. Dennis is not corrupt. And he didn't kill Tim Mackie. Someone else did, and whoever it is, they're trying to pin it on Dennis."

Elsa nodded. "Well, if that's what you think, you need to talk to him."

"I do." Lesley eyed the washing. "Do you mind…?"

"It's not as if I've got anything better to do."

"I thought you had a new client lined up?"

"Only the one. For now. But I'm not busy. You go. Be the knight in shining armour."

Lesley rounded the bed and gave her wife a hug. "Thanks, love. I'll keep you posted. I might be—"

"Back late. I know. I do understand." Elsa stroked Lesley's cheek. "There's no hurry. We've got the rest of our lives."

Lesley felt her blood warm at the thought. She kissed Elsa. "Thanks."

As she closed the door to their flat behind her, her phone rang. It would be one of her team, with an update on Dennis.

It wasn't.

She put the phone to her ear, not breaking stride. "Sir."

"Lesley. Pleasant honeymoon, I trust."

"Very. What can I do for you, Sir?"

Superintendent Anthony Carpenter was Lesley's commanding officer. He'd suspected Dennis, she was sure of it.

He might have been the one who'd ordered the arrest. And now he was going to warn her off.

"A body has been found," he said.

Lesley stopped at the bottom of the stairs, almost tripping over herself in surprise.

Dennis?

Please, no.

"Who?" she whispered.

"Someone you've come across before. A prisoner at HMP Portland. During a routine move, he managed to escape."

"Who?" she repeated.

Not Dennis, thank God.

But someone she'd come across before?

"Kyle Kelvin?" she asked.

"He's at Belmarsh. This one's Trevor Hamm."

"Hamm," she repeated. "Are you sure?"

"No, DCI Clarke. I thought I'd just dig out the name of someone you took down when you were working in Birmingham and pretend he'd died for the fun of it."

Lesley swallowed and hurried to her car, cursing Carpenter.

"Where was he found?" she asked. "How did he die?"

"He's spreadeagled over the old lamp in the lighthouse at Portland Bill. The pathologist reckons he was pushed."

"Right. I'll head over there first thing in the morning." It was 6.30 pm, and her priority was to speak to Dennis.

"I expect you to make your way to the crime scene right away. Local CID have already arrived, but you're the obvious person to act as SIO, seeing as you're the one who put him in that prison in the first place."

CHAPTER THREE

THE CRIME SCENE was half an hour further away than Lesley had expected. Looking at the map before setting off, she'd had it in her head that once she passed Weymouth, she was effectively there.

But no. It took twenty minutes of climbing a vast hill in the dark, then descending again, more slowly, towards the sea, to reach the lighthouse. It stood alone, facing out to sea like it was at the end of the world.

Gail was already there, accompanied by Brett from her team. She was fetching equipment from her van when Lesley arrived. Another car was parked next to it, a blue Honda CRV.

Gail raised a hand to hold her hair, which was being ripped around her face by the wind. "How was the honeymoon?"

"Eventful."

A raised eyebrow. "How so?"

"I'll tell you another time. What have we got?"

Gail frowned and turned back to her van. "What have you been told?"

"I gather we've got an ID already."

"Yeah." Gail lifted a cardboard box. "D'you mind carrying this for me?"

Lesley pushed her handbag back on her shoulder and took the box from Gail. Gail bent to grab two pilot cases by the handles, then used her elbow to close the van door.

"Trevor Hamm," Gail said. "There's talk that you might have come across him before."

Lesley shifted the weight of the box as they walked towards the entrance to the lighthouse. "I was part of a team on the Canary investigation in Birmingham. Three years ago. Hamm was a key suspect, but we didn't manage to arrest him till over a year later, when we finally got hold of evidence that he was trafficking women and children."

Gail winced. "Nasty. And he was sent to The Verne Prison."

"I try to avoid keeping track of where the people I've arrested end up."

They reached the door to the lighthouse. Gail kicked it open. A uniformed constable Lesley hadn't come across before turned to them and stood aside.

Gail gave him a grin as she passed and Lesley followed.

"You keeping a log?" Lesley asked the PC.

"Yes."

"So why aren't you logging me?"

"Oh." His face reddened. "You're DCI Clarke. DC Abbott told me."

"Tina's here?"

"I hear you told her to come back and get Mike to finish her maternity leave instead," Gail said. She stood in the centre of a gift shop at the entrance to the lighthouse.

"Not maternity leave," Lesley corrected her. "Parental leave. I wasn't expecting it to happen so quick."

Her wedding to Elsa had been only six days ago. They'd spent the intervening time in Scotland, where Lesley had managed to stumble across a dead body and solve a murder case with the help of Petra McBride, the psychologist she'd worked with on the Swanage Globe case.

The cogs of police HR departments normally moved slowly. But when Tina Abbot was determined to make something happen, they could be forced to speed up.

"Right," she said. "Where are we going?"

"Through here." Gail gestured towards a door behind her.

"PC...?" Lesley looked at the constable.

"Sorry, Ma'am. PC Filch." He walked around the two women and held the door open for them.

"Thank you." Lesley made her way through, followed by Gail.

The corridor behind the doorway was cold and echoey, the walls painted a sterile white and the floor made of polished wood. She wondered how old this structure was.

"Where did they drag PC Filch in from?" she asked.

"Weymouth nick. Don't be so hard on him."

"I'm not being hard on him. Just expecting him to do his job." Lesley could see an open door ahead of them, police tape spanning the doorway. Beyond it, she could hear voices.

She stopped at the cordon.

"Hello?"

Gail put down her pilot cases. "We've erected a double cordon," she said. "One at this entrance, and another around the bulb. And local CID are in there. They said they wouldn't go until you'd arrived."

"They?"

"One bloke. DI Angus. From Blandford Forum."

"I'll send him on his way, unless he can be of help."

Gail grunted but said nothing.

"That's the bulb?" Lesley put down the cardboard box and looked at the vast glass object in front of them. It was made of multiple lenses and was at least ten feet high. There was no sign of DI Angus. "Why isn't it at the top?"

"They replaced it with LEDs a while back," Gail replied. "They're the ones at the top, actually doing the job of warning boats away."

"So this one is just for decoration." The bulb sat on the floor in the centre of the space. If she hadn't been told what it was, she'd never have known.

"And for the tourists. Besides, I don't imagine they could have got it out if they'd wanted to." Gail pulled the tape aside and carried her cases to an area below a staircase that rose steeply upwards. They were in a space a few metres in diameter, steep wooden stairs spiralling around the perimeter and the vast lens at the centre. Despite the voices Lesley had heard, there was no one in sight.

"We need to go up," Gail told her. "You can't see him from down here."

"Where is he?"

Gail hesitated. "On top of the bulb."

"Ouch."

Gail nodded. "He's a mess. Gareth Bamford's up there already. We're trying to work out how to get at him safely without disturbing the scene."

Lesley looked up. Way above her head was a platform. Was that the top of the lighthouse building, she wondered, or did it keep on going?

She could hear voices again: three men and a woman.

"I suppose we'd better head up," she told Gail.

Gail looked down at Lesley's shoes. "It's steep."

Lesley was wearing low heels. She hadn't stopped to change into the walking boots she'd bought after her second case in Dorset. "I'll be fine. You'll see."

CHAPTER FOUR

"Just humour me," Gina told Rick. They were in his car, heading for Harborne police station.

"I don't see how you can possibly help them. They'll have coppers all over Dorset by now. They've probably found him."

She shook her head as they passed through a green light on the Harborne Road. "Park in St Johns Road car park," she told him.

He sighed. "I still think this is a dumb idea."

Gina tightened her lips as Rick found a spot. "They need to know what kind of man he is. And I want to know what's happening." She took off her seatbelt and turned to her husband. "What if he comes back here? What if he does the same to Danny as he did to Susie?"

Rick closed his eyes. His face was grey and the skin around his eyes sagged. He'd aged a decade in the two and a half years since their daughter had decided she couldn't live with what had happened to her and taken her own life.

"I just don't see why we have to dredge it all up, love. That's all."

Gina put a hand over his. He flinched.

"I'm not dredging it up," she said. "There's nothing to dredge up. It's always with me. From the moment I open my eyes in the morning to when I finally take my sleeping pills and close them at night. How can talking to the police possibly make things any worse?"

"I just think it will."

"Then you can stay here. You don't have to get involved."

He looked at her. "I'd rather do that. If you don't mind."

Gina felt her jaw clench. "I can't force you to do anything." She opened her car door and got out, before he could see her tears.

She hurried across the car park. Couldn't he see how much she needed him? Regardless of what Rick felt about 'dredging it all up', doing this alone would be that much harder.

But she had to do it.

The police station was a broad building at the end of a street of terraced houses. She pulled in a deep breath on the pavement, then strode up the path and pushed the glazed doors open.

A man in his forties was at the desk, wearing police uniform. He had a sergeant's shoulder pips.

"I was a witness in the Canary court case," she told him. "I might have information that could help you find Trevor Hamm."

He frowned. "Sorry?"

"The Canary case. Organised crime, three years ago. They colluded with local businessmen and politicians to groom young people and…" she couldn't say it. "My daughter was one of them. Susie O'Toole. I spoke for her at the trial."

"Ah, yes, Canary. This isn't a public police station, Madam.

I'm sorry. You'll need to report it to your local station. What's your address?"

She shook her head. "I know this isn't a public station. But Force CID are stationed here. They dealt with the initial investigation. There was a detective I spoke to, here. DS Uddin. Can I speak to him please?"

The sergeant shrugged. "I'm sorry, Madam, but DS Uddin has transferred to Police Scotland."

Gina felt like she'd been winded. She'd had a plan. It had involved DS Uddin, who'd been so kind.

But now... now what?

The sergeant caught the look on her face and gave her a sympathetic smile. "What's your name?"

"Gina O'Toole. Mother of Susie O'Toole."

He tapped some keys on his computer. "I'll find someone who can talk to you. Give me a few minutes." He pointed towards a row of chairs against the far wall. "You can wait there, if you'd like."

"Oh." Gina looked from him to the chairs, back at the sergeant and then towards the chairs again.

He'd fetch an administrator. Someone to fob her off, pretend to listen but ultimately to get rid of her.

Still, she had to try.

"OK." She took a seat and crossed her ankles, her heart racing.

The last time she'd sat in this waiting room, Susie had been alive.

Don't cry.

She had to hold it together.

A door opened and a woman came through. She was tall, with long red hair. She looked at the sergeant and he nodded towards Gina.

The woman approached Gina, a sympathetic smile on her face. "Hello, Mrs O'Toole. You say you spoke to Mo Uddin before?"

Gina half stood up. "DS Uddin, yes."

"Then hopefully I can help you. I was a colleague of DS Uddin's, before he transferred to Scotland. My name's Detective Inspector Zoe Finch."

CHAPTER FIVE

THE STAIRS WERE as steep as Gail had promised. Lesley stopped about two thirds of the way up, her breathing heavy. This was worse than the time she and Dennis had climbed the stairs up to the obelisk above Swanage.

Tina was with Brett and Dr Bamford the pathologist, on a platform over the lens. They leaned against a railing, looking down. Lesley followed their gaze.

She gasped.

Spreadeagled over the top of it, blood oozing from beneath him, was a man. He lay face down, his legs and arms draped over the glass.

The lens itself was intact. If he'd fallen – or been pushed – onto it, the force of the impact hadn't broken it.

Lesley supposed that a lighthouse lens would have to be made of pretty thick glass.

She looked up. Somewhere above her head was the new, more modern bulb. LEDs. Less romantic but probably easier to control and certainly less energy-hungry.

She approached Tina and her companions. "Evening, everyone."

Tina looked up and smiled. "Boss." She turned just as a man came down a further set of stairs, leading right up to the top of the lighthouse, Lesley guessed.

She approached him. "You must be DI Angus."

He gave her an insincere smile. "Blandford Forum CID. And you are...?"

"DCI Clarke." She looked him up and down. Thinning light brown hair, suit which wasn't cheap but didn't quite fit. Blue tie with a faint stain. Every inch the detective.

"Ma'am," he said. "I don't know you."

No, you don't. "Major Crimes Investigation Team. I'm SIO."

He raised his eyebrows. "Fair enough." He made for the stairs leading down.

She looked at him again. He was wearing no protective gear, not even gloves. "How long have you been in CID?"

"Twelve years."

"And you don't think to bring a protective suit."

"I haven't touched the body."

Yes, but you've touched pretty much everything else.

The man was showing no sign of wanting to hang around, and based on her first impressions, she was happy for him to leave. "Well, thanks for your time. We can take it from here."

"OK." He looked between the rest of the group and headed down the steps.

Lesley listened to his footsteps recede. She looked over the barrier to see him appear at ground level, pause a moment to look at the lamp then leave through the door she'd entered by. She winced as he pulled on the doorhandle.

"I hope we've got his prints," she said to Gail. "There'll be a lot of elimination to do."

"I know."

Lesley turned to Tina. "Good to see you, Tina. Mike at home with the baby?"

Tina responded with a grin. "I'm back for three months, then he'll do a month, and then we'll both be back."

"Sounds like a plan." Lesley looked past Tina at the pathologist. "Dr Bamford. You've been here long?"

"About half an hour. Not long enough to get close to him."

"And we've got no idea how we're going to get him down," Tina added.

"Not without the risk of breaking the glass and giving him cuts that have nothing to do with his death," Bamford said.

Lesley looked down at the victim. From the rear, she wouldn't know his face. But he was wearing prison uniform. An orange one-piece that no one in their right mind would ever choose voluntarily.

So whoever had helped him escape, if anybody had, they hadn't brought him a change of clothes.

She turned her head this way and that to try to get a better angle. No matter how hard she tried, she couldn't match the body below them to the face of Trevor Hamm. The build was right though: stocky.

"Is the ID definite?" she asked. "It could be someone else who's been dressed up to look like an escaped convict."

Gail was next to her. "We're not a hundred per cent yet. But we've managed to scrape some blood off the lens, and we're comparing that to the records we already have from Hamm. We'll know within the hour."

Lesley looked down to see trickles of blood running down the sides of the lens. It would take some cleaning.

"Thanks," she said. "That has to be the priority, along with establishing a cause of death."

"It looks pretty obvious," Brett said. "He was pushed off—"

"Not necessarily," interrupted Tina. "The barrier here doesn't seem to have been disturbed. If someone pushed him off, he'd have put up a struggle."

"He might have been unconscious," Lesley said.

"He *might* already have been dead." Dr Bamford gave Lesley a look. "Shall we keep the speculation until we have hard evidence?"

Tina flushed. Lesley gave Bamford a wry smile. "Fair enough. How are you going to get to him?"

"Good question."

"We're trying to source some scaffolding," said Gail. "Build a platform, so we can access him by climbing up from below."

"How long will that take?" Lesley asked.

"It's Friday night. We're relying on a scaffolding supplier being available on a Saturday morning."

"So we're not going to get to him tonight?"

"Sorry." Gail sniffed.

Lesley blew out a breath. She checked her watch: 8.30pm. Elsa would be in front of the TV, waiting. It was the night after her honeymoon, for God's sake.

Trevor Hamm, I hated you back then and I hate you even more now.

"OK," she said. "Are there any more forensics?"

"We've examined the steps," Gail said. "And the platform. Looking for anything that might have been left behind by him or his attacker."

"And?"

"Nothing obvious. I wouldn't have let you up here otherwise."

"Is there a possibility he simply jumped off?"

Dr Bamford pointed down at the body. "See that staining on the back of his neck?"

Lesley leaned over further, causing Tina to flinch. She gave the PC a reassuring smile and tried to make out the stain the pathologist was referring to.

"I can't see it," she said.

Bamford handed her a pair of binoculars.

"Really?" Lesley asked. "You carry these?"

"We do," said Gail. "You never know."

"Sometimes I think your van is like Mary Poppins's bag." Lesley took the binoculars from the pathologist and focused on the body. Sure enough, there was a dark stain on the back of his neck, at the point where the collar of his prison uniform ended.

"What about it?" she asked.

"Whatever that is," Bamford said, "I don't think it was self-inflicted. It certainly wasn't due to the fall."

"No?" Lesley put the binoculars to her eyes again. "What about broken glass bouncing up, piercing his skin from above?"

"The glass is too thick for that," said Gail. "It hasn't broken."

Lesley scanned the lens. Gail was right.

She stood up. "So we think we're looking at a premeditated killing here."

"Once I've been able to get closer, to examine his injuries, I'll be able to tell you more," the pathologist said.

"And we'll keep looking for traces of a struggle," Gail added. "Or any fibres or prints left behind."

"Good." Lesley looked at Tina. "You've got a baby to get home to, and I've got a new wife." She turned to Gail. "Are you going to make any progress on the scaffolding this evening?"

"No."

"In that case, finish up with your initial investigations and then we'll reconvene in the morning. PC Filch can secure the scene. He's not going anywhere."

"The body will start to decompose," said Bamford.

"He's going to decompose whether we stand here or not. I'd love to be able to wave a magic wand and transport him to your morgue, but whoever threw him over this railing was determined to thwart us. You can adjust for an extra night when you calculate time of death, can't you?"

"I can."

"Good. I'll see you all back here at seven am."

CHAPTER SIX

DESCENDING the stairs was considerably easier than ascending had been. Lesley went after Gail and Brett, letting Tina and the pathologist follow after her.

At the bottom, they paused to look up at the lens. The body was invisible from this angle.

"How was he spotted?" Lesley asked.

"The lighthouse attendant goes up twice a day to check that safety rails and the like are in place," Tina said. "He looked over and saw him."

"And the place is open to the public?"

Tina nodded.

"In that case, we need to establish when the last public tour took place today. He would have been brought up at some point between that ending, and his discovery."

"Unless he came up on one of the public tours," suggested Tina.

"What, in that get-up?" Lesley frowned. "I reckon someone snuck him in here while the place was open, then took him up after the tours had finished. Question is, was he carried up, or did he walk?" She turned to Gail. "Any sign of shoe prints?"

"The stairs are covered with them. It's going to be a struggle isolating specific ones. That's why we let you up there."

"Of course." It was never easy.

"OK," Lesley said. "We need to examine the area outside. Tina, do you know if Stanley's still in the office?"

"It's almost nine pm on a Friday night, boss."

"But there's a murder investigation on."

"To be fair to him, he doesn't know that yet."

Lesley sighed. "OK. We need to speak to the lighthouse attendant. Find out if there's CCTV, and who was on duty this afternoon. We'll need to speak to them."

"If they're still here," Tina told her, "I can do that."

Lesley eyed her. "You're sure?"

Tina squared her shoulders. "Boss. Mike has Louis. I'm one hundred percent committed to this investigation."

Lesley thought back to when Sharon had been tiny. Work had been a sanctuary from the sleepless nights and incessant crying. Not to mention Terry's grumpiness.

"Of course you are," she said. "I'm sorry I doubted you."

"Boss." Tina tuned away and opened the door through to the gift shop.

Three people stood in front of the shop counter: PC Filch, a man in a prison guard's uniform, and another in a suit.

Lesley exchanged glances with Tina, and they emerged into the shop. She pulled on her most sincere smile.

"Gentlemen," she said. "This is a crime scene. If you don't mind..."

The besuited man turned to her. His smile was even more

insincere than her own. "My name's Crawford. I'm from the Home Office. We need to talk."

CHAPTER SEVEN

"Come through here." Zoe exchanged glances with PS Jenner at the front desk, then led Gina O'Toole through to one of the small rooms at the front of the building they used for conversations with the public. These rooms were rarely used.

"Thanks." The woman's voice was small and thin.

Zoe gestured for her to take a seat. "Can I get you a cup of tea or coffee?"

"Are you sure?" Gina visibly relaxed. "Tea would be lovely, thanks. I haven't eaten."

"I'll see if we've got biscuits too, then. Won't be long."

Five minutes later she was back with a tea for Gina, two sachets of sugar, a packet of Hobnobs and a black coffee for herself.

She held out the pack of biscuits and Gina took two. Zoe put the packet down. She hated Hobnobs, was glad to get rid of them.

"So," she said. "You talked to Mo during the original investigation."

"DS Uddin, yes. He was kind. It felt like he cared about what happened to Susie."

"That's Mo all over. I'm sorry he's not here to talk to you now. What is it you feel you can help us with?"

Gina crunched on a biscuit. "That man. Trevor Hamm. I saw him on the news."

"You did?" Zoe had been meaning to go home hours ago, but Carl was working on an investigation in Coventry, and she knew he'd be out late. It made sense to catch up with paperwork instead of sitting in an empty house.

Gina nodded and rubbed her lip with a fingertip. "They say he escaped."

"Hamm? Are you sure?"

She thought back to the trial. Hamm hadn't been arrested in the Canary investigation, but later, after they'd found evidence of him trafficking women and children from Romania. It had been Mo, Zoe's second-in-command and oldest friend, who'd made the arrest.

Gina nodded.

"OK." Zoe took her phone out and scanned the news sites. Sure enough, Hamm's face was all over them.

She'd worked on both cases. Why hadn't she been told?

Because it wasn't her business.

And there wasn't much she could do to help this woman, other than to offer her reassurance. She'd read Gina O'Toole's witness statement during the Canary trial. Her daughter, Susie, had been groomed by Hamm and his associates. She'd been sexually assaulted by at least one man, probably many more. The girl had been unable to talk about the details at the time.

How old had she been? Fourteen? Fifteen?

She'd be eighteen or nineteen now. An adult. Hopefully not a damaged one.

"How is Susie now?" she asked as she sipped her coffee.

Gina's mouth fell open. "You don't know."

Zoe felt her skin bristle. "I'm sorry. Don't know what?"

Gina looked down. She tugged at her right thumb. The skin on it was raw. "She died. She... she took pills."

Zoe closed her eyes. *Idiot.* She should have done some research before coming down here.

"I'm so sorry."

Gina nodded.

Zoe said nothing, instead allowing the woman to sit in silence for a moment. There wasn't much to say. Still, she was itching to open up her phone. To read the news reports.

Had they caught him yet? Had he made it off the Isle of Portland?

Could he be heading back to Birmingham?

No.

He wouldn't be that stupid.

"Gina," Zoe said, her voice low. "I understand why you wanted to come here tonight. Why you wanted to talk to DS Uddin. And I'm sorry he isn't here. But is there anything specific you want to talk to me about, that might help us track Hamm down? To put him back behind bars?"

Gina looked up. "He phoned us."

"He did *what*?" Zoe clenched a fist on the table.

"A month ago. We had a call, said it was from a prison. I'd never heard of the place at the time. I looked it up, afterwards. That's how when I saw the report that someone had escaped from there. I thought it might be him."

"Did you speak to him?"

A nod, followed by a sob. Zoe placed a hand on the table, close to Gina's.

"Not for long," Gina said. "They asked if we would take a reverse charge call. I was confused, it didn't occur to me he might have got our phone number."

"You did nothing wrong."

"I hung up almost straight away."

"Almost?"

Another nod. Gina wiped her face, which was wet with tears. "He said he'd be back. That's all. 'I'm coming back', he said. Then I hung up."

CHAPTER EIGHT

LESLEY LOOKED at the man in the suit. "And you're from…?"

Crawford pulled a business card from his inside pocket and handed it to her. The suit was an expensive one, she noticed. He indicated his colleague. "This is Don Scott. From The Verne prison."

Lesley turned it over in her hand. It had the crest of the Home Office on it. But it was just a business card.

"How do I know you are who you say you are?"

"He's wearing a prison officer's uniform. I think that's pretty conclusive."

Scott drew an ID badge from inside his coat. Lesley bent to check it. She shook her head.

"Given the situation we find ourselves in here, I rather think a prison badge doesn't prove anything."

Whoever had busted Hamm out was clever. Whoever had killed him was cleverer still. Impersonating a Home Office official and a prison officer would be nothing.

"Very well," he said. "The prison is a ten-minute drive from here. Follow us, and we can talk inside."

Lesley narrowed her eyes. She didn't have time for this.

"I'll make a call," she said. "You wait here."

Lesley pushed open the outer door to the lighthouse and pulled out her phone. She dialled the switchboard at Dorset Police HQ in Winfrith.

"Can you put me through to HMP The Verne, please?"

"Er. Yes. Give me a moment."

Lesley turned to watch the door to the lighthouse. It remained closed. Gail, Brett and Dr Bamford were still in there. She wondered what was happening.

Come on.

"His Majesty's Prison The Verne," came a voice. "Who's calling, please?"

"My name is DCI Clarke of Dorset Police. I'd like to speak with your governor please."

"One moment."

Lesley waited as the line went quiet.

"DCI Clarke." A man's voice.

Lesley straightened. She wished she'd brought a heavier coat; it was fully dark now, and the wind was attacking her from all directions.

"Thanks for taking my call," she said. "Can I ask your name?"

"Certainly. Thomas Gordon, governor of the prison. You'll be calling to check the identity of Don Scott and his companion."

"You were expecting my call."

"You have a reputation as a cautious woman, DCI Clarke. An astute one. But I can confirm that my colleagues are who they say they are. And they *do* need to talk to you about the case you're leading on."

Word gets around here fast, Lesley thought.

"Thank you," she said. "So what can you tell me about Hamm's escape?"

"He was being moved to Dorchester for a parole hearing. All the usual security measures had been adopted and we took the precaution of changing the time of the journey at the last minute. A Range Rover rammed the van head-on as it approached the causeway to the mainland. Another vehicle, a van, blocked us in from the rear."

"Us?"

"I wasn't there, Detective. But Don Scott was. He can fill you in."

"Surely he's being allowed time off to recover?"

"Don isn't that kind of man, DCI Clarke. I couldn't allow him back in with the inmates, but he refused to go home."

"How did they get access to Hamm?"

"Haven't you seen the news reports?"

"No." Lesley wasn't about to tell this man she'd been on her honeymoon.

"They shot the officer in the passenger seat. Scott was in the rear of the vehicle, he didn't witness that. But there were members of the public around. Three men forced the driver to stop the vehicle and open the rear doors, at gunpoint. We hadn't thought an armed escort necessary, so we couldn't—"

"What happened to the driver?" Lesley asked.

"No shots were fired. He's at home, potential PTSD."

She nodded. "What time was all this?"

"Five forty-seven this morning. Hamm was expecting to be moved later on. His lawyer turned up at nine am. She wasn't happy."

"And he made off in one of the vehicles?"

"Yes. We were lucky; there was a police car heading down the mainland and it blocked the road into Weymouth. So they had no choice but to go back onto the island."

Lesley frowned. "Did your officers recognise any of them?"

"They all wore balaclavas, DCI Clarke."

Of course they did. She sighed.

Hamm had been in a vehicle heading back onto the Isle of Portland. It was, what, four miles long and two wide?

"How did you lose him, Mr Gordon?"

"Touché. They abandoned the vehicles at the Circle of Stones and managed to lose themselves in the quarry on the west of the island."

"Circle of Stones?"

"You're not local."

"I'm based out of Winfrith."

"Ah. Well, you have a fair bit to learn about Portland, DCI Clarke. It's small, but it's got plenty of nooks and crannies. And the people here don't have a lot of respect for the authorities. Not when they come from the mainland."

"Is the road still blocked?" Maybe they could keep Hamm's killers from leaving the island, Lesley thought. But she'd got onto the island without noticing anything, so it must have all been cleared.

"That wasn't possible. The road reopened within half an hour."

Damn. They could be miles away by now.

"One of my officers will visit you tomorrow," Lesley said. "We'll need a formal statement. And if you could provide the names of all Prison Service staff involved in the transfer."

"Of course. I'm happy to chat to you."

Chat to you?

The man had just allowed a prisoner to escape custody and then be killed. How could he be so breezy about it all?

"Thank you." Lesley pocketed her phone and headed back to the building. Crawford turned towards her as she entered.

"I vote we stay in here," she said, "as it's bloody freezing out there. So how can I help you both?"

CHAPTER NINE

Nine pm was the time at which Dennis habitually commenced his bedtime routine. He liked this, the familiar ordinariness of it. First he made sure the washing up was dried and put away. Next he made his way through the house, turning off lights and pulling plugs out at the socket. Dennis wasn't a man for standby or constantly plugged-in devices. A waste of power, and a fire hazard too.

The routine then shifted upstairs; brushed teeth, pyjamas, the latest edition of *Readers Digest* for ten minutes, then lights out. Pam would have her library book, a tiny light clipped to its cover so she wouldn't disturb him.

But tonight, Dennis couldn't face it. It was 9.30 and Pam was already upstairs. In bed, no doubt. But he was sitting in his armchair, staring at a blank TV screen, the standby light winking at him and all the lights on.

Pam had been quiet since he'd come home. She'd clearly decided that she wasn't going to ask him about what had happened, but instead wait for him to tell her when he was ready.

It wasn't like Pam. Normally she knew everything about Dennis, even before he did.

But this was different.

Arrested for murder.

Charged, too.

Charged.

He could still barely believe it.

DI Gough had turned up at his house, while he'd still been on his way home from the DCI's wedding. He'd waited, with poor Pam. Sitting here, in this very chair, with his wife. Not telling her what he was here for. Just waiting.

What kind of man did that?

On Monday morning, he would be appearing at the Magistrates Court. He'd been there plenty of times before. He'd given evidence, back when he was working in Uniform and then in local CID. Any evidence he'd had to give in more recent years had been in the Crown Court. But the Magistrates Court wasn't new to him.

But still.

He'd never sat in the accused's seat. Never listened to them reading out his own name. Announcing to the world that he had allegedly killed Tim Mackie, his friend and mentor.

He slumped back in the chair.

What would he do?

People would be there. People he knew. People who'd respected him. And they'd all think him capable of murder.

And then...

Then there would be the Crown Court. A murder case would be referred instantly. It was a formality.

How long would he have to wait? And would he be allowed to do so at home, or would the magistrates decide he was too much of a risk, and lock him up?

He'd seen this process a thousand times. He knew that if a suspect was allowed to go home after being charged, then the chances are they would be allowed to do so again after appearing in front of the magistrates. But that didn't stop him worrying.

And if they found him guilty...

He swallowed down a mouthful of bile. His stomach lurched.

Prison.

Dennis couldn't be in prison.

He was an old man. Less than a year from retirement.

He was a quiet man, the kind of man who read the *Readers Digest* and made sure his slippers were waiting for him in exactly the same spot every evening.

And, worst of all, he was a police officer.

Prison, for him, would be dangerous.

Maybe that was why Pam wasn't talking about it. Maybe she couldn't contemplate it either.

Maybe she was just as scared as he was.

CHAPTER TEN

"OK," Lesley said. "Gail, Brett, Tina and Gareth, you head home like I said. I can deal with this."

"Are you sure, boss?" Tina asked. "I'm happy to—"

"It's over an hour's drive back to Sandford for you," Lesley told the DC. "Get home. I'll call you if there's anything I need you to do. But there won't be."

"If you're sure..."

"I'm sure." Lesley looked at Crawford. "It's just me you need to talk to, I imagine."

"The SIO."

"That's me."

Gail picked up a case she'd placed on the floor and approached Lesley. "Are you going to be alright?"

"Of course. I'll see you in the morning, like we said." Lesley wondered who was looking after Gail's son. His granny, no doubt. Or maybe this was one of the nights he spent with his dad.

Gail surveyed her. "Make sure you get home to your wife before midnight, yes? You're not a pumpkin."

"Isn't it the other way around?" Lesley shook her head, too tired to argue. They'd split the journey back from Scotland into two chunks, but the second day's driving had been long and stressful, roadworks on the M6 and an accident on the M3. They'd set off at nine this morning and she'd only been home an hour before she'd had to set off again.

"Whatever," she said. "See you in the morning."

Gail, Tina and Brett left the lighthouse. Dr Bamford gave Lesley a nod of acknowledgement as he passed her.

"We'll get to him, first thing," he said. "Hopefully I'll be able to determine cause of death."

Lesley wasn't as confident, but she wasn't about to contradict the pathologist in front of the Home Office men.

"Thanks," she said.

He closed the outer door. She was alone with the suit and the prison officer.

"So," she said. "How can I help you?"

"We have information about Hamm that might help your investigation," said Crawford. "But we'll need to work jointly, to coordinate our efforts."

Lesley rolled her eyes. She'd seen this coming. Work jointly. That meant they would take over. The Home Office had no idea how to run a murder inquiry. They'd trample all over it, contaminating evidence, mishandling witnesses.

"What's the information?" she asked them.

"You're agreeing to coordinate our efforts?"

She gave him a tight smile. "The more, the merrier." She knew if she refused, she'd be overruled, anyway. Easier to go along with him and then just get on with the job while he wasn't looking.

"Good. In that case, you need to know that Hamm's escape was planned."

"I've just spoken to Thomas Gordon, who filled me in. That isn't exactly a surprise."

Crawford didn't stop for breath. "We've interviewed two inmates and managed to glean some information about the conspiracy."

"What kind of conspiracy?"

"His associates rammed the prison van."

"And they shot one of Mr Scott here's colleagues. I know all this. Surely your conspirators gave you more than that?"

Crawford frowned. He was leaning against the counter of the gift shop, a rack of postcards behind him. "They were planning to take him back to Birmingham. A safe house had been identified."

"Why? Why go back to the one place where every copper knows him?"

"I imagine that's a job for West Midlands Police to work out."

"Do you know who in West Mids was running this? Hamm was the boss of his operation. Who there would have wanted to get him out?"

Crawford tugged at his tie. "Again, one for the West Midlands force."

Lesley looked at him. She knew plenty of detectives in Birmingham. She'd have her answer by the morning.

She cocked her head. "How come you let him get away? Portland isn't exactly a big place."

"We weren't expecting Hamm or his associates to remain on the island. There isn't a permanent police presence. And prisoners are moved all the time. It's not like local police can afford to put the extra resource in."

"That's true."

Lesley turned to see PC Filch looking at her.

"Are you still here?"

He gave her a small salute. "You told me to mind the crime scene, Ma'am. I'll be relieved at midnight."

"How much do you know about Hamm's escape? Did anyone from Dorset Police manage to track him down, while he was still alive?"

Filch looked down, shaking his head. "Not that I know of."

Crawford took a step towards Lesley. "We want your help identifying and capturing the people who helped him escape."

"Who probably killed him," Lesley added.

"We can't assume that."

"No? Hamm's operation in Birmingham was disbanded. All of his nasty little mates are in prison or dead. So if someone wanted to get him out, it was a rival. And it stands to reason they'd bump him off."

"We have no intelligence on rivals."

"No. But West Midlands Organised Crime unit will."

"We need to speak to them."

"Oh, no you don't." Lesley jabbed a finger at him. "They know me and they trust me. I'll be the one talking to them."

He met her gaze. "I'll need you to share any information with me."

"I can do that."

"Good," he replied, not noticing that she'd said *can* and not *will*.

She turned to Filch. "You're local. How do you think they managed to lose themselves?"

"It's surprisingly easy to get lost in the quarries. When you're in the middle of them, it feels like you're miles away from anywhere. And there are gaps, created by the rocks. Almost like caves."

"OK. I suppose it doesn't really matter right now how local police and the Prison Service managed to lose Hamm. What's important is finding out if anyone saw him with his killer."

"We propose a press conference," said Crawford.

"It'll cause panic."

"It'll help us find witnesses."

Lesley wasn't so sure. She looked at Scott. "They must have devised quite a plan, to evade your officers in a place like this."

The prison officer's jaw tightened. "They must have done."

"And you only found out about all this today. A bit late."

"We weren't expect—"

"We're passing on information," Crawford interrupted, "in the hope that it might help your investigation. Not to invite criticism, DCI Clarke."

"I imagine not. So they busted him out of the van, disappeared in the quarries and then what?"

"I'm afraid we don't know."

"No. Well, whatever they did, he ended up here. Dead over that lamp."

Crawford nodded. Lesley wondered who else knew about the nature of Hamm's death.

"Anything else you can help me with?" she asked him.

"How much do you know about Hamm's criminal history? His associates?"

She smiled. "A lot."

"You've researched."

"I've done more than research. It was one of my team that arrested him. So I know who the people are who are likely to have helped him escape."

"A new organised crime gang in Birmingham."

"Indeed. And I also know exactly who might be able to tell me who's in charge of it."

Lesley's phone rang. She looked down at it and resisted a laugh.

"Speak of the devil."

CHAPTER ELEVEN

"You GOT any idea what all that was about?" Tina asked Gail as they walked to their respective vehicles.

"Not a sausage," Gail replied. "But you know Lesley. She'll deal with it."

Tina nodded. She was tired. Louis had slept badly last night and while Mike was officially in charge now, her instincts were still working to keep her awake whenever her son was.

She yawned. "I'm off home then."

Gail gave her a smile. "Give that baby of yours a cuddle."

Tina felt her body deflate. "The only way I'll see him before leaving in the morning is if he doesn't sleep through."

"And you want him to sleep through."

"Of course." She sighed. "This is so hard."

Gail cocked her head. "Of course it is. But it's not forever. Louis'll get used to being with Mike in the day. He'll start sleeping better soon. And at some point, you'll suddenly realise you're not sleepwalking through a fog of fatigue every day."

"Does that ever happen?"

Gail laughed. "Tim's six, and he still has his moments. But

I get a full night's sleep nine nights out of ten now, and he's at school. That makes it easier to juggle."

Tina felt a stab of guilt. "I'm sorry. I'm being insensitive. It must be that much harder as a single parent."

Gail shook her head. "We all play the hand we're dealt, and we all cope with it in our own way. You've been back at work for two days. Give it some time."

"Yeah." Tina felt stupid.

"And don't worry, we won't be traipsing out here to Portland for long."

"No? That body's going to take some moving."

Gail hefted a pilot case into the back of her van and closed the back doors. Brett was in the front, wiping down windows that were already starting to frost up.

"Didn't you know? The DCI arrested the victim, back when she was in Brum. She'll crack this case open quicker than you can say Canary."

"Canary?"

"The name of the original investigation. Look it up, when you get home. If you can keep your eyes open."

"I will. Thanks." Tina went to her car and peered out of the windscreen. The wind lashed at the cliffs beyond the lighthouse, and all she could hear was the sound of the sea and the gale.

What a place to die.

Mind you, it didn't sound as if Trevor Hamm was a victim deserving of all that much sympathy.

CHAPTER TWELVE

Zoe was in her office in Force CID, deep in Harborne police station in Birmingham. The last time she'd spoken to Lesley, it was because the DCI had asked her to help investigate a sensitive case: DCI Mackie's death. Lesley's Super had got wind of it and warned them of the consequences if they were reported. But he'd never reported either of them, and that still niggled at her.

This time, however, she had a legitimate reason to speak to her former boss.

"Lesley," she said. "I heard you got married."

"Got back from my honeymoon today. But enough of the niceties. Is this about Trevor Hamm?"

Zoe gripped the phone. "He escaped."

"He's done more than escape. He's bloody dead."

Zoe almost dropped her phone.

"Dead? How?"

Shit.

If he'd been killed by police in the course of recovering him, there would be an inquiry. And consequences.

"Someone dumped him in a lighthouse at the arse end of nowhere," Lesley said.

"He wasn't killed by the police?"

"Why would he be killed by our lot?"

"I thought... he's a dangerous criminal, there'd have been an armed response..."

"We didn't catch up with him in time. Either whoever helped him bust out only did it so they could kill him, or someone else who wanted rid of him got wind of it and intercepted them."

"He's at a lighthouse, you said. He fell from cliffs? Are you sure it wasn't accidental?"

"He's *inside* the lighthouse. Still is, we can't work out how to get him down. He's on top of an old lamp they keep here for the tourists. Massive great thing. I'll send you a photo. Anyway, there's a chance it could have been accidental. But my Spidey-senses are telling me not."

Lesley's intuition was rarely wrong.

"How can I help?" Zoe asked.

"What's going on up in Brum these days?" Lesley asked. "Since Trevor Hamm went down."

"His operation has been largely taken over by another gang. Brum Boys. They were on the up when we were investigating Hamm, now they're in the process of filling the gap he left."

"Any of his lot working for them?"

"Most of them are in prison. Or dead. So no, none of the key people. Not that we're aware of."

"But there might be others," Lesley said. "People who were further down the chain with Hamm, trying to work their way up."

"There might be." Zoe hadn't had much to do with Brum

Boys; that was Organised Crime's job. "You want me to speak to Sheila Griffin?"

"It's OK, I'll need to speak to her DCI."

"Fine."

"So what was it you called me about, Zoe?"

"I've got a witness here at Rose Road. Her name's Gina O'Toole."

"I remember her. Her kid was one of the victims."

Zoe shivered. "The kid died."

"Shit. Did she have injuries? I can't remember the detail."

"She killed herself. Overdose. Couldn't handle the memories."

"Poor kid. That bastard Hamm. I tell you, if someone else hadn't thought to shove him onto that lamp, I'd have bloody done it myself."

Zoe heard voices in the background. "Have I caught you at a bad time?"

"No, I've just got two bods from the Home Office wanting to work collaboratively."

Zoe smiled. She knew what *work collaboratively* meant, when it came from the Home Office. And she knew how Lesley would respond to it.

"Are you alright to talk?"

"I am. What happened to Gina O'Toole? Please tell me those bastards haven't hurt her."

"She got a call from Hamm. He said he was coming to Birmingham."

Silence.

"Lesley? Are you there?"

"Keep that to yourself for now, Zoe. Send me Gina's statement, I know you'll have taken one. I'll be in touch."

CHAPTER THIRTEEN

LESLEY STOOD next to the bed and peeled off her jumper as quietly as she could. She let it fall to the floor instead of opening the wardrobe with its squeaky hinge.

Elsa was asleep across from her. She was a dim shape in the darkness, her dark hair spread across the pillow. Lesley smiled, looking down at her. This wasn't how she'd envisaged tonight.

There was a bottle of Champagne in the fridge, a box of chocolates in her bedside drawer. She'd been planning on surprising her new wife.

But instead, she'd surprised her by not only getting herself involved in a murder investigation on their honeymoon, but by coming home and plunging straight into another one.

And this was going to be quite a case.

Elsa rolled over. "Lesley?"

"Shh. Go back to sleep."

Elsa's bedside light went on. She sat up, plumping the pillows behind her and yawning. "I waited up. I wanted to see you. Sorry."

Lesley knelt on the bed and kissed Elsa's hand. "You didn't

have to wait up. It's my stupid fault, for running off the day after our honeymoon for work. I'm sorry."

Elsa squeezed her eyes shut then opened them. "You don't have to apologise, sweetie. I know what your job's like."

"Still..."

Elsa put a hand on Lesley's knee. "You're a DCI, and a bloody good one. They want you heading up all the nasty cases. I saw it on the news. Is it the same man who escaped from the prison?"

Lesley nodded. "Are they reporting his death yet?"

"I don't know. I only saw the seven pm bulletin."

"I'm sure they will be soon. It's not like we can keep it quiet."

"Who found him?"

"The lighthouse keeper," Lesley said as she put on her pyjamas and slid into bed.

"Not a member of the public, then."

"No. And the lighthouse is privately owned, so her employers won't be chuffed."

"A female lighthouse keeper, I like that."

"She isn't really a lighthouse keeper. More a gift shop manager. But yeah."

"They used to ban women from running lighthouses, you know."

Lesley pushed her pillow closer to Elsa's and snuggled up next to her. "How d'you know that?"

"I visited Portland Bill, when I first came to Dorset. Felt like I should do all the tourist stuff." She smiled. "It didn't last."

"So you'll know the lens."

Elsa nodded. She stroked the skin on the back of Lesley's hand.

"He was found on top of it," Lesley said. "Must have been thrown off the viewing platform."

"It's an old Victorian one, if I remember right. They've got LEDs now."

"The glass is strong. Didn't crack under the force."

Elsa whistled. She pulled Lesley closer. "I guess you'll be off out early in the morning."

"I need to get to the crime scene, then brief the team. Home Office are breathing down our necks. It took me ages to get rid of them, and I had to promise to share information with them."

"You'll have enjoyed that."

"Totally." Lesley hesitated. "D'you mind if we put the TV on, just for a bit? I want to see if anything else is being reported. There's a Birmingham link."

"There is?"

"Trevor Hamm, the victim. One of my team in Force CID arrested him. He was an organised crime boss."

Elsa's face clouded over. "Birmingham's answer to Arthur Kelvin."

"Worse. He was running a paedophile ring. Trafficking women and children."

Elsa put her hand over her mouth. "There are some horrible people in the world."

"And you represent half of them." Lesley grabbed the remote control and turned on the TV.

Elsa turned to her. "Is that what you think?"

Lesley caught the look on her wife's face.

Shit.

She'd gone too far.

What had she said, exactly? She hadn't been concentrating.

"Sorry, love. That's not what—"

"Everyone deserves a defence, Lesley. Everyone. I don't care who they are or what they've done. It's a tenet of the English legal system. And it's not as if you always arrest the right person, is it?"

"No. I'm sorry." Lesley put out a hand. "Hang on. That's him."

Elsa turned to the TV. "Who?"

"The Home Office man." She looked at Elsa's alarm clock: ten fifty-five pm. "When did he do this?"

Crawford was standing outside what looked like the prison, alone against a stone wall. It was light.

It had been dark when they'd left the lighthouse.

He'd recorded a statement, before arriving? And he hadn't thought to tell her?

"What the…" she began. She stopped to listen.

"The Home Office is doing everything it can to track down the escaped prisoner and find the people who helped him escape. We are confident that they have not left the Isle of Portland and that there is no risk of them accessing the mainland. In the meantime, we urge the people of Portland to come forward if they have any information. If you have seen this man, please call us."

Crawford face was replaced with a photo of Trevor Hamm. Lesley flinched at the sight of him. Large and square with his ruddy tan faded, and wrinkles Lesley didn't remember, he was as ugly as he'd ever been.

Ugly in spirit, even more so.

"Your team arrested him?" Elsa said.

Lesley nodded. "Mo Uddin. One of my DSs. Good officer. You met him, in Scotland."

"I did my level best not to meet any of them."

Lesley looked at Elsa. "Again. I'm sorry."

Elsa cupped Lesley's face in her hand. "I know. And it wasn't your fault you found a body less than a mile away from our cabin. But next time, report it and then leave it alone. Please?"

"I promise."

Elsa kissed her. "Good. But it looks like you're going to have your work cut out with this Crawford guy."

CHAPTER FOURTEEN

THE ROAD to Portland took Lesley west and then south, the sea in front of her as she approached Weymouth. The sun was bright this morning, reflecting off the water. Even she had to admit it was beautiful.

As she reached the coast road and spotted the Isle of Portland curving out at the far end of Weymouth Bay, her phone rang: Carpenter.

"Sir," she said. "I'm on my way to the lighthouse. The CSIs have found a scaffolding contractor, we'll be able to get at the body this morning."

"Good," he said. "I need to talk to you about the Home Office."

Lesley's shoulders dipped. Carpenter never backed her up on anything, and she had a feeling he wasn't about to start now.

"Jacob Crawford arrived last night," she said. "I asked Tina to look him up, and he doesn't work for the Prison Service, but for the National Crime Agency. I'm not sure why he's—"

"Lesley, shut up. I know who Jacob Crawford is, and I know his agenda. I want you to keep him at arm's length."

Lesley looked at the phone in its cradle. Had she heard right?

"At arm's length, Sir?"

"You heard me. Don't say no to him. Make it look like we're cooperating. But only share the bare minimum. Give him an inch, and he'll take a mile."

Lesley decided not to ask why Carpenter was asking her to resist Crawford. Better not to challenge him.

"Not a problem, Sir," she said. "At some point before Monday, I also need to talk to you about DS Frampton. I was on leave when he was arrested, and—"

"No, DCI Clarke. You do not need to talk to me about Dennis Frampton. And I don't want you getting involved."

"He's a key member of my team."

"He's suspected of being corrupt. You want to avoid him."

"With respect, Sir, he hasn't been charged with any offences relating to corruption. And I know Dennis. He's—"

"Lesley, are you listening to me?"

"Sir." Weymouth Harbour was to her left. She crossed a ridiculously complex traffic lights system to take the A354 for Portland.

"Leave it alone," he told her. "You don't want to be associated with him."

Carpenter might work like that, but Lesley didn't. Dennis had shown her loyalty in the past. He'd given Elsa the benefit of the doubt when others had suspected her links to the Kelvin family were stronger than they really were. And he'd been the best DS she could have hoped for, over the last year and a half. Two years, almost.

"Sir," she said as Chesil Beach appeared on her right. She drove onto the causeway, Portland rising up in front of her.

"I don't want you contacting him, you hear me? If I hear you've—"

"I understand, Sir."

Lesley believed in procedure. It had led to run-ins with Zoe, when they'd worked together. Zoe didn't always follow the rules, and she'd put herself at risk because of it. Lesley preferred to stick to procedure. To run through a case logically, follow the evidence instead of intuition, and do absolutely nothing that might put a conviction at risk.

But this was different. This wasn't a case she was running. And it was Dennis.

"Update me when you're at the scene," Carpenter told her. "The Chief Constable is taking a keen interest in this one, he's concerned about links to other forces. I want to know as soon as we get any closer to finding out what happened to Trevor Hamm."

"So do I, Sir."

CHAPTER FIFTEEN

Tina stood at the bottom of the scaffolding, listening to the voices above her. Gail was up there, with Dr Bamford and Brett. The two men who'd erected the scaffolding were gone, and the place echoed with the three voices.

"Shall I come up?" she called.

Gail's face appeared over the edge of the scaffolding. She wore a white hard hat. "There isn't room for anyone else. In fact, Brett, I think it'd be safest if you went back down."

Tina stood back as Brett climbed down the ladder attached to the structure. When he reached the bottom, he rubbed his hands together and gave Tina a grin.

"We're getting there," he said. "Gail's sending down some samples from the surface of the glass. And the doc says he's close enough to work out if the victim died from the fall."

"Good." Tina wished she could go up there. She wanted to see for herself. And she knew that the boss was on her way, too. She'd want to see.

Her phone rang: Stanley.

"Stan, what have you got?"

"Meera and I have been going through information on all Trevor Hamm's associates and enemies. Most of his mates who aren't dead are banged up. He's like a curse."

"What about his enemies?"

"A few of them are dead, too. But there's another gang in Birmingham. The Brum Boys."

"That's a gang? Sounds more like a boy band," she replied. "What do we know about them?"

"Not much. There've been a couple of arrests, looks like low level stuff. Newspaper reports."

"We'll have to speak to Organised Crime."

"Which means DI Gough," Stanley said.

Tina pulled a face. She didn't much relish the idea of working with the man who'd arrested the sarge.

"Surely there's someone else in Organised Crime we can talk to," she said.

"Strictly speaking, we do need to talk to Gough. He's our liaison."

Tina looked at Brett. There was a shout from above and Gail's head appeared again.

"We've got a cause of death," she called down. "Well, we've been able to rule a few things out."

"Stan, I've got to go," Tina said. "Don't call Gough until I've spoken to the boss. She might have people in Birmingham she can talk to."

"Tina, d'you think it's wise for us to be getting mixed up with the sarge's problems?"

Tina bristled. The sarge's problems were the team's problems, as far as she was concerned. "Don't even think it, Stan. The sarge didn't do it, and the boss'll work out who did. You mark my words."

A grunt. "I hope so."

Beside her, the ladder shifted. Gail was coming down. Brett went to hold onto it.

"I've got to go, Stan." Tina hung up just as Gail reached the ground.

"Thank God for that," she said. "I should have mentioned I suffer from vertigo."

"I'd have stayed up there," Brett suggested.

"I'm fine. I wanted to see." Gail looked at Tina. "How long till Lesley gets here?"

"She's on her way. What's the cause of death?"

"It's not the fall."

Tina felt her eyes widen. "It's not?" She looked up at the top of the lens, and the viewing platform high above. "You sure?"

"I'm not," Gail replied. "But the pathologist is. He's managed to get a look at the victim's chest, and there's no bruising. If the fall had killed him, there'd be more than bruising. There'd be busted ribs, severe bruising. Possibly other breaks. But apart from some minor damage to the ribs, there's barely anything."

"Which means he was already dead," Tina said.

Gail nodded. "Our victim was already dead when someone pushed him off that viewing platform."

CHAPTER SIXTEEN

"ZOE," said DS Sheila Griffin, "I think I know what this is about."

Zoe sat back in her chair and smiled. She was in the team office with Connie and Rhodri. She had a private office connected to it, but she rarely used it; she preferred to be with her team. And both Connie and Rhodri knew what was going on with Trevor Hamm.

"Trevor Hamm," Zoe said into the phone. Connie looked up from her screen and grimaced, causing Rhodri to chuckle. Zoe frowned at him.

"Trevor Hamm indeed," replied Sheila. "My Super's already had a call from the Dorset force."

"From Lesley?"

"No. A Superintendent Carpenter."

Zoe wrinkled her nose. Lesley had told her all about Carpenter, and the man sounded thoroughly unlikeable. He was the one who'd threatened the pair of them, so she wasn't really inclined to think favourably of him.

"OK," she said. "Any chance you can share what they've been asking?"

"Nobody told me not to. They want to know who in Birmingham might have wanted Hamm dead. And who might have wanted to get him out of prison."

"We're thinking those might be separate things?"

"From what I can tell, there are two hypotheses. One: whoever busted him out also killed him. Two: one party busted him out and then a second party intercepted them and killed him."

"So we could be looking at half of Birmingham's organised crime suspects."

"I think they're focusing on the Brum Boys. Seeing as Hamm's old lot are mostly dead or in prison."

"There'll be a few of them with a grudge. We didn't catch every one, I'm sure. Which is what I'm calling you about."

"We're putting together a dossier for the Super. You want me to share it with you? It's not exactly pleasant reading."

"Please," Zoe said. "And I want to look at potential connections between Hamm and organised crime in Dorset."

"You think someone down there might be responsible for this?"

"It's unlikely. There's a Kelvin family, but the kingpin's dead and most of the rest are in prison, too."

"Sounds like your old DCI's hit rate is just as good down there as it was here."

Zoe nodded. "And there's always the possibility this could have been instigated by one or more of Hamm's victims. He..."

She'd been about to tell Sheila about what Gina O'Toole had told her. But if she shared that with Sheila, it would get to Carpenter. And she knew Lesley didn't trust him.

"He what?" Sheila asked.

Zoe felt bad not telling Sheila what she knew. But Gina's evidence was relevant to the murder enquiry. Not to any organised crime investigations.

"Sorry? Oh, nothing. Look, if you could send me that dossier it would be great. I'll look into information about his victims, we've got it all from Canary and from the Osman trial."

Ian Osman had been a bent DS who'd temporarily worked with Zoe. It was during his trial that they'd finally tracked Hamm down and arrested him.

"You found yourself a new DS to replace Mo yet?" Sheila asked.

"Not much point. My team's going to be disbanded when I move up north."

"So Carl convinced you."

Zoe's partner Carl had been offered a promotion, in Cumbria. He'd been working on her for months, and after realising half her colleagues thought she might be as bent as the DS who'd worked for her, she'd decided to make the leap.

"He did. We need to find a place to live, I've applied for a transfer up there, just waiting to find out if I got it. So it's not exactly a done deal."

"Good luck with it. Tell me when the leaving do's booked."

Zoe chuckled.

From the corner of her eye, she spotted Connie shifting in her chair. Her transfer and Mo's move to Scotland meant Connie and Rhodri had a choice: work for DCI Frank Dawson, or move to another unit. She knew both of them were pursuing options outside Force CID.

"That won't be for a while yet, Sheila. Thanks for your help."

Zoe hung up. She pulled up the Canary file on her computer and went to Susie O'Toole's statement.

Poor kid. What Hamm and his mates had put her through was unthinkable.

But what was special about her and her family, to Hamm? Why had he taken the trouble to call them and threaten a return to Birmingham?

CHAPTER SEVENTEEN

LESLEY PARKED in the public car park in front of the lighthouse. Last night when she'd left, it had been deserted. Today, it was full.

She blew out an exasperated breath and took in the surrounding scene. The cars didn't belong to tourists, here to visit the lighthouse. They belonged to news organisations.

A crowd had gathered near the entrance to the lighthouse, and two TV vans were parked close to it. She could make out microphones, cameras and arguing.

And right at the front of it all, Sadie Dawes from the BBC.

Lesley smiled. She might have known Sadie would be here.

But they didn't even know how Hamm had died yet. And she wasn't aware his death had been made public.

It seemed it had. Crawford's work?

She scanned the car park for the dark Audi he'd been driving the previous night. There was no sign of it. At least he wasn't planning to stage a press conference at the lighthouse.

She stretched her arms out, brushing the roof of the car. She counted to ten, then opened the car door.

Here goes.

Lesley marched towards the lighthouse, avoiding eye contact with anyone in the vicinity. A group of people stood by one of the TV vans, sorting through equipment. When they spotted her, one of them called over to the main pack. Sadie turned, brightened at the sight of Lesley and pushed through the crowd towards her. The other journalists saw what she was doing, turned and followed.

Lesley chewed her lip. She still didn't make eye contact.

"DCI Clarke!" It was Sadie. Lesley kept her eyes down and carried on walking. Saying nothing.

She looked ahead of her, at the closed – hopefully locked – door to the lighthouse. She wondered if PC Filch was in there, keeping the press out.

She hoped he wasn't alone.

A hand landed on her arm. "Is it true Trevor Hamm's in there?" A man's voice. Lesley didn't look round.

She pushed through the crowd, then stopped at a buzzing overhead.

She looked up and had to fight to stop herself shouting in exasperation.

There was a bloody drone over her head. Filming everything, no doubt.

There were families out there, glued to their TVs, desperate to know what had happened to Trevor Hamm. People like the O'Tooles.

They needed compassion and respect. They needed to be informed of events in an appropriate manner.

But it was turning into a circus.

She shook her head and resumed walking. The pack was in front of her now, blocking the door.

"Excuse me," she said. "I need to get through."

"DCI Clarke, is it true that you were responsible for arresting Trevor Hamm in Birmingham?" came Sadie's voice.

Trust Sadie to get to the bottom of the story. She was annoying, but she was good.

Lesley looked up, meeting Sadie's gaze. "I'll be back out later to give you an update. But in the meantime, I need to speak to my team. Please, let me through."

Sadie narrowed her eyes. The young woman was no more than a metre away. Lesley gave her the most imperceptible of nods.

"OK," Sadie whispered. She stood back. "Let the DCI through," she told her colleagues. "Let her do her job."

Lesley allowed herself to breathe. *Thank God.*

She'd have to face them again shortly, but for now she had work to do.

CHAPTER EIGHTEEN

"I HOPE you don't mind us doing this on a Saturday morning," the DI said. "But we have quite a full caseload right now."

Dennis nodded. "And I hear you've lost two of your team to other forces."

DI Collingwood's cheek twitched. He'd be wondering how Dennis knew that, no doubt. Structures and roles in the Professional Standards Division weren't exactly publicised. But Dennis was an experienced copper. He knew what was going on across the Dorset force.

"I know it was Organised Crime who arrested you, but you'll understand we need to talk to you as well. It's standard procedure when any serving police officer is arrested."

"I know." Dennis also knew that DI Gough had been overstepping his boundaries by making the arrest. He should have left it to PSD.

They were in a windowless interview room in Bournemouth Central police station. Dennis had recognised the duty sergeant on his way in and given him an awkward acknowledgement.

"So what is it you need to ask me about?"

"You've been charged with the murder of former DCI Tim Mackie."

Dennis felt his stomach clench. *Keep calm.*

"I have."

"It's been established that after DCI Mackie's retirement, he continued working on one investigation."

It wasn't a question. Dennis said nothing.

DI Collingwood looked at him. Dennis licked his lips and stared straight ahead.

"Can you confirm that DCI Mackie was still investigating activity by the Kelvin family?" Collingwood asked.

"I can."

"And how is it that you know this?"

"The DCI contacted me. He asked me for information about the ongoing investigation by the Major Crime Investigations Team."

"And what, specifically, was this investigation relating to?"

"There'd been a series of robberies targeting industrial units in Poole. They belonged to various of Arthur Kelvin's businesses. We believed there was an organised crime element to them."

"So the MCIT was investigating the robberies? Not the organised crime activity? After all, that's a job for the Organised Crime unit."

"It is."

"You haven't answered my question, DS Frampton."

"MCIT was investigating what it needed to in order to trace the individual or individuals who had stolen from those units."

"Who reported the robberies? Was it Kelvin?"

Dennis shook his head. "One of his employees." At the

time, they'd been surprised that the crimes had been reported. Kelvin was the sort of man who dealt with that kind of thing himself, rather than bringing in the police. The assumption had been that the employee who'd made the report hadn't known what kind of organisation she was really working for.

"Who was in charge of the investigation into the thefts, DS Frampton?"

"Before his retirement, DCI Mackie was. Then it passed to me."

"Not to another DCI? Or to a DI?"

"There was a vacancy. It wasn't filled until three months later, when DCI Clarke joined the unit."

Collingwood nodded. "Did you continue to work with DCI Mackie because you thought you weren't capable of conducting an investigation that had previously been overseen by a DCI?"

"I was confident I could run the investigation. It was just a series of robberies."

"The case file says aggravated robbery."

"Yes."

"So not the straightforward case you're making out."

"No."

"Dennis, why aren't you telling me everything?"

Dennis looked at the man. "That's not true."

Collingwood gave him a long look. He stood up from his chair, across the table from Dennis. Next to him was a female detective who'd introduced herself as DC Dugdale and not spoken since. Collingwood turned his back to the table and pressed his fingers against the wall.

He turned back to Dennis, still standing.

If you're attempting to intimidate me, you won't succeed.

Dennis looked up at him, his face impassive. Or so he hoped.

"DS Frampton, how did you feel about DCI Mackie continuing to do police work after his retirement?"

"I didn't think it was wise."

"No. Illegal, in fact."

"He never made out that he was still a serving officer."

"He had you to do that for him."

Dennis said nothing.

"DS Frampton, did you speak to witnesses or interrogate evidence on Mackie's suggestion?"

Denis swallowed. "It was a case I was already heading up. He had suggestions, ideas. It was nothing I wouldn't have done anyway."

"No?"

"No."

"So why did you resist working collaboratively with Organised Crime on this investigation?"

Dennis felt his foot twitch. "I didn't resist anything."

"Organised Crime requested oversight of the case. They wanted to take it off you. You insisted that the MCIT should keep it. Why?"

"It was an investigation into aggravated robbery. Not organised crime."

"That's pretty naïve."

"I was given a case to investigate. I investigated it."

"Did you have an ulterior motive for hanging onto this case, Dennis?"

"No."

"You're sure?"

Dennis met the man's gaze. "Of course."

"Very well. Tell me about DC Johnny Chiles."

"What about him?"

"He was corrupt. You covered for him. With the collusion of your DCI."

"DCI Mackie knew nothing about what happened with Johnny. And Johnny was not corrupt."

"He was coerced into providing information for the Kelvins after they recruited his brother to their operation."

Dennis said nothing. Again, this wasn't a question.

"And you covered it up and helped arrange for DC Chiles to be transferred to the Met."

"The transfer was Johnny's idea. He—"

"Not only that, but you did so with the collusion of your DCI."

"I've already said. DCI Mackie didn't—"

Collingwood slammed his hand on the table. "Not DCI Mackie, Dennis. DCI Clarke."

CHAPTER NINETEEN

"It's chaos out there," Lesley said as she walked through the doorway into the body of the lighthouse. The tape had been removed; the site was secure, with only half a dozen people inside.

Gareth Bamford was packing up a case in front of her while Gail stood near him, calling up instructions to her team on the top of the platform. Tina was with her, making notes in a pad.

"Lesley," said the pathologist, "you've had a chance to chat to the press then."

"Not so much chat as tell them to bugger off. Who told them we were here?"

"None of us," Gail said.

Lesley shook her head. "Well whoever it was, I'm going to have to speak to them on my way out. Have we got anything useful I can tell them?"

"We've certainly got useful," Gareth said. "Not sure you'll want to tell the press, though."

"That sounds promising."

"He didn't die from the fall." The pathologist looked upwards. "He was pushed off the upper platform, but he was already dead. There's no bruising on his torso, only minor cracking to the ribs. If he'd died from that fall, he'd be in a much worse state."

"So how did he die?"

"I haven't managed to work that out yet. There are no visible injuries, not fatal ones, at least. He might have been poisoned."

"That sounds very Agatha Christie, for a man like Hamm."

"If it was the same people helped him escape as killed him," Tina pointed out, "it'd be easy to give him something. All they have to do is offer him a drink."

"You're right," Lesley said. "Dr Bamford, how long before we can get a toxicology report?"

"We'll need to get him to the morgue first."

"We're working on that," Gail said. "Gav and Brett are up there now. We've got the scaffolding guys coming back with a winch. We'll get him down."

"Be careful," Lesley told her. "We don't want to do any damage that might confuse the post-mortem."

"Don't worry," said Bamford. "We've got hundreds of photos, and I've made copious notes. If any damage is done to him, I'll know what it is."

Lesley nodded.

"And we won't damage him," Gail added. "We know what we're doing."

"That you do," said Lesley. "I don't suppose you've managed to find any other forensics? Anything left behind by his attacker?"

"Sorry," Gail said. "Like I told you last night, there's shoe prints everywhere. DI Angus's fingerprints, we've ruled those out. And we haven't found any fibres. Looks like whoever brought him up here was careful."

"We've spoken to the company that runs the lighthouse," Tina added. "To find out if there's CCTV."

"And?"

"There are cameras, at the front of the building. Another set round the back. Nothing inside."

"So all we'll be able to get is them bringing him in."

"He was wearing that jumpsuit," Gareth said. "He won't be hard to spot."

"Cameras are black and white," Tina told him.

"Typical," said Lesley. "OK. Have you asked for copies of the footage?"

"It's being sent to the office. All footage from the time Hamm escaped to the time he was found."

"Good."

"Meera's going to look at it." Tina looked at Lesley for a moment. "I haven't met her before. Is she...?"

"D'you think I'd have brought her onto the team if she wasn't a good detective?"

"No." Tina didn't look convinced. "No, you wouldn't." She nodded.

Lesley raised an eyebrow. Meera had worked with DC Mike Legg, Tina's husband, in the past. Was this a simple case of jealousy?

"She's just with us temporarily," Lesley said. "Until you and Mike are both back full time."

"Yeah."

"We needed another person."

"We did."

"Right. Glad that's sorted." Lesley looked up at the scaffolding. She could hear voices: Gavin and Brett discussing how they were going to get the body loaded onto the winch.

Rather them than me.

But there was no need for her to hang around and supervise. Everyone here knew what they were doing.

Back at the office, on the other hand, she had Stanley and Meera: the two newest members of the team. And she hadn't had a chance to speak to either of them since taking on the case.

She also had Dennis to think about. And Carpenter's threat.

"OK," she said. "Tina, I'll call you when I get back to HQ. I want you in on a team briefing."

"No problem, boss."

"Thanks. Can someone tell me when the body's been moved and is heading to the morgue?"

"Will do," said Gail.

"And I'll need to know when we've got that tox report."

"Of course," said Gareth.

"Thanks. Time to face the ladies and gentlemen of the press." Lesley sighed.

CHAPTER TWENTY

LESLEY PUSHED her shoulders back as she opened the door to the lighthouse. The wind blasted her from the side, almost making her stumble. The air was cold and sharp and the car park looked desolate, like something out of a post-apocalyptic movie.

She pulled on a tight smile as the press pack advanced on her, trying not to look like she wished they'd bugger off and leave her alone.

She raised a hand. "I'm going to make a brief statement, then I'd be grateful if you could let me and my team get on with our jobs."

Questions rang out. She ignored them. Sadie was at the front, looking at her with a question in her eyes.

Lesley frowned at her, then raised her chin to speak over the crowd.

"As has already been briefed to the press, Trevor Hamm managed to escape from custody while being transferred from HMP The Verne yesterday. I can now tell you that we have found Hamm's body inside the lighthouse. We are treating his death as suspicious. That's all I can tell you at this time."

The pack surged forward.

"Did armed police kill him?"

"Did he push himself off the cliffs?"

"Was it organised crime?"

"How did he escape?"

"What about his victims? Have you told their families?"

That last question was from Sadie. She had a point.

Lesley looked at her and nodded. "We will be speaking to them."

She'd need to make some calls, on her way back to the office. Start with Zoe, who was better placed to contact the families.

She could have refused to divulge the identity of the body. She could have refused even to say there was a body. But the journalists weren't stupid. They knew that the pathologist had been inside, and the CSIs. They knew that Lesley would only be here for a serious crime.

It was more respectful to the families, and easier with the press, if she gave them just enough information.

The rest would be communicated to the families directly. Although not too much of it; they couldn't rule out the possibility that one of Hamm's victims, or their family, might have been involved in his death.

With a well-planned prison break, however, it was unlikely. This was the work of organised criminals.

"Now please," she said. "Allow us to get on with our investigation into the escape and into Hamm's death. If you need any further information, speak to our press team."

More questions. Lesley ignored them. She didn't want to give out anything else until she'd spoken to Zoe.

And, reluctantly, to Carpenter.

She dropped her shoulders and pushed through the crowd. Moments later she was at her car.

As she put her hand on the door handle, she heard heavy breathing behind her. Someone running to catch up.

Leave it, she thought. *I've told you, you're not getting any more.*

"DCI Clarke!"

Lesley closed her eyes. It was Sadie.

She turned. "I can't tell you any more right now. You know as well as I do that it's above my pay grade."

Sadie shook her head. "That's not what I wanted to talk to you about."

The journalist looked over her shoulder. Two more men were advancing on them.

"Not here," she said. "Not now. But I've got information which might help Dennis Frampton."

CHAPTER TWENTY-ONE

Having a detective in her living room again made Gina feel cold. They'd sat here before, more than one of them. The only one who'd been kind to her, who hadn't just barked out questions and expected her to answer as if as she didn't want to curl up and die, had been DS Uddin.

This woman had been his boss. Gina hoped she'd be as sympathetic as he had been.

"I'm really sorry to have to dredge all this up," DI Finch said. "But I've got news which I wanted you to hear from me and not on the TV."

The door to the hall fell open and Danny ran in.

"Mum! He's dead!"

Gina frowned at him. "What? Who?"

The detective shifted on the sofa. She looked irritated.

"Mrs O'Toole," she said.

"Gina," Gina corrected her.

"Gina, that's what I came to tell you. Trevor Hamm has been killed."

Gina felt her body turn slack. "Killed?"

The detective nodded.

Gina could feel tears coming.

Tears?

Why would she want to cry? For that man? That man who'd put them through so much? That man who'd as good as killed her Susie?

"You'll be experiencing conflicting emotions," the detective told her. "Confusing ones. It's a shock, when a person dies who's done something to you of the magnitude that Trevor Hamm did to your family. It brings all the feelings rushing back."

Gina blinked. "Is that why I want to cry?"

"It is." The detective put her fist to her chin. "I'm sorry."

Gina shook her head. "Don't be. It's not your fault." She hesitated. "Danny, where's Dad?"

"I don't know."

"I'm sorry, Detective. I don't want Danny hearing all this."

"Mum, I deserve to—"

She turned to her son. "Don't worry, love. I'm not going to hide anything from you. But you need to hear it from me, not from the police. Go and find your dad. I'll be as quick as I can."

Danny sniffed then left the room, calling "Dad!" as he did so. Gina heard Rick's voice from upstairs and let out a breath in relief.

"Carry on," she said to the detective. "Please, though, be quick."

"I will. We found Trevor Hamm's body in a lighthouse on the Isle of Portland, just a couple of miles from the prison and the spot where he escaped. We're treating his death as suspicious."

"The same people got him out then killed him?"

"It's a possibility, but not the only one."

Gina nodded.

"We have to consider the possibility that this might have been done by someone who wanted revenge on him."

Gina felt her skin turn cold. "You're not suggesting..."

"No. I'm not. But if there's anything you might have heard. I know you've kept in touch with the families of some of the other victims. If anyone has said anything about a possible escape or attack..."

"No one's said anything like that. And we're just... we're just normal people. We don't do that sort of thing."

"I know. I'm sorry I have to ask you. But I don't believe Trevor Hamm was killed by any of his victims or their families."

"It'll be other men like him," Gina said. She could hear her voice breaking. It killed her to know there were more men like Trevor Hamm out in the world. She looked towards the door. *Rick, I hope you're looking after Danny.*

The detective stood up. "Is there anything else relating to the phone call you got, that you think might be helpful?"

"I've told you everything I know."

"You didn't get any other strange phone calls? No silent calls, withheld numbers?"

"Not that I can remember."

"Gina, do you mind if I ask your phone provider for a record of calls made to your number?"

"Of course. Me and Rick have got mobiles, and there's the landline. That's what he called on."

DI Finch nodded. "What about your son?"

"He doesn't have a phone. We won't let him."

Danny had kicked up such a fuss about not being allowed a phone. But it was through her mobile that Hamm's men had got to Susie. She'd been groomed, or at least that's what the police had told her. Gina hadn't been able to take it in.

"I'll leave you and your family to your weekend. If you think of anything that might be helpful, please call me." The detective handed over a card with her phone number and the West Midlands Police crest on it.

Gina nodded. "I'm sorry."

The detective was at the door. She stopped, her hand on the wood. "You've got nothing to apologise for, Gina. I'm only sorry that the system has let you down like this."

CHAPTER TWENTY-TWO

"Morning, Stanley. Meera, good to have you on board. I hope Stanley's looking after you."

Meera smiled across the desks. "He got me a coffee when I arrived, Ma'am."

Lesley looked at Stanley and raised her eyebrows. "Never did that for me."

"I'm sorry, boss," Stanley said, "I—"

"I'm pulling your leg, Stanley. And Meera, less of the ma'aming."

"Sorry. Boss."

"Good. What have you been up to while I've been at the end of the universe?"

"Er...?" replied Stanley.

"Portland Bill. Haven't you noticed that the closer you get to the lighthouse, the more you feel like you might fall off the edge of the world?"

Stanley shrugged. "Never been, boss."

"You've lived in Dorset how long?"

"All my life."

"Thirty-two years. And you've never thought to go to Portland."

Another shrug. "There're people in Portland who've never set foot on the mainland, boss. No reason it can't work the other way round."

"People who've never left the 'island'?" Lesley waggled her fingers in air-quotes. She was getting used to islands that weren't really islands. Purbeck, Portland. "It's only a couple of miles long."

Stanley shook his head. "Don't ask me. They must like it there." He grimaced.

"Hmm." Lesley didn't comment on the wisdom or otherwise of *liking it there*. From what she'd seen, Portland was a bleak place, with more seagulls in evidence than people.

"OK," she said. "Enough of the grockle chatter. Let's see where we are." She walked into her office, waiting for the others to follow.

Lesley's office was a glass box to one side of the team office. It was separated from the large team room by a glass partition and from the car park below them by a wide window. It got bloody freezing in here right up until April, and then it steadily progressed to sauna temperatures throughout the summer. And it gave no privacy.

The board was to one side of the room on a stand, its back turned to them. Lesley pulled it out and turned it to face them.

Someone had been busy. Trevor Hamm's photo had been pinned to the top along with images of six others.

"Stanley, can you get Tina on speakerphone?"

Stanley pulled out his mobile and dialled Tina, then placed it on Lesley's desk.

"Tina," Lesley surveyed the board as she spoke. "You there?"

"I'm in an office at the lighthouse, boss."

"Good. Any new developments?"

"The press are dispersing. Seems you got through to them."

"Well that's something. I'm in my office with Stanley and Meera. Who's added these to the board?"

"Me," said Stanley.

"Good. Ugh. I remember these bastards." Lesley approached the board and surveyed the photos. Howard Petersen, Jory Shand, Robert Oulman, Simon Adams, Kyle Gattis and Adam Fulmer.

"We got all the files on Hamm from HOLMES," Stanley said. "This lot are some of his key associates."

"Where are they now?"

"Petersen, Shand and Oulman were arrested as part of Canary."

"I know that. I was there."

"Petersen was killed, by Hamm's group," said Meera. "Shand got off with a suspended sentence, and it looks like he's kept his nose clean since. Oulman got a three-year sentence for money laundering."

Lesley nodded. She remembered watching the trial. "The other three?"

"Simon Adams was one of Hamm's deputies. He was imprisoned following the death of the West Midlands Assistant Chief Constable."

"For theft. It was a family member who killed him."

Meera frowned.

"So what did Hamm's gang have to do with that?" Tina asked from the phone.

"ACC Jackson was corrupt," Lesley said. "He'd been tipping Hamm off to investigations that might compromise him. His killer found out."

Stanley whistled. Lesley gave him a glance but said nothing.

"If I remember right," she continued, "Gattis was sent down for impersonating a prison officer and Fulmer for people smuggling."

"If Gattis has impersonated a prison officer before, then—" began Stanley.

"He's still in jail," Meera interrupted. "Winson Green in Birmingham."

"Nowhere near Portland," Lesley said. "Are any of them in The Verne?"

"None of them," replied Stanley.

"Is anyone with a prior connection to Hamm in The Verne?"

"Not that we know of. Although he might have made connections after he got there."

Lesley tapped her fingertips against her chin. "I want to know about the regime at The Verne. How much opportunity Hamm will have had to make contacts there. Whether he was involved in planning his escape, or it was done for him."

"Or *to* him," suggested Meera.

"Indeed." If the same people had busted him out and killed him, it was unlikely he would have been behind it.

"There's the Brum Boys," said Stanley. "New organised crime group, muscled in on Hamm's territory after his arrest. They were already operational, but smaller."

"And have they taken over all aspects of his operation? The people trafficking? The kids?"

Meera shook her head. "From HOLMES, it looks like it's mainly drugs they're focused on. No evidence of trafficking yet. Prostitution, yes, but no international operations."

Lesley sighed. Sometimes it seemed like they talked about

these organisations as if they were legitimate international businesses.

Men like Trevor Hamm – and local crime boss Arthur Kelvin, whose killer she'd recently had to identify – hid their crimes behind legitimate businesses. But they were nothing of the sort.

"OK," she said. "We need to know more about these Brum Boys. I'd like one of you two to talk to a DI in the West Midlands called Zoe Finch. She was part of my team when I was up there, and she knows these bastards inside out. If I know Zoe, she'll have spoken to her contacts in Organised Crime and she might be able to fill us in on the details without going round the houses."

"I can do that," said Meera.

"Good. Stanley, I want you on witness statements. The Home Office did a press conference last night, in their infinite wisdom. I'm sure half of Portland will've been ringing in with alleged sightings. Find out where the calls have gone to, make sure we have sight of what's coming in. And report back if anything seems legit."

"Boss." Stanley made a note in his pad. "We got any forensics or the PM results yet?"

"Gail can't find anything useful so far," Lesley replied.

"They're making progress with moving the body," Tina said.

"There's CCTV," added Meera. "We're still waiting for that to come in."

"I sent it to the team inbox," Tina said.

"Thanks." Meera glanced towards the outer office, no doubt eager to get back on her computer.

Lesley nodded. "You go through it. I also want to know if

any traffic cameras picked up the escape. Where exactly did it happen? Any lucky passersby manage to get phone footage?"

"We can look on social media," said Stanley.

"Do that."

And what was Lesley going to be doing?

She wasn't sure. She still needed to speak to Dennis, despite Carpenter's warnings. And she needed to brief Carpenter on the case.

She rubbed her cheeks. Carpenter. Might as well get him out of the way first.

CHAPTER TWENTY-THREE

It was going to be easier to lie to Carpenter over the phone than face to face.

Lesley drove out of the police HQ car park, going over the calls she had to make in her head.

First, there was Carpenter to placate. Then she needed to speak to Dennis. She wanted to check in with Zoe and see if there was news on the Birmingham angle of the case, as well as warning her she'd be getting a call from Meera. And finally, there was Sadie Dawes.

What did Sadie know about Dennis, and would it help his defence?

Or had Lesley misjudged him all long? Had Sadie uncovered evidence that pointed to Dennis killing his former boss?

He'd certainly been acting strangely enough in recent weeks. When they'd disbanded the investigation into Mackie's murder and DCI Phipps had returned to Hampshire, Dennis had brightened, getting back to work at his usual pace and with no more mysterious absences.

But since their last case – Arthur Kelvin's death – Dennis

had gone back to being the anxious, worried man he was a year ago.

Arthur Kelvin was connected to Mackie's death. Lesley could feel it in her blood. But did that mean Dennis was in all this deeper than she'd thought, or would it help her get him off?

Her phone rang.

"Tina. Have they managed to get him off that bloody lens yet?"

"He's on his way to the morgue as we speak. Gail and her team have still got the scaffolding up and they're examining the lens for any evidence. They're also going over the platform above it again."

"OK. Let me know if they find anything."

"Will do. You want me to stay here?"

"I know it's not the best spot to find yourself stuck in on your first few days back—"

"It's alright, boss. I'd rather be at the crime scene than stuck in the office."

"Really?" Tina was normally good at the 'stuck in the office' stuff.

"I've been stuck indoors with Louis the last three months. Having a baby in the winter's no fun. It takes an age to get him all wrapped up to go out, and then he fills his nappy and I have to start all over again."

Lesley stopped at red lights: the level crossing in Wool. She grimaced at her phone in its cradle.

"I don't envy you."

"It's fine. Worth it, isn't it?"

It was. Sharon was a million times more rewarding now she was a young woman. And Lesley saw more of her too, since the divorce from Terry.

"It is."

"Don't tell Mike, but I'm feeling a bit smug about him being back there and me being at work."

"Well, all I can say is it's good to have you back."

"It's good to be back."

Four cars ahead, Lesley could see the barriers being raised.

"I need to go, Tina. Keep me updated."

"Will do, boss."

As Lesley drove over the crossing, she hit speed dial for Carpenter. She sat up in her seat and gripped the steering wheel tighter.

"Detective Superintendent Carpenter's Office."

"Carla, it's Lesley. Can you put me through?"

"One moment."

Lesley tapped the steering wheel as she waited, running through the conversation in her head.

"Lesley. Why haven't you put a leash on those Home Office arseholes yet?"

OK.

That wasn't what she'd been expecting.

"What's happened, Sir?"

"Crawford's done another press conference. He's given the press details about how we found Hamm's body. The kind of thing that if we'd kept it under wraps, might help us solve the crime."

"What kind of details?"

"The fact that he was already dead when he was pushed, for one."

"*What?*"

How had Crawford known about that? The only people present when Gareth Bamford had examined the body up close had been Gail's team, Tina and herself.

So who was talking to Crawford?

And if he'd returned to the crime scene, why hadn't Tina told her?

"Leave it with me, Sir."

"No, Lesley. This goes above your level. I need to involve the ACC. And speak to our press office."

"Are you suggesting a press conference of your own?"

"Dear God, no. What d'you take me for, a total idiot? No, we need to calm things down. Stop all the speculation."

"Generally the best way to stop speculation is to be honest."

"In a murder inquiry, DCI Clarke, you only release the information you need to. Specific details of the crime can be used to help identify a suspect."

"I do know that, Sir. But there will be information that Crawford has not passed on to the press."

"We don't know that right now."

Lesley sighed. "Do you need me to find out who's talking to him?"

"No. Leave it alone. It's a political minefield, and I know what you can be like."

She glanced at the phone. *If you're going to criticise me, at least do it straight.*

"Sir, I have other calls to make relating to the case. We may need to send detectives up to Birmingham to interview some of Hamm's former associates and victims."

"You have contacts up there."

"I do. I was involved in Hamm's arrest, as you know."

"Very well. I'll authorise a team of no more than two going up there. But talk to me first, so we can square it with senior officers in West Midlands."

Lesley sighed. She didn't need to work up and down the chain of command to go to Birmingham and work with Zoe.

Not from a practical perspective, and not from a procedural one. Carpenter was covering his arse.

"Thank you, Sir."

She hung up, grateful at least that Carpenter hadn't mentioned Dennis.

CHAPTER TWENTY-FOUR

"DCI Clarke has got nothing to do with any of this." Dennis tried to stop his feet shifting under the table. DI Collingwood looked at him, an eyebrow raised. The man had a faint birthmark the shape of half a star on his chin, and Dennis was struggling not to stare at it.

"You two have become close since she transferred down here from the West Midlands. Did you know that her boss up there had to go into witness protection after he gave evidence against an organised crime group he'd been helping?"

Dennis almost bit his tongue. He knew nothing of the sort.

But just because Lesley had worked for a corrupt officer, didn't mean she was corrupt herself. His experience was that she was the kind of DCI who leaned heavily on procedure and doing things by the book. And she was too abrasive for organised crime to want to work with her.

"I did not," he said. "But that has nothing to do with DCI Mackie's death. If that even happened, it took place before DCI Clarke started here."

"True. Let's go back to DCI Chiles. When did you

discover that Johnny was feeding information to an organised crime group?"

Dennis had no idea how PSD had got hold of this. As far as he was concerned, he was the only person Johnny had spoken to. And it had only happened a few times. Johnny had left for the Met before it had had a chance to ruin him.

He swallowed.

Johnny had been a trusted colleague for years. It had taken all the reserves Dennis had to promise Johnny he wouldn't betray him. Not to the DCI, not to anybody.

"DCI Clarke did not know that Johnny was talking to the Kelvins."

"That wasn't what I asked you."

Dennis pinched the flesh on the ball of his thumb, under the table.

Lying would be pointless.

He wondered if Professional Services in the Met had spoken to Johnny. He hadn't heard from his old colleague in over a year.

"I discovered that Johnny had been compromised when we were investigating the Ameena Khan and Harry Nevin murders."

"And you covered for him."

"He requested a transfer. I supported that."

"So that you wouldn't have to report him."

"So that he would be removed from the influence of the Kelvins." Dennis looked at his interrogator. Had the Kelvins got to Johnny, in London? Was that how PSD knew?

"Where is Johnny now?" he asked.

"Never mind that. How much did DCI Clarke know about all this?"

"I did not tell her my suspicions."

"Again, not what I asked. What did she know?"

"I'm not sure." Dennis thought back to the conversation he'd had with the DCI. She was an astute woman; she would have been able to read between the lines. But nothing had been said.

He shook his head. "I did the wrong thing, not reporting what I knew about Johnny Chiles to my commanding officer. I realise that."

"Bit late now."

"DC Chiles was – is – a good detective. He had found himself in an impossible position."

"That's how corruption always starts, DS Frampton. Is that how it started with you? You found yourself in an impossible position? Couldn't afford the mortgage, perhaps? Wife spending money you weren't earning?"

Never. Pam was one of the most financially careful women he knew. She kept a record of all their transactions and knew the balance of their bank account to the nearest penny.

"No," he said, trying to keep his voice level.

"Maybe it was to do with your son, Jacob." Collingwood gestured to his colleague, DC Dugdale. She placed a sheet of paper on the table.

A bank statement.

Dennis narrowed his eyes and looked at it. He said nothing.

"Can you describe the document in front of you, DS Frampton?"

"It's a bank statement."

"A bank statement for whose account?"

"Jurassic Holdings Limited."

Collingwood picked up the paper. "That's the name of the company. It's a savings account. Do you know who owns, or rather owned, Jurassic Holdings Limited?"

"I'm afraid I don't."

"Of course you don't." Collingwood took a pen from the inside pocket of his suit, underlined a row in the statement, and put the sheet of paper back down. He jabbed the spot he'd underlined with a finger. "Whose name is that?"

Dennis leaned over. He felt his throat close up. "Jacob Frampton," he said. He felt sweat prickle on his forehead.

There was more than one Jacob Frampton, surely.

"Your son's name is Jacob Frampton."

"It is. But that doesn't—"

"We checked the account details, and this transaction does indeed go into your son's account."

Dennis made an involuntary sound. He felt sick.

"Can you explain that?"

"Not without knowing what this Jurassic Holdings is. My son is a financial advisor. There's no reason why—"

"Jurassic Holdings was owned by Arthur Kelvin. We're not sure who owns it now he's dead. His family, I imagine. But this bank statement shows money going from a company owned by the biggest crime boss in Dorset, a man who you were investigating and who we believe is connected to the death of DCI Mackie, to your son."

Dennis nodded. His feet were numb.

"Can you explain that, DS Frampton?"

CHAPTER TWENTY-FIVE

LESLEY PULLED up a few houses along from Dennis's and on the opposite side of the road.

She scanned the quiet street for vehicles looking like they might belong to the police. There was nothing.

Good.

She stretched her back as she got out of the car. She was still paying for the drive back from Loch Lomond, earlier in the week.

Dennis's front garden was as neat and tidy as ever. She knew that at the weekends he weeded the block paving and that once a month, he got the pressure washer out. His car was on the drive: clean and tidy.

Hopefully, that meant he was at home. She knew he hadn't been kept in custody, and she hoped being at home would help him to adjust to what was happening.

The door opened and a short middle-aged woman with wavy grey hair and a pale apron stood in front of her.

"DCI Clarke," she said. "It's kind of you to come."

Lesley smiled. "How are you?"

"Bearing up." Pam Frampton looked along the street as if expecting to see someone there, watching her. "You know how it is."

Lesley didn't know how it was to have your spouse arrested, despite a fleeting moment during her last case when she had thought Elsa might be a suspect. But she nodded in sympathy.

"Can I speak to him, please? He's not ill, I hope?"

Pam's face dropped. "I'm so sorry, DCI Clarke."

"Oh?"

"I'm so sorry. He's gone out."

Lesley frowned. "I hope he comes back soon. They've tagged him, haven't they?"

"Oh, I don't think that will be an issue." Pam's face grew more grave.

"Where is he? What's happened?"

"He's being questioned."

"Organised Crime already spoke to him. Surely—"

"Not by the organised crime men. By Professional... Professional..."

"Professional Standards."

"That's it." A grave nod. "They took him this morning." Pam clutched her apron. "Is that alright, DCI Clarke? Should he not have gone with them?"

"They're Professional Standards. When they knock on your door, you go. But I'd be grateful if you could tell me when he returns."

"Of course."

"And don't tell anyone I came by."

"Oh. Of course. No." Dennis's wife closed the door.

Lesley turned back to her car. She wondered where Dennis

had been taken. Was he in an interview room in Dorset Police HQ somewhere, being treated like a criminal?

Dennis was no criminal.

She slid behind the wheel and started the ignition. She'd just turned out of Dennis's quiet road when her phone rang.

"DCI Clarke."

"DCI Clarke, it's Sadie. I was expecting a call."

"You were next on my list. What's this information you've got?"

"I've been looking into DCI Mackie's death."

"Since over a year ago. You've made a bloody nuisance of yourself."

"To be fair, that is my job."

"True. What have you got on Dennis?"

Silence.

"Sadie?"

"Sorry. There's someone waiting for the phone."

"Don't tell me you're in a call box."

"In Weymouth."

Why was she not using her mobile? This wasn't exactly Watergate.

"I'm heading over that way," Lesley said.

"I can imagine."

"OK, Sadie. This is what we'll do. You sit tight in Weymouth. I've got some people I need to speak to, in connection with Trevor Hamm's death. I'll call you when I'm done and we can talk. And you'd better have something useful for me, or—"

"We can meet at Portland Bill. I'm heading back over there now."

Lesley sighed. "Don't interfere with the CSIs' job, will you?"

"What makes you think I'd do that?"

When they'd been investigating a double murder on Brownsea Island, Sadie had hired a boat and managed to get in the way when Lesley was about to apprehend a suspect. Sadie was good at interfering.

"I'll see you in the car park."

"Too public," Sadie told her. "Turn off before you get to the car park and go past the bird observatory. I'll see you there, by the beach huts."

"What beach huts?" There was no beach by the lighthouse.

"The ones that look like someone planted a shanty town of sheds at the top of the cliffs."

Lesley couldn't remember any huts. But last night it had been dark, and today she'd been distracted.

She'd find it.

"Very well. And this had better not just be your way of getting to me so you can find out more about Trevor Hamm."

CHAPTER TWENTY-SIX

"Want to help me look at the CCTV?" Meera asked Stanley. "I've just picked it up from the team inbox."

Stanley looked across to her. Meera had moved from the spot she'd occupied while temporarily assigned to them as part of DI Varney's team. Now she was formally one of them, she no longer sat at the separate bank of desks but had taken Mike's place next to Stanley. The sarge's desk, next to Tina's, was empty, but no one was about to sit there.

"Yeah," he said. "How many cameras have we got?"

"Four. Two at the front, two at the back. Which ones d'you want?"

"I'll take the back." The front seemed more obvious, but if Stanley had to smuggle a body into a lighthouse, he'd go round the back. "I assume there's an entrance at the back."

She shrugged. "I guess we're about to find out."

Stanley nodded agreement then opened up the team inbox on his computer. Sure enough, there was an email from the lighthouse manager with four files attached. He saved them to the case folder then opened the first.

The camera was positioned on the back of the building, at an angle which showed the ground immediately to the rear of the lighthouse and some of the area behind it. He could make out the cliffs and the sea behind at the bottom right of shot.

"I'm on the back," he said. "Five thirty am on Friday."

Meera's gaze was on her screen. "I've got the same time, on the front."

"What time did Hamm escape?"

"Seventeen minutes after this."

"So we need to skip forward." Stanley grabbed his mouse.

"Just because he couldn't have been at the lighthouse yet, doesn't mean his attacker might not have gone there before-hand to prepare."

"Or attackers."

"Or attackers."

"OK," Stanley said. "I'll hit play, then."

He started the video and Meera did the same. He glanced sideways and noted the expression on her face as she watched. Her eyes were wide, like she was making sure everything went in.

Three minutes later, all he'd seen was a pair of seagulls making their way along some rocks behind the lighthouse. Their feathers were being buffeted by the wind.

Rather them than me.

"Shall we run it on double speed?" he suggested. "I don't think we'll miss anything."

"OK." Meera clicked her mouse and Stanley did the same.

Still nothing. The seagulls walked faster now, but they were still seagulls. Not criminals, unless shitting on people's heads or nicking their chips counted as a crime.

"I'm speeding up more," he said. They switched to eight

times normal speed. Stanley narrowed his eyes to make sure he didn't miss anything.

"Hang on," Meera said after thirty minutes or so. "I'm slowing down again."

Stanley checked the time stamp: 6.22 pm. He clicked his mouse and switched to regular playback. The back of the lighthouse showed no sign of movement; even the birds had gone.

"I've got a vehicle turning up," Meera said. She had her hand on the edge of her monitor.

Stanley pushed his chair towards her desk. "What kind of vehicle?"

"SUV of some description. Hang on." She zoomed in and read out a registration plate.

"On it." Stanley went back to his desk and typed it into the system.

"There's people getting out," Meera said.

Stanley was still working his way through registration plates. "Can you check that number again?"

"The plate?"

"Yeah."

Meera frowned at her screen then read it out again.

"You're sure that's what you can see?"

"I am. Let me watch while they get out."

Stanley typed in the plate again. Maybe he'd done it wrong.

"Nope," he said, leaning back in his chair.

"Nope what?"

"Nope, that reg doesn't exist."

"You what?"

"No record of it. It's a forged plate."

"At least that tells us these must be organised criminals."

Stanley looked across at Meera's screen. A figure had

emerged from the vehicle, which could now be clearly identified as a Range Rover.

Original.

The person that had got out had their back to the lighthouse and their hood pulled up. They wore a thick black coat that made them look like they'd had too many roast dinners.

"Can you see anything from the back?" Meera asked, her gaze not leaving the screen.

"Sorry. Just a seagull crapping on a rock."

A smile twitched on her lips, but she didn't look across.

Focused. Determined. The kind of colleague who could either be an asset, or a right pain in the arse, depending on how ambitious they were.

His recollection was that her colleague, DC Young, had been the ambitious one. She'd been so far up the DCI's arse he was surprised she could see.

"Uh-oh," Meera said.

Stanley left his fruitless vehicle check and pushed across to her desk. "What's happening?"

"What d'you think that is, in the boot?"

He leaned in. "Could be Hamm. Might just be a holdall or something." The shape was too dim.

"I know what you mean."

"If they're going to get him into that lighthouse, they'll have to take him out. And then we'll get to see his face."

"Let's hope so." Meera put a finger in her mouth and started chewing the edge of a nail.

"Here we go," Stanley said. Another figure had emerged from the passenger door and was bending over the shape in the boot. Like the first person, this one wore a heavy dark coat, and Stanley couldn't see their face.

"I reckon they know there are cameras," he said.

"They're not exactly hidden."

"They aren't."

Meera pointed at the screen and pulled in a breath. The two men had pulled the shape out of the boot.

"That's a body," she said.

"It is."

"But whose?"

Stanley gave her a look. "It's not as if there's more than one of them in that lighthouse."

"It's black and white. Otherwise we'd get a flash of that jumpsuit."

"They've wrapped him in something," Stanley pointed out. "We might not."

Meera's gaze flicked to the top of her screen. "This is 6.34 pm. What time does the place close to the public?"

"Five pm. Over an hour earlier."

"The car park's deserted."

Stanley pointed at the screen. "There's a car there."

"Maybe someone who works there."

The two men lifted the shape – the body – from the boot of the car and hoisted it up. Quickly, they carried it towards the door to the lighthouse.

"They're just going to walk in the front door?" Stanley said.

"Looks like it."

The door opened and a woman stepped out. She wore a uniform and a grim expression that Stanley could see even on the low-resolution image. She gestured into the building, then at the men, then back into the building.

"She's an employee," Meera said.

"Can you zoom in on her?"

Meera nodded and clicked her mouse a few times. Even at top resolution, Stanley couldn't make out much of the woman's face. But he was sure she was wearing a uniform. Most likely the lighthouse uniform.

"We need to track her down," Meera said.

"We do."

The lighthouse woman held the door open as the two hooded men shuffled past with their load. Stanley watched as the three of them disappeared inside, then looked at Meera.

"They've got someone on the inside," he said.

CHAPTER TWENTY-SEVEN

"My son is a financial advisor," Dennis said. "He could well have been doing some work for the Kelvins."

"Where is your son based?"

"London."

"And the Kelvins are based in Dorset. Why don't they use someone local?"

Dennis met DI Collingwood's eye. "You'd have to ask them that."

It wasn't exactly uncommon for people in Dorset to hire professionals from London, after all.

He stood up. "Is this all you have?"

DC Dugdale jerked in her chair. Collingwood looked at Dennis. "Where are you going?"

"You didn't arrest me," Dennis said. "I'm speaking to you as a courtesy."

"If you killed your senior officer, then we need to be involved."

"You and DI Gough think I killed DCI Mackie because

Arthur Kelvin was paying my son money. I don't see how that adds up."

"There are phone calls."

"Between me and him, on the day he died. Yes. I've already told you he was still investigating the Kelvins, and I was helping him."

Collingwood looked uncomfortable. Dennis stayed where he was. His heart was pounding and he ached to pick up that bank statement and look at it again.

Jacob, what in goodness name were you doing?

"Your son will be called as a witness when your case goes to trial. In the meantime, you cannot speak to him."

Dennis blinked. He didn't speak to Jacob all that much; it was Pam who answered the phone.

"Very well," he said.

"And neither can your wife."

He pursed his lips.

He needed to hire a lawyer. The lawyer would be able to speak to Jacob, and find out what was really going on.

They had nothing.

"Have you spoken to my son?" he asked the DI.

"Organised Crime have."

"And?"

Collingwood smiled. "We're not about to share information from another witness with you, DS Frampton."

"No." Not yet, Dennis thought. But when it came to trial, if it ever got that far, they'd have to disclose what they had.

"So. Are you going to sit down again?"

"I came here today as a courtesy. I'm entitled to a solicitor."

"You are."

Dennis eyed him. "In that case, I'm asserting my right to pause this interview until I have a solicitor present."

Collingwood leaned back. He had pronounced five o'clock shadow, even at lunchtime. He shared a look with DC Dugdale. "Very well. You can make the phone call, and we'll wait for you in here. Fran, can you escort DS Frampton to a phone?"

"I can." DC Dugdale stood up.

Dennis shook his head. "I want time to find the most appropriate solicitor for the case."

"Dennis, I know you've been permitted to stay at home until your trial, but we can't have you slowing things down. Go and make a phone call now, and hopefully your solicitor will be with us in an hour or so."

Dennis pursed his lips.

He only knew the names of two criminal lawyers. And neither woman would be his first choice.

CHAPTER TWENTY-EIGHT

"Your prison has had quite a week." Lesley sat in a threadbare chair opposite the governor of HMP The Verne, smoothing her trousers down her legs. His office was large but unkempt, with a hint of damp.

Thomas Gordon steepled his hands in front of him, spinning lightly in his chair. For a man who'd just lost a prisoner, he seemed very relaxed.

"Oh, we'll cope. But of course, I'll do anything I can to help the murder inquiry. You do realise that the Home Office are also mounting an investigation into the escape?"

"I've met Jacob Crawford."

"This prison and its staff have nothing to account for. We did our job, followed procedure. It was a Protektis vehicle which was compromised in the attack."

Lesley resisted rolling her eyes. *That's it,* she thought. *Blame someone else.*

She gave him the sweetest smile she could muster. "I'm sure the Home Office will get to the bottom of it." A dangerous criminal had been allowed to escape and had wound up dead.

Careers would end over this. She imagined questions were being asked of ministers right now, not that she cared.

"So," he said. "Your responsibility is the murder case. And you think I can help you."

"To find out who killed Hamm," she replied, "we need to establish who wanted him out of jail, and who wanted him dead."

"The 'who wanted him out of jail' element is for the Home Office."

Lesley shook her head. "The two might be the same. They might be connected. It's safe to assume his death is directly related to his escape, so we'll need information about that."

A sigh. "Very well. We've mounted our own internal investigation, of course."

"And?"

"We haven't found evidence of any other inmates being involved. Hamm kept himself to himself. He was housed in a secure wing and didn't make any friends."

"What about phone calls?"

"Phone calls?"

"How often was Hamm allowed to make external phone calls?"

"Once a day. It's every prisoner's right."

"Do you monitor phone calls?"

"Not the content. Prisoners have to provide us with the numbers they're calling. We put through the call, and then leave them to it."

"Even the high-risk prisoners like Hamm?"

"It's procedure, DCI Clarke. Same for all inmates."

"I'll need a list of the numbers Hamm was approved to call while he was incarcerated here."

"Why?"

"How carefully did you check the list of numbers for Hamm?"

"He handed over a list when he arrived with us, and we checked it before he was allowed to make any calls."

"He called one of his victims."

Gordon shook his head. "No. He didn't."

"I have a statement from the mother of one of the children he abused, saying he phoned her."

"I'm sorry, DCI Clarke, but that couldn't have happened. We have very—"

"Governor Gordon, I really don't care about your procedures or your checks. Somehow Trevor Hamm got hold of the number of a victim's family and called it. Somewhere, your processes went wrong."

Gordon stared back at her. "Who?"

"Just provide us with the list of numbers Hamm called, please."

He eyed her for a moment. "OK."

"Good. Are you absolutely sure no one inside this prison was involved with Hamm's escape?"

"No one that we can find. Like I say, he didn't make friends."

"Is there anyone else here who was associated with Hamm in Birmingham?"

"No brummies at all."

"Really?"

"Really."

"They don't have to be brummie to have been part of his operation."

"DCI Clarke, we're stretched for resources as it is. We don't have the time to find out if our inmates were pals on the outside. If they were, it soon comes out in the wash."

I bet it does.

"So did Hamm have anyone in particular he spoke to, among the inmates?"

"No one. He kept himself to himself."

Lesley cocked her head. "He spoke to no one?"

"Not that any of my officers witnessed."

Either they weren't looking very hard, or the governor was covering something up. Lesley found it difficult to believe Hamm had never spoken to another inmate.

"OK," she said. "What about the escape? Did you have cameras on the van he was travelling in?"

He shook his head. "Not our van."

Lesley resisted an urge to punch the desk between them. "Whose van, then?"

"Protektis. If there were cameras, they'll have the recordings."

Lesley stood up. "It seems we need to speak to them, then. I don't suppose you've got a contact for the prison, at Protektis?"

"We have." Gordon scribbled on a pad and tossed a piece of paper across the desk.

Lesley picked it up. *Giulia Russo, prison liaison.* That would be her next point of call.

CHAPTER TWENTY-NINE

TINA WAS COLD. The lighthouse building was thick-walled and barely heated, and any warmth would travel straight up to the top and out via the glass.

She rubbed her arms, wishing she'd worn something more substantial than her oldest suit. When she'd joined CID she'd bought three new jackets and two pairs of trousers, along with some smart shirts. But since Louis's birth, none of those fitted; she was reduced to wearing the suit her sister had bought her when she'd first joined the force. Not much point, she'd argued, since she'd be in uniform. But Sam wasn't to be argued with.

She checked her watch: just gone 1pm. Mike would be putting Louis down for his afternoon nap, maybe taking him for a walk in his pushchair to help him get off.

Despite herself, she was missing her son. She kept imagining what he and his dad would be doing, picturing herself curled up on the sofa with him curled in her arms. Being at home alone with a baby had driven her potty, she knew it. But it was amazing how the mind managed to filter out the crappy stuff and remember the good.

Still, the effect wasn't so powerful that she had any intention of having another one any time soon. It would take reserves of energy Tina didn't possess.

"Tina?" Gail put her head around the door leading to the gift shop.

"Yes?" Tina realised she was miles away. "Sorry."

"We've got something that might be useful."

"Oh. What?"

"A footprint."

"I thought we had hundreds of those."

"This one's different."

Tina followed Gail into the gift shop and through to a tiny room off it. They were at the front of the building now, no longer in the lighthouse itself.

Brett was in a corner, firing off photographs, his camera pointing towards the floor.

"The manager told me they had decorating work done, started on Friday," Gail said, "and there's a paint print there."

Tina looked where Gail was pointing. She shifted around the CSM and waited for Brett to move aside.

The print was hidden from view behind a pile of boxes. It was smudged; something had been put on top of it.

She looked around the room. "Pale grey. Same colour as the walls."

Gail nodded. "It's the new colour. They hadn't finished." She gestured towards one wall, which was pale blue at the top. "Whoever left that, they trod in the new paint."

"Which means that footprint was left after Friday. And the lighthouse hasn't been open since then."

"Exactly."

CHAPTER THIRTY

LESLEY DROVE AWAY from the prison. The road was narrow, with a steep incline to one side. She glanced towards the Marina and the mainland beyond, clearly visible from here.

There was only one road on and off the peninsula. It should have made the place secure. But clearly someone had thought it possible to get Trevor Hamm onto the mainland.

They'd failed, although they'd managed to get away themselves. Either that, or leaving Hamm where he was, dead, had been their intention all along.

But who were they?

She hit hands-free on her phone.

"Stanley, I need you to call Protektis. A woman called Guilia Russo. She's their liaison with HMP The Verne, they're responsible for the transport vans. If anyone's got CCTV footage of the escape, it'll be them."

"Right, boss. We've got CCTV from the lighthouse too."

"Anything useful?"

"Very useful. Two people bringing Hamm's body in via the front door at 6.34 pm."

"The front door?"

"Looks like they had someone on the inside working with them. There's a woman in a lighthouse uniform opening the door for them."

"Surely she'd have known about the CCTV? Bit stupid to let yourself be filmed."

"You can't see her face."

"How d'you know it's a woman, then?"

She reached the main road running from the mainland to Portland Bill and indicated left.

"Stanley?"

"Er... her shape. It's clearly a woman."

"Send it to me. I'm heading to the lighthouse now, I'll get a list of staff there."

"We've already got one, boss."

Lesley smiled as she pulled out, making for the lighthouse. Mist had descended, lending the place an eerie feel.

"Tell me you've got photos, too."

"HR files," Stanley said. "The lighthouse company are very keen to help us."

"I bet they are."

The sooner the lighthouse was finished with as a crime scene, the sooner they'd be able to get paying customers back in. Lesley wondered if the fact a body had been dropped onto the lamp would increase the interest, or diminish it.

Increase it, most likely. People were ghoulish.

"OK, send it over. I'll talk to Tina, see if she recognises any of them. And we'll want to get anyone looking like the person on the CCTV in for questioning."

"I'll talk to Uniform."

"Thanks."

Lesley hung up and rang Tina.

"I'm heading your way. I'll need you off the crime scene in the morning and interviewing potential suspects. Stanley's told me there's CCTV of a member of lighthouse staff letting two men in with Hamm's body."

"OK. That's a breakthrough."

"Let's hope so. Are you close to being done there?"

"We've found a shoe print. In some paint that could only have got there in the last few days."

"Where?"

"The gift shop."

"OK. It might be irrelevant. But ask the lighthouse manager to get her staff to provide the shoes they've been wearing to work, so we can eliminate them."

"Or not."

"Or not indeed," Lesley said.

"I'll see you here in a bit," Tina replied. She sounded tired.

"Yes." Lesley passed a road sign: a mile to the lighthouse. Five minutes until she was due to meet Sadie.

"I'll be with you in fifteen minutes," she said. "There's fog descending, it's slowing the traffic."

"OK, boss. See you shortly."

Lesley put her foot down and took the hill leading over the tip of the peninsula towards the lighthouse. She didn't like lying to Tina, but at the same time, she didn't want to involve anyone she didn't have to in whatever Sadie was up to.

CHAPTER THIRTY-ONE

LESLEY PULLED off the road by the white tower of the bird observatory and took the track leading around it towards the cliffs. Soon she was driving through the beach huts, wondering if any of their owners were around.

It was an incongruous spot to find a set of beach huts. No beach, for starters. The huts were arranged in rectangles, groups of them facing each other around rectangles of grass. Not in rows facing the beach as they would have been up the coast in Weymouth. She imagined that, battered by winds like the ones she'd experienced here, they gathered around for shelter instead of facing outwards for the views.

She pulled up behind a Skoda parked between two huts and got out, hoping the car was Sadie's.

A text arrived: *I'm on the coastal path. Next to a curved row of huts.*

Lesley looked around, one hand on her head to keep her hair from blowing into her face and the other over her eyes to shield them.

Up ahead, a path ran along the clifftop. She'd head that way, find the row of huts.

She walked through the huts and emerged onto the path, which led from the lighthouse along the cliffs. Sadie sat in the shelter of a hut ahead of her, the rightmost one in an arc of them that faced out to sea. Lesley wondered if their owners had drawn the short straw, or if they were just hardier than most.

No point in calling out: the wind would blow her voice away. She approached Sadie and stopped next to the journalist.

"Hello."

Sadie looked round and up at her. She wore a thick grey beanie into which she'd tucked her hair. Her cheeks were pink from the cold wind.

"I thought you'd never make it."

Lesley gestured up towards the lighthouse. "I *should* be in there. I hope this is going to be quick."

Sadie stood up. They were inches apart, a necessity given the force of the wind. "Dennis Frampton was arrested for Tim Mackie's murder a week ago," she said.

"That's not exactly news," Lesley replied.

"He's going before the magistrates on Monday."

"Again, not news. You said you had something that could help him."

"I spoke to Detective Superintendent Phipps. From Hampshire."

Lesley pulled her coat tighter around her shoulders. "The man who was given oversight of the investigation into Mackie's death."

"And who went scurrying back to Hampshire after less than a month."

"Again," said Lesley, "not news. What did you talk to him about?"

A lock of hair had escaped from Sadie's hat. She pushed it back inside, her nose wrinkling. "He was scared. Did you know he'd moved to Winchester after retiring?"

"It's his business where he lives."

"He was bloody hard to track down. He's not on the electoral roll, uses a PO Box for his mail."

"He's an ex-copper. I imagine there are plenty of people he's not too keen to have get in touch with him."

Sadie shook her head. "I think he was intimidated. Forced to close the case and go back to Hampshire."

Lesley felt her stomach dip. "By whom?"

Sadie cocked her head. "I think you've got your own suspicions."

"Sadie. Did you come here to try and get information out of me? Because if that's—"

Sadie put a hand on Lesley's arm. "Have you heard of Rowan Angus?"

"Yes."

"You have?"

"I've met him," Lesley replied. DI Angus's name seemed to be popping up a lot lately.

"He's a DI in Blandford Forum. Used to be PSD, left them without any explanation."

"A cover-up?"

"He maintains his innocence."

"Don't they all?" Lesley looked over towards the lighthouse. "You think he's involved in all this?" Her mind went back to DI Angus walking around the crime scene without protective clothing.

"He was being set up. That's what he claims."

"And what's that got to do with Dennis?"

"I think that the same person who set him up is the person trying to pin Mackie's murder on Dennis Frampton."

"Where's your evidence?" Lesley asked.

"I spoke to Angus. I was with him the first time I clapped eyes on your mate Zoe."

Lesley felt her cheek twitch. She'd asked Zoe to speak to Sadie and look into Mackie's death, back when they'd been investigating the death of one of Elsa's colleagues. Carpenter had given her a reprimand over it, although he'd never turned it into anything formal.

"Has it ever occurred to you," Sadie asked, "that you and DI Finch should both have been formally reprimanded after you brought her in on a Dorset case that wasn't even a case at the time?"

"Again, Sadie. You're speculating. Tell me what you have that could help Dennis."

"I spoke to Jacob Frampton."

Dennis's son. "When?"

"Yesterday. He's legit, Lesley. He had legal business dealings with Arthur Kelvin and the Kelvins paid him for his work. It's got nothing to do with his dad."

Lesley wasn't so sure. It was true that she didn't believe Dennis had introduced his son to the Kelvins, or that Dennis had a direct hand in the money transfer. But she was confident that Kelvin had singled Jacob out because he was the son of a detective.

"I could easily find that out myself."

"And I've seen files that make me suspect Mackie was investigating police corruption."

"You have?"

"I think he was looking at PSD."

"Professional Standards?" Lesley resisted a laugh. How

much of this was based in reality, and how much was Sadie sniffing for a sensation? "If you had something concrete, you'd have broadcast it by now. You wouldn't be talking to me."

"You're right. But I think we can work together."

"Oh you do, do you?"

"Lesley. Do you want to root out corrupt officers in the Dorset force, or not? You did it in West Midlands."

Lesley felt her limbs sag. She'd left West Midlands in the middle of the biggest anti-corruption operation for years. Her own former boss was now in witness protection. She'd expected a quieter life down here.

She pulled her coat tighter – Jesus, it was freezing up here – and looked at Sadie. "Send me what you've got. You have my email address."

"It's a police email address."

"I'm not accepting anything relating to a case via a personal email address. That's a breach of—"

"I know you're not *supposed* to do it, Lesley…"

Lesley narrowed her eyes. Since when had Sadie started calling her by her first name?

"…but sending it to a police email address is unsafe."

Lesley made to turn away from Sadie. She'd been intending to walk up to the lighthouse from here, but with the wind against her that would be a battle. She'd take the car.

"Send me what you've got, Sadie. If I want to know any more, I'll tell you."

CHAPTER THIRTY-TWO

MEERA WAS out of the room getting them both a cuppa and Stanley was working through anything he could find on the lighthouse company and its staff. So far, he hadn't managed to find photos of anyone looking like the woman he'd seen on the CCTV.

They'd run through the rest of the footage, hoping for a good look at Hamm's killers and their assistant emerging from the lighthouse, and had found it forty-six minutes after the group had entered. The car that had brought them remained outside the whole time.

Whoever had killed Hamm, they hadn't been shy. They'd driven right up to the lighthouse building, left a car that was doubtless dripping in forensic evidence outside for almost an hour, then driven off again hours after the place closed for the day.

The other car they'd spotted in the footage had left shortly afterwards, the woman in uniform at the wheel: it looked like she hadn't been working there that day. Moments later, CCTV had caught another car arriving. The woman who'd found the body, perhaps.

Meera had tried to contact the lighthouse management company, but it was a Saturday and no one was picking up. Even though a body had been found on one of their properties.

The door opened and Meera placed a mug on Stanley's desk, just as his phone rang. He picked up the phone and gave Meera a thumbs-up as he answered it. She was alright, was Meera.

"Major Crime Investigations team, DC Brown speaking."

"DC Brown, it's Gareth Bamford. The pathologist."

"Is the post-mortem done?"

"We haven't done the full PM yet. But given the conversation I had with your boss earlier, I ran some toxicology tests first."

Stanley beckoned to Meera to come closer to his desk. She leaned across, a question on her face.

"Post-mortem," he whispered. "Tox results."

She nodded.

"DC Brown? You still there?"

"Sorry," he said. "Just talking to a colleague."

"Are you with the DCI?"

"She's at the crime scene." At least, he assumed she was.

"OK. Only she wasn't picking up her phone."

"Tell me what the results are, and I'll pass it on to her."

"Good. We found MDMA in his system. Lots of it."

"Ecstasy?" Stanley shrugged at Meera, writing it down. "You sure?"

"His creatinine kinase levels were elevated, which is indicative of rhabdomyolysis. Rhabdomyolysis is a common symptom of Ecstasy intoxication."

"Rhabdo..."

"Rhabdomyolysis. It could have led directly to the heart attack, or it could have caused renal failure, which in turn caused the heart attack."

"And that would have happened fast?"

"The concentration of MDMA in his blood is well over what it would take to be fatal. He'd have passed out fast, died not long after. I'll have to do a thorough analysis of his internal organs to know exactly what the course of events was, but I think we can safely say he was given a lethal dose of MDMA, fairly pure judging by the concentration. That's what killed him."

"OK. Thanks."

"How was it given to him?" Meera whispered.

"Er, how would they have given to him?" Stanley asked. He considered. "What does it taste like?"

"They could have made out it was a paracetamol tablet or something. Or they could have mixed it into a drink. It would have been bitter, but not overly so. I don't know if Hamm was on prescription drugs, that would have been a way to make him think it was something else."

"Right." Stanley wrote down *Hamm – prescription?* and tapped his pad for Meera's benefit.

"I'll send you an email with my preliminary findings," the pathologist continued. "I've still got to do the full PM. But for now, I can't see any evidence of defensive wounds. I don't think he was forced to take the drug."

"OK. Thanks."

Stanley hung up. He wrote some notes then pointed at his pad. "MDMA."

"That doesn't exactly narrow things down," Meera said. "You can get it anywhere."

"And if Hamm was broken out by an organised crime gang, they'd probably be manufacturing the stuff somewhere."

She nodded. "How did they give it to him?"

"Pathologist says they could have made out it was something else. If he was on medication, they might have pretended to be giving him a dose of that."

"He'd believe them?"

He shrugged. "If it was the same people who busted him out, then he would have trusted them."

"Maybe." She looked pensive.

"What are you thinking?"

"What if Hamm's escape wasn't staged by his mates at all? What if it was someone who never pretended they wanted him any way other than dead? They might have busted him out without him expecting."

"But there were no defensive wounds," Stanley told her. "And he called his victim's family. Told them he was coming."

She shivered. "Horrible." She gazed at Stanley's pad. "What now?"

"We need the CCTV of the escape. And we need to know if he was on any medication."

Meera nodded. "The boss needs an update, too."

He grinned at her. "You're getting the hang of it."

CHAPTER THIRTY-THREE

LESLEY WALKED BACK to her car, cursing Sadie Dawes under her breath.

She was out here at the arse end of beyond, working on the murder of Trevor Hamm, of all people. She just wanted to get the case wrapped up and go home to her new wife. She didn't need Sadie upsetting things.

But she did want to get to the bottom of Mackie's death. Regardless of what the high-ups said, regardless of the inquest. Regardless of Carpenter's threats.

She sighed and pulled open the car door. She needed to get back to the crime scene. Check out this boot print, and the CCTV. Then she'd think about Sadie.

Just as she was about to get into the car, she heard a voice behind her.

"Help! Someone, help!"

She slammed the car door shut and turned in the direction of the voice, her senses on fire.

Sadie?

No.

It had been a man's voice.

Sadie was nowhere to be seen. The Skoda that had been here when Lesley had arrived was still parked by the huts, but there was no way of knowing whether that was Sadie's car.

She took a few steps away from her car.

"Hello?"

She wouldn't be heard over the wind. She had no idea where the voice had come from. Or if she'd even imagined it.

"Hello?" she repeated, louder. "Is someone there?"

A man appeared around the side of a hut. He stopped, turning from side to side, scanning the area. He spotted her and beckoned wildly.

"Call the police!"

I am the police.

Lesley ran towards him, feeling for her phone in her pocket. Where the fuck was Sadie?

She was panting when she reached the man. He was in his fifties, ruddy-cheeked, his eyes wide.

"Sir." She drew out her ID. "I'm a police detective. What's happened?"

He stared at her for a moment as if not believing her, then pointed towards the huts. "In there," he breathed.

"In there, what?" Lesley looked in the direction he was pointing. A car sat alongside a row of huts. One of the structures had its door slightly ajar.

She could smell...

Oh, shit.

"Sir," she said, putting out a hand. "You stay here. Let me investigate."

The man nodded and sank to the ground. She wondered who he was and what he was doing here. Anything to do with Sadie?

She approached the hut, scanning the empty patch of ground in front of it, the gaps between the huts nearby. There was no one in sight.

Sadie, where the hell are you?

That smell. It was too ripe. It couldn't be Sadie.

But still...

She looked back to see the man on the ground, his arms clutched around his knees.

"Stay there!" she called. "Don't go anywhere."

He rocked back and forth, ignoring her. She had to hope he wouldn't wander off. He looked too shocked to move.

She was at the hut now. Flies buzzed around the door.

She turned away and swallowed. Held her breath.

Resisting the urge to close her eyes, she pulled on the hut door. The space inside was dark. She had to wait a moment for her eyesight to adjust.

But she'd been right.

The smell. You never lost that smell, once you'd experienced it once.

In the far corner of the hut, crumpled on the ground in a manner that made her think of the man outside, was a body.

The way it was folded up made it hard for her to identify it as human, at first. But there was no movement,

And the blood...

She looked down at the floor of the hut. The blood had seeped into the wood.

She couldn't go in. Couldn't disturb the scene.

"Hello!" she called across the dim space. Just in case. "Are you...?"

Are you alive?

Not by the looks of it. But it paid not to assume.

Lesley glanced down at the floor again, traced out a route

in her head, and tiptoed to the body. She pulled down the sleeve of her shirt, inside her coat, to cover her hand, and grabbed the wrist.

It was cold. Wet with blood, and cold. A pulse hadn't beat through this wrist for a while.

Shit.

She retraced her steps, withdrawing from the hut and resisting the need to gag. She was too experienced for this.

Outside, the man was still on the ground. Lesley approached him.

"Did you go inside?"

He looked up. "What?"

Think, she told herself. "I'm sorry." He'd seen the body. He wouldn't be in such a state if he hadn't. "Did you know the person?"

He shook his head.

Well, at least that was something. Combined with his reaction, it made him unlikely as a suspect.

"What's your name?" she asked as she pulled out her phone. Tina was in the lighthouse, with the CSIs. It wouldn't be long before they could get a crime scene set up here.

"Roy," the man said.

"Your surname?"

"What? Ilford. Roy... Ilford." He gasped in a shaky breath. "Is he... is he dead?"

"I'm sorry, Mr Ilford. Yes, he is."

CHAPTER THIRTY-FOUR

Tina's phone rang as she was watching Gail transfer the boot print onto a gelatin lifter and hand it to her colleague, Brett. She checked the display and took the call.

"Boss. Everything OK?" It had been over half an hour.

"I'm at the beach huts. Along the cliffs."

"Sorry, I don't understand. Are you in trouble?"

Gail looked up from her work, eyebrows raised in a question. Tina shrugged. Why had the boss stopped at the huts? Surely her car hadn't broken down. She wouldn't be lost; the lighthouse wasn't exactly hard to spot.

"Do you need me to come for you, boss?"

"Not you. There's a body. IC1 male, twenties or thirties by the look of it. He's been stabbed."

Tina looked at Gail. "A body," she mouthed.

"Stabbed?" she repeated into the phone.

"A member of the public found him inside a beach hut. Looks like he's been here overnight. Have you got Gail with you?"

"I have."

"OK." A pause. "Has she got her whole team there?"

"Brett. Not Gavin."

"OK. Find out where Gavin is, will you?"

Tina put a hand over the receiver. "There's another body been found. The DCI is asking for Gavin."

Gail nodded. "I'll call him. They won't want me there, in case of cross-contamination."

Tina pursed her lips. The CSM was right. If the two crimes were unconnected, then they couldn't run the risk of fibres or DNA being spread from one scene to the other by Brett or Gail. And if the crimes *were* connected, then the only way to prove that was to observe procedure.

She took her hand off the receiver. "Gail's calling Gavin now. He's in the lab at Dorchester, he'll be a while."

"I'll call local Uniform to help secure the scene. There's a shedload of blood, we'll need a spatter expert."

"Spatter," she mouthed at Gail.

"Gav's had all the training."

"Gail says Gavin can deal with that," Tina told the boss.

"Good. Well, let's just hope he can get here quickly."

Gail was gesturing for Tina to pass her the phone.

"Boss, I've got Gail for you." Tina handed it over.

"Lesley, it's Gail. Gavin'll be about fifty minutes. In the meantime, you need to erect a strict cordon around any blood spatter. Don't let anyone walk in it, and try and get samples asap."

Gail paused. Tina could hear Lesley's voice, dull down the phone.

Brett gave her a nudge. "This boot print?" he asked, his voice low.

"Yeah." Tina had forgotten that Brett was still working on the print.

He'd scanned the transfer using his phone and was running an analysis on a laptop.

"Bad news, I'm afraid."

Tina felt her chest sag. "What kind of bad news?"

"It's from a shoe we've got on file."

"What? Whose?"

He pointed at the screen. "We took prints from the officers who attended. That one there's a match."

She looked at the screen. He was right.

She'd been hoping it might be a match for the member of lighthouse staff Stanley and Meera had spotted on CCTV.

"Thanks, Brett."

He gave her an apologetic shrug then went back to his screen as Gail handed back her phone.

"Does the boss think the two bodies are connected?" Tina asked.

"You know Lesley. She's not jumping to any conclusions. But it's not like you get a lot of killings along here."

"Despite there being two prisons on the island."

"I've worked forensics in this county for fourteen years," Gail told her. "This is the first time I've had to come to Portland."

"Really?"

A nod. "I'm sure minor SOCO work has been done here. Just nothing big enough to drag me all the way down from Dorchester. And your DCI says this body is fresh."

"How fresh?"

"A day old, no more."

Tina's gaze went to the door to the inner part of the lighthouse, where Trevor Hamm's body had been found. "They have to be connected."

"Like Lesley says, don't jump to conclusions. I'm sure once you've got an ID on the second body, you'll know if they're linked."

CHAPTER THIRTY-FIVE

MEERA SMILED to herself as she clicked on the link in the email from Protektis. The woman she'd spoken to had been friendly enough, but unwilling to release the video of the escape. She'd insisted that it was a Home Office matter and told Meera to speak to the prison. Tina had cited three separate laws around obstructing an investigation and eventually persuaded the woman – less friendly by this point – to attach it to an email.

The woman had known just as well as Meera that the police were entitled to receive the footage. But she'd probably been leant on by Jacob Crawford and his cronies.

"Stan, can you give me a hand with this?" she asked, then looked at him. "You don't mind me calling you Stan, do you?"

He smiled. "Call me what you like."

"Really?"

"OK. Not *anything*." He frowned. "At police college they called me... you don't need to know what they called me." He licked his lips. "What did you need help with?"

Meera watched her new colleague's face, wondering what

his college nickname had been. Everyone had a nickname in college. Some stuck. Stanley's clearly hadn't. Still, her intrigue was piqued.

"What d'you need me to do?" he asked again., leaning over the desks.

"I've got the CCTV of the escape. There were three vehicles, six cameras. I'll send you three of the files."

"I've got them," he told her. He'd already checked the team inbox. Good man.

"Let's take a vehicle each to start with," she suggested.

He looked across the desks. "You talked them into sending these over. You tell me which ones you want me to take."

"I'll go with the car at the back. You take the van he was inside."

"No problem." Stanley sucked on his bottom lip as he identified the correct file. "I'll start on the internal footage."

Meera put out a hand. "Take the rear one. If someone came for him, that'll pick them up first."

"Fair enough." Stanley's eyes darted from side to side as he switched files.

Meera clicked her mouse to start running her own file and sat back to watch. The camera was mounted on the dashboard of an armoured car that had been travelling behind the van containing the prisoner. She frowned, realising something.

"Was Hamm alone in the rear of that van?" she asked, as much to herself as to Stanley.

"Huh?" Stanley's gaze didn't leave his screen.

"Were there any other prisoners travelling with him?"

"Don't know."

"I guess we'll find out if we watch the video."

"I guess," he agreed.

Meera pressed play again. The car was travelling away

from the prison, the view from the dashboard camera largely obscured by the van in front of it. She watched as they travelled down the narrow road leading away from the prison, turning sharply as they took the switchbacks down towards Fortuneswell and the main road. If you could call it that.

The attack had taken place on the roundabout leading to Portland Beach Road, where the island met the mainland. Meera would have a few minutes to wait.

"Where are you up to?" she asked Stanley.

"Ninety seconds in. They've just turned onto Victory Road."

"I want to see if there's anything behind them." Meera paused her video then checked the files. There was another for the camera mounted on the back of the rear vehicle. She brought it up and placed the two windows side by side. Below those she put Google Maps, so she could follow the route.

She wouldn't get all the detail this way, and would probably have to run through the key moments again. But this let her see the events leading up to Hamm's escape from two angles. And it meant working through twice as much footage in the same amount of time.

"What you looking at?" Stanley asked.

"I've got two windows up. Front and rear cameras from the rear vehicle."

"I'll do the same for the van."

"You want me to pause?"

"I'll fast forward through the first bit. If neither of us has seen anything relevant yet, there's unlikely to be anything I'll miss."

"Don't assume." Meera sipped at her coffee, her eyes not leaving her screen. The convoy took a sharp left-hand bend approaching what looked like a graveyard. The beach was visible beyond the roofs of pale, boxy houses leading down to the sea.

"Stop," she said.

Stanley looked across the desks. "What?"

Meera leaned in towards her screen. She'd paused. "There's a drone."

From the rear camera on the car, she could just make out the movement of a drone hovering above them and to the rear. It was coming from Castle Road and the marina.

It would have been invisible to the drivers.

"Look for a drone," she told Stanley. "Following the convoy. See if it's filming, or if it's involved in the escape."

"I haven't seen a drone."

"It's coming in from the right-hand side. Let's go back a minute, see if we can spot its approach."

Meera rewound one minute, to the previous switchback. "Play."

Stanley grunted and hit his mouse button.

They sat in silence for a few moments, both watching the scene play out. Meera watched as the vehicles turned the bend and descended towards the beach.

"Whoah," said Stanley.

"What?" Meera glanced at him then went back to her own footage.

"Stop."

Meera hit the stop button and looked at her colleague. "What?"

He was leaning forward, peering into his screen. "The drone. It's come in from the side. Hang on." He frowned for a moment, shifting his mouse around and clicking the button. "Yeah. I've got it from the front vehicle too. Rear camera."

Meera stood up and rounded the desks. On Stanley's

screen she could see four video feeds from two vehicles. One of them was partially obscured.

"What's wrong with that one?" she asked.

He looked up at her. "It fired something. The drone. It fired something to take out that camera."

CHAPTER THIRTY-SIX

"Right." Lesley sighed. The man was leaning against the wood of the hut, his head in his hands.

She approached him, her ID held up.

"I'm sorry sir, but I'll have to ask you to move. This is an active crime scene."

He pulled his hands down. "Active? Does that mean...?"

She gave him a reassuring smile. "There's nothing to fear."

Not with the blood so dry, she thought. Well, most of it. The pooling was so deep that the cabin floor was still sticky.

"You're safe, but I need you to keep away from the hut. Is the hut yours?"

"It's my dad's."

"Your dad's?" The man was in his sixties, she reckoned. Skinny, with a grey combover. "Really?"

A shrug. "It's been with my family for decades." He gestured around them. "They all have. I look after it for him. All it's good for, with the weather nowadays."

Lesley had no idea what he was talking about. But she needed to get him away from her scene.

"Why don't you come and sit in my car?" she asked him. Did she have police tape in the boot? Or anything she could use to secure the scene?

It was deserted here. Sadie had long since disappeared, God only knew where. All Lesley had to do was watch the hut until Uniform arrived.

She guided the man back to her car and helped him into the rear seat. There was a Twix in her glove locker. She'd been looking forward to it, but needs must...

She dove into the driver's seat, opened the locker and held it out to him. "Eat this. You need the sugar."

"I'm on a diet."

Lesley looked the man up and down. "No, you're not. Eat this."

He stared at it a moment then took it and peeled back the wrapper. He eyed it like it might singlehandedly turn him into Giant Haystacks, then took a bite. Within seconds he'd wolfed the whole thing down.

Lesley's stomach gurgled. *Lucky bastard,* she thought. Or maybe not.

She turned to look in the direction of the hut. It was obscured by its neighbours.

Damn.

"I'll need you to stay here while I make sure no one else goes into your father's hut. Please, don't go anywhere."

He gave her a silent nod. His face, ruddy when he'd first approached her, was pale.

She'd need to call for an ambulance, too.

She dialled Tina.

"Tina, any idea how long Uniform are going to be?"

"They're on the island, boss. Ten minutes."

And there was her thinking that getting around Portland would take no time. "I'll need an ambulance too."

"You've found a second victim?"

"The witness. He's in shock."

"How much did he see?"

"I haven't established that yet. I need to secure the scene."

"You sure you don't want my help? I'm only just across the—"

"You've been all over that lighthouse," Lesley reminded her. "I can't have any more cross-contamination than we've already got."

A notorious organised crime boss had died. Another body had turned up within metres of the first. Lesley had been investigating the first murder and had been part of the man's original arrest. She needed to stick to procedure for this one.

"I've got to go, Tina. Tell me when you've got an ETA on Gavin."

"Thirty minutes last I heard, boss."

"Which was how long ago?"

A pause. "Twelve minutes."

Good. She didn't have long to wait.

"Thanks."

Lesley was nearly at the hut. She plunged her phone into her pocket and pushed back a lock of hair that kept blowing into her eyes.

Bloody wind.

Why didn't people dump bodies in nice calm spots down here? Why was it always windswept cliffs or blustery hillsides?

She'd give anything for the bottom of a canal or a rotting industrial site right now.

OK. Secure the scene. She hadn't found police tape in her boot but there was a bag that Elsa had brought home from the garden centre, with twine for the plants she was planning to cultivate on their balcony. It would have to do.

Lesley looked around, searching for something she could secure the twine to. The nearest anchor was the door handle of the next cabin along.

She walked to it, checking the ground for blood. It had seeped out from under the cabin where the body had been found, but it hadn't reached its neighbours.

She secured one end of the twine to the door handle, then paced towards the first hut, keeping her steps steady. As she reached the hut, the door blew open.

Fucking wind. She'd been sure she'd secured the door.

She pulled on plastic gloves then approached the door. It banged back and forth, hitting her on the shoulder.

Ouch.

Lesley rubbed her shoulder, then regretted it. She had plastic gloves on. She'd transfer fibres.

So be it. God only knew what the wind had ripped from her clothes and scattered to the four winds.

Grabbing the handle, she pushed the door closed, struggling against the gusts. Just before the door was fully closed, she realised that the body inside had shifted.

Lesley stopped, her hand on the door. The wind seemed to die down.

No.

She narrowed her eyes.

First Trevor Hamm, and now...

It couldn't be.

No. She was wrong.

She held the door firm, staring into the hut. Wishing she could go inside.

Her breath had slowed, her skin grown cold.

She thrust the door closed.

She could wait. She *would* wait.

Forensics would get here, and the pathologist. They would examine the scene properly, put down protective plates. Then and only then would she be allowed to approach the body.

To identify it.

Because Lesley knew who she'd seen in there.

She knew who their second victim was.

CHAPTER THIRTY-SEVEN

STANLEY LEANED over Meera's desk. The two of them were watching together now, tracking the progress of the drone on Meera's screen. It had moved to the side of the convoy, following it without any sign of the drivers noticing.

They had two windows open: the rear view from the back vehicle, and the rear view from the van. The drone hovered behind the convoy, floating in mid-air. The weather had been calm on Portland, and it avoided being buffeted by the wind. But when they reached the road across to the mainland, the wind would pick up. Even Stanley, who'd never been to Portland, could work that out from looking at a map.

"Shit," Meera breathed. "That's another one gone."

"I'll check the front ones." Stanley went back to his desk.

Meera put out a hand. "It's OK. I'll bring it up on my screen. With two down, we've only got four feeds to follow now."

He nodded. "How come no one at the prison told us about this?"

She shrugged. She'd replaced the dead feed from the rear

of the back vehicle with one from the front of the lead car, alongside the one from the rear of the van.

Stanley pointed. "What's that?"

The vehicles were approaching the main road now, Chesil Beach visible from the front feed.

"Vehicles."

"Vans," he said.

Meera squinted. "They're going to block the road. What did the prison governor tell the boss about the escape?"

"They blocked the road off the island, made it impossible for the vehicles to pass."

"They engineered a crash," she added.

"Yeah."

Meera flicked between more of the feeds. Another one was obscured now.

"Hang on," she said. She rewound to the moment where it went out. "The drone."

Sure enough, the drone had fired something at the camera, just before it disappeared.

"What *is* that?" he asked.

"Paint, maybe?"

"Or some kind of projectile to destroy the camera."

"We'll need to get access to those vehicles."

Stanley nodded. "Go back to where we were. The crash."

Meera clicked her mouse and the two of them watched the feed from the very front camera, alongside that from the front of the van that Hamm had been travelling in.

"How come no one in the prison vehicles has spotted them?" Stanley asked.

"They're just sitting there. It's only cos we know what's about to happen that we think they're dodgy."

He snorted. It looked pretty dodgy to him.

As the cars descended the hill, the vehicles because clearer. An SUV and a van, parked on either side of the road. The van was white, with no markings. Of course.

"Wait for it," Meera said.

"Can you slow it down?"

"Let's watch at normal speed first."

Stanley wanted to object, but she had a point. They could watch events unfold in real time, then go back and examine it second by second.

The prison convoy reached the bottom of the hill and slowed for the roundabout. There was one car in front, a hatchback.

"Is that one of them?" Meera asked.

"Dunno."

The hatchback paused for longer than seemed necessary, then drove off across the roundabout. It took the road towards Weymouth, just as the SUV, a Range Rover, started to move. It turned in the road and approached the convoy, coming at the front vehicle head-on. The white van drove past it and the convoy, turned, then started following the convoy.

The screen erupted into static as the Range Rover made contact with the front car in the convoy. The van behind it took the wrong side of the road, approached the prison van at speed then disappeared into the bottom of the shot as it made contact.

Both screens went blank.

Meera brought up each feed one by one. The only one working now was from the back of the front vehicle. They could see the white van blocking the road at the back.

Stanley held his breath as they watched. The view was at an angle, the ground to one side and the sky off to the right of the image.

"The front car's gone over," Meera said.

"And the van." Stanley pointed. The prison van was visible on the edge of the shot, lying on its side.

"What security measures do prison vans have for accidents?" Meera asked.

"They can't be opened from inside," Stanley told her. "You need one of the guards to open it."

"So they can't just ram the van and expect to get Hamm out."

"No."

"They're about to bloody well try," Meera said.

Stanley's mouth was dry. He swallowed as he watched the feed. A shape moved in front of the camera, briefly obscuring it.

"What's that?"

'Someone's got out of the front vehicle," Meera said.

"A guard."

She nodded, her gaze steady on the screen.

Stanley watched as the figure grew smaller, approaching the van.

"Shit," he said. "They had someone on the inside."

"We don't know that yet. They could be going to secure the van."

"They didn't though, did they?"

Another figure appeared in shot, dressed all in black with a balaclava. It held a gun. It looked like a shotgun, short barrel.

The guard turned towards the second figure.

"Not a bent guard, then," Meera said.

"A threatened guard."

They watched as the figure in the balaclava stepped closer to the guard, gesturing with the gun. The guard walked out of shot.

"He's gone to the back of the van," Stanley said.

"How come we didn't know about this?" Meera asked.

On screen, nothing was happening. The guard and the person in the balaclava were out of shot, presumably opening up the van and getting Hamm out.

"We need to find out who that is," Stanley said.

"You reckon?" Meera turned and gave him a sarcastic smile.

"And we need to talk to the guards."

"We certainly do. Hang on."

Someone was in shot, the man with the balaclava. He held a second person next to him.

"Hamm," Stanley said.

The second figure wore prison uniform.

"Where's the guard?" Meera asked.

Stanley shook his head.

The two figures stood in front of the van, facing each other. It looked like they were arguing.

"Why are they hanging around?" Meera asked.

After a moment, Hamm jabbed a finger into the other person's chest.

"What's going on?" Stanley breathed.

"It's almost like he doesn't want them to bust him out."

"Or he doesn't trust them."

Hamm withdrew his finger and grabbed the balaclava.

"He's about to..." Meera began.

"Take it—"

"There." Meera froze the screen. Hamm had ripped the balaclava off the other figure's head. The owner quickly pulled it back into place. Then there was what looked like more shouting. After a moment both of them looked off to one side, then ran out of the shot. A car passed behind the skewered prison van, heading towards the island.

"They've taken him back onto the island," Meera said.

"Towards the lighthouse."

"Yeah. Question is, can we enhance the image enough to identify that person when Hamm rips their balaclava off?"

CHAPTER THIRTY-EIGHT

"Everyone. One at a time."

Lesley ran a hand through her hair. She was in her car, parked outside the huts. Roy Ilford had been taken home by Uniform and told to expect a visit for a formal statement. Given the identity of the victim, she was confident he wasn't a suspect.

"Sorry, boss," Stanley said.

"It's fine. You've all got things to report. Tina, you first."

The team were all on speakerphone. Tina had set up a conference call and patched Lesley in.

"Thanks," said Tina. "I'm at the lighthouse still. We found a shoe print but it's a match for DI Angus. It's not a lead."

"Shit," hissed Stanley.

"Let's not overreact," Lesley said. "A case like this is going to have plenty of leads. Not all of them will take us anywhere. Anything else, Tina? Any other forensics?"

"Sorry. Looks like whoever left Hamm here was ultra-careful. There's nothing inside, but we do still have the CCTV. The insider."

"We do. Are you done at the scene now?"

"Yes."

"Good. So in the morning I want you back in the office and talking to the lighthouse company. We need to know if a member of their staff matches what's in that footage."

"It's not much to go on," said Stanley. "It was dark a—"

"Let's not decide to fail before we've even tried, eh?"

"Do you want me to stay over here?" asked Tina. "I can base myself a—"

"You've got a four-month-old baby at home, Tina. And I imagine Mike is missing you."

'He is." There was a smile in Tina's voice. "They both are."

"Good. Get yourself home, give that boy a cuddle. Not Mike, the other one."

Lesley heard laughter down the line: Stanley. She smiled.

"OK. Stanley and Meera, what do you have for me?"

"You go, Stan," Meera said.

"It's OK, you can."

Lesley rolled her eyes. She opened her glove locker, then remembered she'd given the Twix to Ilford. *Damn*. She put a hand on her stomach. She'd have to find a chippy on the way home.

"Meera, just go for it," she said, realising her voice sounded harsh.

"We watched the footage of the escape," Meera said. "There were three vehicles, six cameras. When they were almost at the spot where they took him, we saw a drone."

"It fired something at the cameras," Stanley continued. "Took them out."

"This isn't a spy movie, Stanley. Can you be more specific?"

"Sorry. I reckon it was paint. I've watched it again. And—"

"So someone sent a drone down there to disable the cameras. Did they get all of them?"

"No," Meera said. "Two vehicles attacked the convoy, an SUV and a van. Someone got out of the SUV and went to the prison van."

"And?"

"They threatened one of the guards with a gun. Presumably the guard did as he was told."

"We need to speak to those guards," Lesley said. "Get their take on it."

"I've spoken to the local hospital," Meera said. "They told me that two guards from the prison came in yesterday. I've got names."

"They still in hospital?"

"They were discharged this morning. Minor wounds. No one was shot."

"No." Lesley would have to speak to the governor again. And by now Jacob Crawford would have stuck his oar in.

She sighed. This needed to go up the chain. To Carpenter.

"OK," she said. "Well, I've got something helpful."

Silence.

"Don't you want to know what it is?"

"Sorry," Tina said. "I guess we were all waiting for you to tell us."

"Of course. So we have a second body, found in the huts by the lighthouse."

"What huts?" Meera asked.

"They're beach huts," Tina said. "They belong to people who live on Portland."

"There's no beach," Lesley told her.

"OK, not beach huts. But that's the job they do. People use them for leisure, to sit on the cliffs and watch the sea."

"Really?" Lesley looked out of her car window at the gale. It was dark now and she couldn't see the sea, but she didn't especially want to.

"Yes," Tina said. "They've been there for generations."

"The witness said the hut where the body was found belonged to his dad."

"What was it you had that was helpful?" Tina asked.

Lesley smiled. She was glad she'd convinced Tina to come back to work. Sure, Mike was a good detective. But he was no Tina.

"Good question. Tina. I've got an ID on the body."

Someone gasped.

"Who?" asked Stanley.

"His name's Samuel Watson. Known as Zee. He's suspected of being part of a Birmingham gang that's been trying to take over Hamm's territory since his arrest. He was a minor foot soldier in Hamm's operation, now trying to set up on his own. His gang call themselves the Brum Boys."

"So you think that whoever killed Hamm, killed Watson too," Meera said.

"I'm not assuming anything right now," Lesley replied. "But it does mean I need to take a trip to Birmingham."

"That's where Watson was last seen?" Stanley said.

"It was indeed," Lesley told him. "I need to have a chat with a former colleague of mine, and find out what she knows."

CHAPTER THIRTY-NINE

The journey home from Portland would take over an hour. Lesley switched on the radio and let it wash over her as she drove. Something about politics: ministers backstabbing each other. It never changed. As long as it didn't impact on policing, she didn't care.

Dennis's house wasn't far out of her way, just outside Lychett Minster. She drove past the sign, unsure if he would want her knocking on his door at this time of night. It was past eight o'clock and Dennis was a man of strict habits. He would be in his slippers by now, feet up and TV on. Winding down for bed.

Or perhaps, given what had happened in recent days, he wouldn't.

At the next roundabout she turned back, retracing her route. At the sign for Lychett Minster she turned off.

She hadn't spoken to him yet. Not since her wedding. Not since his arrest. She owed him that, even if she didn't have any answers for him.

Once again, the door was answered by Pam, Dennis's long-suffering wife. She smiled as she recognised Lesley and ushered her inside.

"I'm so glad you came back," she said, her voice hushed. "He's in a foul mood."

Lesley wasn't so sure that seeing his boss would help with that, but she was here now. "Where is he?"

"Living room, at the front." Pam opened a door.

Dennis was inside, newspaper folded on a table next to him, face raised in expectation.

"I heard you at the door," he said. He stood, his movements slow.

Lesley stopped, the coffee table between them. "Sit down. I shouldn't be here."

"I know that." Dennis sat, his gaze steady on her face.

"Carpenter. He'll..."

"I won't tell anyone you've been here." Dennis gestured towards the sofa next to Lesley. "I think you should sit down."

Lesley did as she was told, wondering whether Dennis had ever given her an order before. "How are you?"

He looked down towards his slippers. "As well as can be, given the circumstances."

She nodded. "You're in front of the magistrates on Monday."

His gaze came up. "You've been kept up to date on proceedings."

"I'm the last person they'd tell. But court dates are public."

"Really? You don't have anything to do with this?"

Lesley stared at him. "How the hell can you think I'm involved in your arrest? I've seen the way your eyes mist over when you talk about Tim Mackie. You didn't have anything to do with his death."

"That's not what PSD think."

"I thought it was Organised Crime who made the arrest."

Dennis shook his head. The door opened and he sat back, his face stern. How much was he telling his wife about all this?

Lesley leaned forward, her elbows on her knees. "Dennis. You have to tell them what you know about Mackie's activities after his retirement. All you were doing was helping him out. What was he investigating? What did he discover?"

Dennis's gaze flicked to Pam. She placed a tea tray on the table and retreated from the room.

Lesley watched as the door closed. "You aren't talking to her about this?"

"She doesn't need to know."

"They've got bank statements showing payments went to your son, and you aren't involving his mother?"

Dennis shook his head. "Jacob has got nothing to do with this."

"You'll have been told not to contact him. He's a material witness."

Dennis chewed his lip. "That doesn't mean..." He looked away.

"Doesn't mean what?"

He sighed. "Let me drink my tea."

Lesley watched as Dennis stood, went to the table, and poured himself a cup of tea. Pam had brought a plate of Rich Tea biscuits. He offered Lesley one.

"No thanks." She eyed the biscuits, then changed her mind. "Actually, I'm bloody starving."

He gave her a look.

"Dennis, I think we're past your swear jar now."

"Maybe." He sat down with his cup and saucer, a biscuit balanced in the saucer. Lesley pushed one of the three biscuits she'd taken into her mouth and chewed.

"You were about to tell me something," she said to him.

"I was." He looked at the door again.

"Just tell me, Dennis. You have to help yourself." She wanted to cross the room, turn him upside down and shake him until the evidence that would exonerate him fell out of his pockets.

"Very well." He nibbled on a biscuit. Lesley swallowed her second biscuit.

"Very well, what?"

"Pam has had a visit from a journalist. While I was out today, talking to PSD."

"Sadie Dawes."

A frown. "You know her."

"She works for the BBC. Everyone in Dorset knows her."

"But you expected her to contact me."

"She's been sniffing around Mackie's death since before I arrived here. I thought she suspected you, at one point."

His face darkened. "She followed me. Not long after you... after you took over. I thought the same."

"But now?"

"She's spoken to Jacob."

Lesley sat back. "When?"

"I don't know."

"Hang on." Lesley put down her cup. "Exactly when did Sadie come here?"

The journalist had been in Portland this afternoon, talking to Lesley. But she'd left before the second body had been found. It had taken hours for Uniform to arrive and for Lesley to be comfortable leaving them at the scene.

"This afternoon," Dennis said. "Around four pm. She left minutes before they brought me home."

Coincidence, or did Sadie have a colleague watching Dennis?

"She spoke to your wife," Lesley said. "Not to you."

"Yes."

"So why isn't your wife in here, telling me about it?"

"She doesn't want to get involved."

From what Lesley had seen and heard, Pam Frampton was not the kind of woman who would shrink from a fight.

"That makes no sense."

"It involves our son, boss. She's scared."

"It also involves you, in case you hadn't noticed. Surely she should be scared of you being convicted of murder. If you don't get bail—"

"I know the risks for a copper on remand, boss. That's why I contacted Sadie."

"You called her back?"

A nod. "She can help me. Us. Jacob knew nothing about all this, until she called him. But he worked for the Kelvins. Legitimate work, in London. My son's a financial adviser. They hired him. Paid him via a legitimate bank account."

Lesley looked at him. "So it wasn't a bribe."

"It wasn't a bribe. Jacob can provide all the documentation. It's a red herring, boss."

"I spoke to Sadie too. Not long before she came here."

Dennis rubbed his nose. "You approached her."

"She called me. She told me she wants to send me something. She's looking at... at other officers."

Dennis opened his mouth, then closed it.

"You want to know who," Lesley said.

"It's not my place."

Lesley resisted the urge to grab Dennis by the collar and shake some sense into him. "Of course it's your bloody place."

His cheek twitched. "Maybe. In that case, who does she suspect?"

Lesley leaned back in her chair. Dennis would be questioned again. By PSD and potentially by Organised Crime. The less he knew, the less he could tell them. The man was just too damn honest.

"Don't worry about that, Dennis. I'm going to contact Sadie, and I'm going to find out what she knows."

CHAPTER FORTY

Tina had spoken to the regional manager of the company that managed the lighthouse, and arranged for all of the staff to report to Portland Lighthouse at 9 am. For most professions, the fact it was a Sunday would be an issue. But this was a tourist attraction, and they were used to being busy at the weekend.

She drove up the hill leading into the Isle of Portland, ignoring the view to her right in favour of concentrating on the road.

"Blimey," said Meera. "I saw it on the CCTV but it's different in person."

Tina smiled, her eyes still on the road. "We've still got ten minutes or so of driving. Don't get too excited."

"You're sure they'll all be there? If it was me who'd been caught in that CCTV on Friday, I'd be halfway to Mauritius by now."

Tina glanced at her. "Mauritius?"

A shrug. "I've got an auntie who lives there. Always fancied it."

"Bit different from Portland Bill."

"It certainly is." Meera craned her neck as they took the bend at the top of the hill, peering past Tina towards the mainland.

The view stretched out below them, Tina knew. She'd taken a look for herself yesterday. Chesil Beach arcing off to the west and Weymouth Bay to the east, with the coastline reaching round to Durdle Door and beyond. She wondered why more grockles didn't come here in search of the view.

They crested the hill and approached a roundabout, signs to the prison on the left.

"That's where he came from," Meera breathed.

"Not originally," corrected Tina. "He came from Birmingham. It was the DCI who arrested him."

"And now she's heading up there to interview his cronies." Meera wrinkled her nose. "Lucky Stanley, getting that one."

"It was always going to be Stanley. You're... I don't mean this disrespectfully, but you're new. And I'm..."

"You've got a baby."

Tina glanced at the other woman. "You got kids?"

"Yeah. A four-month-old."

Tina felt her mouth fall open. She closed it. "So how come you're not being treated with kid gloves?"

"I didn't give birth. My wife did. Jill."

"Ah. What's that like?"

Meera tensed. "What's what like?"

"Watching your partner go through that. Louis's birth was horrible. Emergency C-section. But I was more worried about Mike passing out than I was about myself."

Meera laughed. "Suzi came out easy. A quick birth, not that Jill'll say that's easy. She tore. Badly."

Tina winced. That was one benefit of what had happened when Louis had been born. "She a copper, like you?"

"A DI."

"And you're the one still at work?"

"We saved up, beforehand. She wants to breast-feed right up to six months."

"I thought I wanted to do that. Then I realised how bloody painful it is."

Meera smiled. "I'm glad I haven't had the pleasure." She pointed out a sign. "Lighthouse is right at this roundabout."

"Thanks." Tina took the turn. They were in what seemed to be a village. Tina hadn't realised there were so many houses on the island.

"So how many people are we talking to today?" Meera asked.

"Six, if they all turn up."

"I thought you were confident they would."

"I don't want to be cocky."

Meera eyed her. "I get the feeling you're a bit of a dark horse."

Tina clutched the wheel tighter. "What d'you mean?"

"You make out like you think you've failed at something. Like this. You know full well they'll all turn up. You told them what you needed to, to make it happen. Is it a real lack of confidence, or are you just trying not to appear smug?"

"I... I'm not sure." Truth was, when Tina had moved from Uniform to CID, she'd suffered from excruciating impostor syndrome. But she was learning fast, and she knew the boss had more respect for her than for Mike. Eventually she was going to leapfrog him. She wasn't looking forward to his reaction.

"Here we are," she said, glad to end the conversation as

they reached the lighthouse. "We need to get an alibi from each of them, and poke it a bit."

"Ask them to recount it backwards."

Tina stopped the car. There were five cars outside the lighthouse. Further away, in the public car park. "Sorry?"

Meera put a hand on the back of Tina's seat. "Ask them for their alibi, then get them to run through what they were doing on Friday, but backwards. If they've made the story up, they'll struggle."

"Good idea." Tina smiled. Maybe having another woman on the team wouldn't be so bad. "Let's try that."

CHAPTER FORTY-ONE

LESLEY GAZED out of the window, a coffee in her hand. She needed to get into the office, but it was Sunday. No one would notice if she waited for Elsa to wake.

She downed the last of her coffee and turned towards the kitchen for another cup just as Elsa entered, still in her dressing gown.

"Hey," Lesley said.

"Hey." Elsa put an arm around Lesley and kissed her. "I didn't hear you get up."

"I didn't want to disturb you."

"I don't mind." Elsa eyed Lesley's mug. "You want another one?"

"Please." Lesley handed it over.

Elsa went into the kitchen and started up the coffee machine. It was complicated, a wedding present. She turned on the radio: Fleetwood Mac.

"They played this at the wedding." Elsa looked at Lesley, smiling.

Lesley went to the kitchen and took Elsa in her arms. She brushed Elsa's long hair out of her face. "They did."

"You've got to go into work today?"

"I'm SIO on a double murder enquiry."

"I know." Elsa sniffed, pulled out of Lesley's arms and went to the coffee machine. She inhaled. "It's a bugger to use, but it makes damn good coffee."

"It does."

"I'm sorry I was asleep when you got in last night. How was Dennis?"

"How you'd expect."

"Stoic."

"That's Dennis." Lesley took the coffee that Elsa offered her.

"Has he got a solicitor?"

Lesley paused, her mug midway to her mouth. "You're offering?"

"That's not what I said."

Lesley sipped the coffee. "I don't know."

"He must have. They've interviewed him, what, twice? And he's up before the magistrates tomorrow."

Lesley nodded. "He must have. Still..." Dennis was stubborn. He was the kind of man who still believed innocent people didn't need lawyers.

Oh Dennis, I do hope you're protecting yourself.

"You want me to ask some of my contacts, see if anyone's been hired by him?"

"Would they tell you? You're a bit close to it all."

"Who's hired who is no secret." Elsa raised her eyebrows. "As you well know."

Elsa had worked for Arthur Kelvin, a local organised crime

boss, until she'd left her previous firm. Now she was trying to set up on her own.

Lesley sighed. "See what you can find out. Keep it subtle."

"Of course. If he doesn't have someone…"

"*Now* you're offering."

"I know some of the people involved. If the case hinges on the fact that Mackie was investigating the Kelvins, my experience could be of help."

"Or it could be the exact opposite."

Elsa shook her head. "Arthur Kelvin's dead now. There's no conflict."

Lesley grabbed her wife's wrist. "And you need clients."

"It's Dennis. I'll do it pro bono."

Lesley cocked her head. "You'd do that?"

"I've seen how worried you are about him. He's on a DS's salary. Of course I would."

"You're trying to set up a business."

"That's not the issue here."

Lesley put down her empty mug. It was nine am: she needed to get moving. "It's kind of you, sweetie."

"It's selfish. I want you to be happy. And you won't be until Dennis has been cleared."

'You're confident he will be."

"Of course I am. So are you."

Lesley drew in a breath. She looked at her wife, who was eying her over the rim of her mug.

Elsa was a good lawyer. She'd been headhunted by Harry Nevin, invited to join one of Bournemouth's most prestigious firms. And she was motivated.

"OK," she said. "Find out if he's got representation. And if it's any good. If not, then maybe you're the right person to help him."

CHAPTER FORTY-TWO

Tina and Meera sat in the cramped office of the lighthouse gift shop, a list of staff members in front of them. The space was echoey, despite its size, and Tina was convinced their interviewees would be able to hear her stomach rumbling.

All she'd had for breakfast was a slice of toast while she fed Louis then expressed more milk for Mike to use while she was gone. She'd grabbed a cereal bar on her way out but then left it in the glove locker. And what with allowing time for the feed and the pumping, she'd been up since six.

She put a hand on her stomach as their third interviewee came in. So far, they'd interviewed the manager, Callum, who seemed ridiculously young to be in such a role. He'd been working at the lighthouse on Friday and had gone home to his girlfriend and a takeaway pizza afterwards. When they'd asked him to recount the evening backwards, he'd done so with no hesitation, listing the TV programmes he'd watched, the beers he and his girlfriend had enjoyed and the time the pizza had turned up. When he'd got to the bit about the extra pepperoni for the second time, Tina's stomach had almost drowned him out.

The second in the hot seat had been Harvey, a middle-aged man who'd shifted in his chair and sweated the whole way through. Tina and Meera had repeatedly exchanged glances, convinced that his behaviour made him suspicious. But when they'd asked him to recount Friday evening backwards, he'd happily worked through the gaming club he'd attended, listing what they'd played, who'd won which games, and going through the attendees in the right order of arrival and departure both forwards and backwards. Either he had a brain for that kind of thing, or he was telling the truth.

Now their third interviewee, Dawn, was taking the chair opposite them. She was in her late thirties, with long dark hair and a blank expression. Tina wondered if she used Botox.

"Thanks for speaking to us," Meera began. "We're trying to get some more information on what happened here on Friday, and to establish where each member of the lighthouse team was on Friday evening."

"Why?" the woman asked. She scratched her forehead, leaving a red mark. The flesh was clearly numb: Tina had been right.

"As you know, a body was found here on Friday evening. We have CCTV footage showing it being left earlier in the evening."

"What time?"

"We'll come to that," Tina said. She looked down at her notes: shifts at the lighthouse. "You were working here on Friday, is that right?"

"Just until early afternoon. Callum was on his own for the rest of the day."

"Did anything unusual happen while you were here on Friday?"

"What kind of unusual?"

Tina shrugged. "Any disturbances. Suspicious behaviour. Members of the public trying to access restricted areas."

The woman looked from Tina to Meera. "Nope." She licked her lips.

"What time did your shift finish on Friday?" Meera asked.

The woman leaned back and looked up at the ceiling. "My shift finished at two. I left at two thirty."

"Do you normally stay for longer than your shift?"

"A delivery of books came in. We sell history books, about the island. Callum asked me to help him with them."

"OK," said Tina. "So you left here at half past two. What did you do then?"

Dawn blinked. "I went to visit my mum. She lives in Osmington."

"Where's that?"

A cough. "Past Weymouth. Half an hour away, maybe a bit more."

Tina nodded. "You went straight there?"

"No. I had shopping to do for her. She's not been well."

"No?" Meera asked.

"No."

"So where did you go for the shopping, and what time did you arrive at your mum's?"

"I thought you said the body was left here at night. I got to my mum's in the afternoon."

"Humour us. Please," Tina told her.

The woman sighed. "OK." Her eyes went upwards again. "So I left here at two thirty. I stopped off at the Asda in Rodwell. That took half an hour. It's a thirty, forty-minute drive to my mum's. So I would have got there at quarter to four. Give or take."

"You're saying you would have got there at that time, or that you did get there at that time?" Meera asked.

Dawn eyed her. "I did."

"And how long did you stay with your mum?"

"Am I a suspect or something?"

"We're interviewing all the lighthouse staff. The team here would have had access to the lighthouse overnight, so it makes sense to—"

"But I didn't have access. Only Callum has keys."

"We've spoken to Callum too."

"Good."

"How long were you at your mum's, Dawn?" Meera asked.

Dawn licked her lips. "Until late evening. I cooked her tea, ate there."

"What did you cook?"

"Burger and chips. From the freezer aisle at Asda."

"And you left... when?"

"Nine. Ish."

"You live in Weymouth, is that right?"

"It is."

"So you got home at what time?"

"Half nine, twenty to ten. I watched a bit of TV, then went to bed."

"Can you remember what you watched?"

Dawn narrowed her eyes. "The news."

"The news."

"Yeah."

"What did you see reported on the news?"

"The prison break, of course." Dawn placed her elbows on the table and leaned forward. "Are you done?"

"Not quite." Tina looked down at her notes. "You had a busy afternoon."

"I did."

Meera leaned in. "Can you recount what you did backwards, starting from when you went to bed?"

"What?"

"Take us through the evening and afternoon backwards."

"Why?"

"Please."

"OK." Dawn cleared her throat. "OK." A pause. "I went to bed about ten. Before that I watched TV." She gave Tina a look. "The news. Prison break. I drove back from my mum's."

"What time did you leave your mum's?" Meera asked.

"About... half nine."

Meera smiled. "Keep going."

Tina noted what Dawn was saying in her pad.

"I cooked tea for mum, burger and chips."

"Before that?"

"I drove to hers from work. I... I picked up a prescription for her."

"Where?"

"Her local chemist. Of course."

Tina sat back. "Did you go anywhere else?"

"I helped Callum with a delivery, then left here late and went to my mum's." Dawn narrowed her eyes at the two detectives. "Yeah. That's it. Told you I could remember it backwards."

Meera's face was impassive. Tina wondered if she played poker.

"Thanks, Dawn," Meera said. "If you can ask the next person in after you, that would be great."

CHAPTER FORTY-THREE

LESLEY WAS en-route to the office, to pick Stanley up. The two of them had a long day ahead of them: the drive to Birmingham, various meetings and interviews there, and the drive back. She wished she had an excuse to stay longer. Her daughter Sharon was still up there with her dad until the middle of next week, and Lesley was missing her.

Her phone rang as she drove through Lychett Minster: unknown number.

"DCI Clarke," she said.

"DCI Clarke, it's Thomas Gordon. From HMP Portland."

"Governor Gordon. We've watched the video of the escape. You're presiding over a right shitshow right now, aren't you?"

"I see you've had a second body turn up. I could say the same about you."

She stuck her tongue out at the phone. "The second body is one of the men who helped your prisoner escape."

"Is it?"

"I can't tell you more than that. But I'm heading to Birmingham today to find out more."

"Hamm was from Birmingham."

Lesley turned off the A35. *State the bleeding obvious*, she thought.

"He was," she confirmed. She wondered if Gordon knew she'd been part of the team who'd arrested the man. "Anyway, what can I do for you? Tell me you've got evidence of a plot to bust Hamm out from amongst your inmates."

"Nothing as dramatic as that."

"You've got something, though. Or you wouldn't be calling me on a Sunday morning."

"I wouldn't. It's the phone call."

"Phone call?"

"You said one of Hamm's victims reported that he'd called her."

"Gina O'Toole. *Mother* of a victim."

"You know what I mean. I've had my team go through phone logs and there was no call."

Lesley turned right at the roundabout leading to Police HQ. She should have called ahead to Stanley, had him waiting outside. "What do you mean, no call? Gina would have no reason to lie."

"I'm not saying she's lying. But Trevor Hamm didn't call her number. And neither did anyone else at this prison."

"You've checked your records?"

"DCI Clarke, this is how it works. When an inmate arrives here, they provide us with a list of phone numbers. Normally wife, girlfriend, sometimes both. Family. We check the numbers and add them to an approved list. To stop the exact thing your Gina O'Toole claims Hamm did. No one wants prisoners ringing their victims. Or their former associates, for that matter."

"In which case, Hamm had access to a mobile phone."

"I've seen the transcript of the call. It includes an exchange with the switchboard operator, asking if the recipient is prepared to take a reverse charge call."

"Which means it *did* come from your prison." Lesley parked outside the HQ building and peered up at the window to her office. *Stanley, are you watching?*

"It didn't come from any landline in this building," the governor replied. "I think it was faked."

Lesley shook her head. "Hamm faked a legitimate call from the prison phones?"

"Or someone else did. Maybe to put the wind up your victim."

"Victim's mother."

"Victim's mother. Or they did it to get the police thinking Hamm was planning his breakout, when maybe he wasn't."

The door to the building opened and Stanley walked out. Lesley tapped the steering wheel.

"You're suggesting Hamm wasn't in on the escape," she said, her mind racing. Gordon had a point. Why would Hamm agree to be broken out by people who would go on to kill him?

If the same people who'd broken him out *had* killed him...

"That's for you to determine," the governor told her. "I'm just providing information. But I don't think it was Hamm who made that call."

CHAPTER FORTY-FOUR

"Dear goodness, woman," Dennis said. "It's Sunday. When will they leave me alone?"

Pam stood in front of him, her expression anxious. "I'm sorry, love, but this one isn't police."

"Press? If it's that Sadie Dawes again—"

"It's not Sadie Dawes. It's your DCI's wife."

"Sorry?"

"Elsa Short. She wants to talk to you."

Dennis was still getting used to the boss having a wife. Just as he'd got used to the girlfriend, and now here she was, one of a pair of wives. Dennis didn't have any problem with it, it was up to the DCI who she lived with, but he still forgot from time to time.

He was about to ask Pam what Elsa Short wanted to talk to him about, but then he realised. And he didn't know whether to be appalled by the woman, or impressed.

He sighed. "Send her in."

He folded his newspaper and placed it on the side table

beside him. He shuffled in his chair and adopted a neutral expression, his face just ready as the door opened.

"Dennis." She stood over him, all thick dark hair and London confidence. He bristled.

DS Frampton, he was about to reply, then realised he wasn't allowed to use his rank while all this was ongoing.

"Ms Short," he replied. "What can I help you with?"

She smiled. "This isn't what you think it is."

"Oh? What do I think it is?"

She nodded towards the sofa, raised her eyebrow and sat down at his nod. She arranged herself tidily, her legs together, her palms on her knees.

"You think I'm here to talk you into hiring me. You think I'm looking for a client, given that my business is struggling to get off the ground."

'I'm not sure I'd put all that much thought into it."

She shook her head. "I would like to represent you. But if you'll let me, I don't intend to charge you."

He gritted his teeth. "You're offering me charity. Was this your wife's idea?"

"She resisted it."

"She did?"

"She did, at first. Then she saw that it makes sense."

"I don't see how."

She shuffled forwards, her knees still together. "I have experience with Arthur Kelvin. DCI Mackie was investigating his activities before his death. There's every chance Kelvin, or one of his associates, is responsible for Mackie's death. I know who some of those associates are."

"As does your wife."

"She does, yes. But..." She licked her lips. "They're more likely to trust me."

"Not when they find out you're my lawyer, they won't."

"People don't need to know that, not yet. I'm told you have someone representing you."

"Christopher Regis."

"Of Parnell & Regis."

"Yes."

She sniffed. "They aren't as good as me."

Dennis resisted a smile. "Modest, aren't you?"

"I'm a woman trying to build a legal practice from scratch. I need to be comfortable blowing my own trumpet."

"Very well. Let's say you were to become my solicitor. What do I tell Regis?"

"You've reached a crucial stage in the case. It's not uncommon to hire a new brief."

"Really?"

"And I'm working for you pro bono. Any solicitor will know what that's worth."

"I suppose. So what do you intend to do to advance my case?"

"I'll need you to talk to me. To tell me everything you know about what Tim Mackie was doing after his retirement. I'll speak to Sadie Dawes, and find out what she knows—"

"She's a journalist. I wouldn't hold your breath."

"I can do some sniffing around amongst Kelvin's associates. See if there was any talk of Mackie before he died."

Dennis clasped his hand together. "Were you even in Dorset when it all happened?"

"I was. Had been for almost a year."

"Do you remember it?"

"It was barely reported at the time," Elsa said.

"Exactly."

"You're suggesting someone leaned on the press?"

Dennis looked towards the door. He could hear Pam clattering around in the kitchen. Making as much noise as possible, so he'd know she wasn't about to burst in.

Pam was nothing if not discreet. Practical. Supportive. But sometimes he wished she'd be a bit less solid.

"I spoke to Superintendent Carpenter at the time. He was anxious to have Mackie's death recorded as a suicide. To keep things quiet."

"You think he was involved."

"I have no evidence for anything," Dennis told her. "But I do know that someone somewhere is hiding something."

She nodded. Her hair was incredibly thick, her skin pale against it. He could understand what the DCI saw in her.

"I've got my first hearing with the magistrates tomorrow," he told her.

"I know that. It's routine. They'll refer to the Crown Court. I'll do some digging, and build a solid enough case to go back to the CPS."

"What about PSD?"

"Sorry?" She frowned.

"Professional Services Department. They're convinced of my guilt. Even if the courts don't find me guilty, I stand to lose my job. My pension."

"You won't."

"No?"

She stood up. "You had nothing to do with Tim Mackie's death, Dennis. You don't mind if I call you Dennis, do you?"

"No," he said. He didn't have much choice in the matter, it seemed.

"Good. I'm going to get them to drop the case before it even reaches court. And I'll get you reinstated in your job."

CHAPTER FORTY-FIVE

"So," Lesley said as they filtered off the M40 onto the M42, "what's our plan?"

"I thought you'd have that worked out already," said Stanley. He was at the wheel, having swapped with her at Cherwell Valley Services.

"I've got some ideas. But it's useful to know what you think."

"Well, there's the family to speak to."

"Watson's family."

"Yeah."

"He's got a girlfriend and a brother, as far as I'm aware."

"The brother..."

"He's dodgy too." Lesley pulled down the sun visor and checked her face. She looked tired. This wasn't how she'd expected to spend the weekend following her wedding.

"So we don't want to talk to him."

"His brother's dead. We talk to him, either way. I want to see the look in his face when he talks about Zee. Work out if he's responsible."

"For his own brother's death." ˎ

"These are not nice people, Stanley."

"No."

"Not as bad as Hamm, though."

They turned off the M42 onto the M6. The traffic was building, even on a Sunday afternoon. This wasn't Dorset.

"You investigated him?" Stanley asked. "When you were up here?"

"I did. There was an operation. Canary. We were investigating a group of men who were abusing children. Hamm was suspected of providing the children, for money." She pulled in a breath. "We were able to arrest three of his 'clients', but didn't have enough to arrest him. He was a slippery bastard."

They reached the Aston Expressway and she looked out of the window. The Aston Villa ground slid by on their right. She'd often taken this route in. Despite hooking up and over the city, it was quicker than fighting their way through the south of the city to reach the Force CID offices in Harborne.

"But you got him eventually."

"There was an air crash. A terror attack at New Street Station." Lesley's hand went to the back of her neck, where she'd been injured in the explosion, the injury that had led to her being transferred to Dorset. It seemed a lifetime ago. "Hamm was trafficking women and children from Eastern Europe. There was a girlfriend. She helped us put together enough evidence to arrest him." She looked at Stanley, trying to push some lightness into her voice. Trying to forget the explosion, the sight of a colleague being blown up in front of her. "It was Zoe's team that got him. That's who we're going to see."

"DI Finch?" Stanley checked his rearview mirror, then indicated to leave the motorway. They filtered onto the Aston Expressway. Lesley could smell the city. It felt heavy.

"Zoe," she replied, looking out of the passenger window over the grey mass of the city. "And DS Sheila Griffin, from the Organised Crime unit. She's been investigating the gang who took over, after Hamm and his mates were taken off the streets."

"The Brum Boys."

"That's them." She tapped the window. The glass was cold. "Zee Watson is on file as a suspected gang member. West Midlands have been watching him for a couple of years. Nobody expected him to turn up dead in Dorset."

"He was breaking Hamm out," Stanley said. He'd shown her the CCTV, the image of Watson approaching the prison van. There was a moment when he lifted his balaclava.

"Only problem is," Lesley told him, "I've no fucking idea why."

He didn't answer, too focused on the roads.

"Have you driven in a city before?" Lesley asked him.

"Exeter, a couple of times."

"A proper city. Not a glorified town with a cathedral."

He shook his head.

"I'm sorry, Stanley. I should have taken over. I'll do the first section, on the way back."

He was sweating, she realised.

"OK, boss." He checked his rearview mirror again, his movements jerky. "Thanks. You were saying, about not knowing why Watson would want to break Hamm out."

"It makes no sense," she said. "Watson and his mates took over Hamm's territory after he died. Hamm being in prison was the best thing that happened to them. Why would they want their old rival back out?"

"Maybe he broke Hamm out so he could kill him."

"That makes no sense either. Why go to all that trouble when Hamm is nice and tight in a high security prison?"

Stanley shrugged.

"Left hand lane here," she said. They were at the Five Ways roundabout, having taken the underpasses through the city. "You want the turnoff to Harborne."

They'd practically pass her old house. Terry's house, now. She should stop off, speak to Sharon.

No. Her mind was on the case. She was in no mood for a social call on her daughter, who might not even be in.

And besides, she didn't want Stanley meeting her ex-husband.

"Hopefully we'll get some intelligence from Zoe and Sheila," she said. "Find out what was going on up here. Why Watson wanted Hamm dead."

"Which way?" They were at a set of traffic lights.

"That way." Lesley pointed. Harborne was just over a mile away. It felt strange coming back. She'd expected it to feel like a blanket. Instead, it felt like a cold bath.

"Keep going straight until you reach the Green Man pub, then turn right at the lights. The satnav's got it right."

"Satnav's just confusing, on roads like this."

OK. I get the message. "Like I say, Stanley, I'll take over on the way back." Lesley looked at him. Was he nervous about meeting her old colleagues? Concerned they'd think he was a yokel?

She thought of her own attitude when she'd arrived in Dorset. The way she'd looked down her nose at the team. Especially Dennis, with his swear jar and tweed coats.

Dennis.

How was Elsa getting on? Had she convinced him to hire her?

She smiled. Elsa could be persuasive.

"We're here, boss. Is there a code, or should I wait?"

"Wait. We want them to know we're here."

"Right." He stopped the car at the gates to Harborne Police Station, his face pale.

"It'll be fine, Stanley. Let me do the talking, and you take notes."

"Sounds about right, boss."

"But if you think of anything, jump in. I brought you here for a reason."

He frowned. Probably trying to work out what that reason was.

Truth was, she wasn't sure herself. But she was glad she wasn't alone.

CHAPTER FORTY-SIX

Tina shrugged her coat off as she and Meera walked into the office. The building was cold and dark today, most of its inhabitants enjoying a Sunday at home.

Not them. They had a murder investigation to pursue.

"Thanks for letting me stop off," she said to Meera as the DS sat at her desk.

Meera looked up. "I know what it's like. I'm impressed that you're working, with such a little one. I don't think you'd catch Jill doing what you're doing."

Tina smiled. Did it make her a bad person, that she wanted to be at work when she could be at home with her husband and baby? It wasn't that she preferred work. Just that she needed both.

"Don't look like that," Meera said. "I'm here with you, aren't I? And you got me to stop off so you could give him a feed."

Tina nodded and sat down. Meera had driven back, her driving smooth and confident. She'd done the response vehicle training, just like Tina had. It had only taken them thirty-five minutes to get back, and they hadn't broken a single speed limit.

"OK," Meera said. "Let's see what we can find out about Dawn Stephens."

Tina nodded. "She said her mum lives in Osmington."

Meera was barely listening, her eyes on her screen. "Hmmm."

They'd stopped off at the mum's address en route, too, to find no one in. Dawn had said her mum was ill. So where was she?

"We'll need to go back to her," Tina said. "Get the alibi confirmed."

"We won't. You heard her getting it wrong."

Meera was right. Tina had replayed the recording on her phone in the car, the two mistakes Dawn had made when recounting her alibi backwards. The timing was the sort of mistake anyone might have made, but the fact she'd mistaken a supermarket trip for a visit to the pharmacy was more suspicious. And then she'd given herself away at the end. Asking if she'd remembered it right.

They'd interviewed three more staff members after Dawn, and none had been suspicious.

"I'm bringing up the CCTV again," Tina said. She clicked on the file from the lighthouse and fast forwarded to the point where the person in uniform had appeared.

She watched as the group went into the lighthouse, Hamm's body between them.

The shape fitted. Not too tall, not too large. But not slim either. Just like Dawn.

"We need more," she said across the desk.

"I know. I'm on PNC now, seeing if we can find her."

"You're thinking she might have a record?"

A shrug. "Not a record, necessarily. But any contact with the police can help us get a feel for her." Meera looked up. "Can you try calling the mum? I'm worried her daughter will get to her before we do."

"She might have already." But Tina was already dialling the number.

She waited as it rang out.

"Hello?" A small voice. Croaky.

"Mrs Stephens?" Tina asked.

"Yes. What are you selling? I'm not looking for double gl—"

"I'm not a salesperson," Tina told her. "My name's Detective Constable Abbott. I work for Dorset Police."

"Is this about Mrs Henderson's break-in last week? Someone already knocked on my door."

The woman had an accent: not Dorset. It was familiar.

"It's not, Mrs Stephens. I hope you don't mind, but I need to ask you what you were doing on Friday evening."

"Sorry? It was Wednesday, the break-in was. Are you saying there was another one?"

"No. It's just—"

"In which case, I'm sorry, but I won't be able to help you. What happened to Mrs Henderson made me nervous. So I went to my friend Freda's on Friday night. She let me stay in her spare room."

"On Friday?"

"Yes. Sorry. I know you're probably looking for witnesses, but—"

"You're saying that on Friday evening, you were out all night?"

"I went to Freda's at five. She likes to eat early. Do you need me to talk to someone about Wednesday?"

The accent had become clearer, as Mrs Stephens grew

more anxious. Tina could place it now. And she knew who it sounded like.

"Thanks, Mrs Stephens," she said. "You've been very helpful."

She hung up.

"Brummie," she said.

Meera looked up. "What?"

"Dawn's mum. She had a Brummie accent. Sounded just like the boss."

"Plenty of Brummies retire down here."

Tina stood up, suppressing a smile. "And she was out on Friday night. Stayed at a friend's."

"Just when Dawn said she spent the evening with her."

"Exactly." Tina clutched the back of her chair. "We need to talk to Dawn again."

"We certainly do. I've got more."

"What?"

Meera beckoned. Tina hurried round the desks to look at Meera's screen.

"She's got a brother," Meera said.

Tina looked at Meera's screen and whistled. "Suspected gang member."

"Brum Boys." Meera turned to look at Tina, her eyes alight.

Tina could feel her pulse racing. "We need to call the DCI."

CHAPTER FORTY-SEVEN

LESLEY AND STANLEY were back in Lesley's car, heading for the home of Zee Watson's mother. DI Zoe Finch was with them.

"So have you spoken to her yet about her son's death?" Lesley asked, looking in the rearview mirror at Zoe. She was driving, Stanley in the passenger seat beside her.

"No. I wanted to see the look on her face, we'll be doing it together."

"OK." Lesley slowed the car at the roundabout leading to Stonehouse Lane, Old Quarry Park on their left. Green spaces like this had felt expansive when she'd lived up here. Now they just felt cramped.

"You say they?" Lesley asked. "Is there a dad on the scene too?"

"A brother. We reckon he's part of Brum Boys too."

"We've heard about him. He lives in the same house, then?"

"Seems so."

Lesley nodded. "She's going to be wary."

"She is."

"What have you asked her about the circumstances of her son's death?"

"Not much. We asked her what she knew about him being in Dorset, but she claimed she had no idea."

"Where does he live normally?"

"Weoley Castle."

"Not far from his mum."

"Or his brother."

"We're going to need to talk to him too." Lesley turned off the dual carriageway onto Jiggins Lane, heading for Bartley Green.

"That won't be easy. He's not been in when we've called round."

A few minutes later, they arrived at the Watson house: a former council house in a street of properties that had once been identical but over the years had been altered, some more effectively than others. The Watsons' was, surprisingly, the neatest on the street. It had sparkling new windows, daffodils in pots either side of the door and the driveway looked as if it was regularly swept.

"Someone looks after their gaff," Stanley said.

Lesley grunted. "She does."

They stopped the car and spent a minute watching the house, Lesley scanning the windows.

"Stanley," she said, "I want you to keep your eyes open once we're inside. See if you can spot anything indicating anyone in that family might have known Trevor Hamm, or been involved with a gang."

"We've already got enough on that," Zoe pointed out.

Lesley shrugged, her eyes still on the house. It had lace curtains: white, clean. One of them shifted.

"She's seen us," Zoe said.

"We're not in a squad car," Stanley said.

Lesley turned to look at him. "Families like the Watsons, they can spot police a mile off. Three of us, sitting in a modern saloon car in smart clothes."

Stanley's gaze flicked towards Zoe, who was wearing her usual leather jacket and jeans.

"Oi," Zoe said.

"Zoe might look casually dressed to you," Lesley said. "But her jacket's clean. Her jeans aren't ripped. She might as well be wearing a suit."

"OK." Stanley didn't look convinced.

"Right," Lesley said. "Showtime."

She got out of the car and strode to the house, not waiting for the others. She indicated the side gate to Stanley. "Keep an eye on that for a minute or two while we go in."

"I thought you wanted me to—"

"You can follow us in after a couple of minutes. I just don't want anyone using the time it takes us to get inside to make a quick exit."

"No problem, boss." Stanley folded his arms across his chest, watching the side gate.

Lesley turned as the front door opened. A woman in her forties wearing a pristine Take That T-shirt and a pair of jeans as unblemished as Zoe's stood in front of them. She looked them up and down, her expression blank.

"We're not buying."

Lesley held up her ID. "Carrie Watson?"

'That's me." The eyes narrowed. "What's he done now?"

He. Lesley wondered which son she was referring to.

"Do you mind if we come in?"

A sigh. "That means it's bad. I told him, Detective. If he carries on like this, he won't have a home to come back to. He keeps—"

"If you don't mind, I think this is best discussed inside." Lesley had noticed a shadow in the window next door, separated from the Watson house by a low fence. The next door driveway was far less neat than this one.

Mrs Watson's gaze followed hers. "*Him*." She raised her eyebrows. "Come on then. Let's not give them too much entertainment this time."

She turned and disappeared into the house. Lesley signalled for Stanley to stay behind and followed the woman, Zoe right behind her.

The hallway was empty. Ahead of them was a narrow kitchen, to the left a tidy living room. Carrie Watson had already taken a seat on the sofa.

She was clearly accustomed to police visits.

Lesley and Zoe entered the room, Lesley taking the armchair opposite the woman and Zoe sitting on the other end of the sofa. Zoe took out a notepad and brushed her red hair out of her face. Lesley noticed a few tiny strands of grey running through it. That was new.

The fact that Mrs Watson had gone on ahead meant Stanley could stay outside without being separated from them by a closed front door. Lesley looked through the living room door to catch a glimpse of him shifting from side to side, still in the same spot on the front path.

"Mrs Watson," she said. "My name's DCI Clarke. This is DI Finch. My colleague is DC Brown. DC Brown and I are from the Dorset police force. DI Finch is local."

"I've seen you before," Mrs Watson said, looking at Zoe.

Her expression was neutral. She looked more like a regular victim of petty crime than the parent of a gang member.

"Once," Zoe confirmed. "When your younger son was arrested."

"He got off though, didn't he?"

"He received a noncustodial sentence. Community service."

A sniff. "Which he did all of. I made sure of it."

"Thank you."

Lesley leaned forward. "We aren't here to talk about your younger son. David, is it?"

"Day. That's what he calls himself. Just like Samuel calls himself Zee."

Gang names, Lesley thought.

"We're here to talk to you about Zee." She watched the woman's face. "I'm sorry to tell you that we found his body yesterday, on Portland Bill. We believe his death was suspicious."

Carrie stared at them. "Zee?"

Lesley nodded. From the corner of her eye, she could see Zoe looking around the room, taking everything in. The front door closed, gently. She resisted the urge to turn and look; it would be Stanley, taking the opportunity to look around.

She wondered if Day was in the house, or if Stanley had seen him leaving. If he'd been here at all.

Carrie Watson had crumpled. Her face had reddened and her limbs gone slack. Her mouth hung open and a low wail came from it.

"No," she muttered, shaking her head slowly. She looked up, her eyes full of tears. "No."

"I'm so sorry, Mrs Watson."

The woman stood up. She shot out a hand as her balance

teetered. Zoe stood and grabbed it, to be rewarded with a dirty look and a shake that separated the two women.

"No," she repeated.

"Mrs Watson, is there anyone else in the house?" Zoe asked. "Anyone who can support—"

"No!" Carrie brought her hand up, almost hitting her face. "You're wrong." She gave Zoe a long look, then turned and ran out of the room.

"Where's Stanley?" Zoe hissed.

Lesley shrugged. "Inside. Don't know where."

"We don't have a warrant to search this house. If she finds him..."

"It'll be fine. She's the mother of a gang member."

"Who lives in a house like this."

Lesley swallowed. "I'll go after her."

She went to the door, but was met by Carrie coming back the other way, almost crashing into her. She waved an object in Lesley's face.

"See!" she said. She hit Lesley with the object. It was a card.

Lesley grabbed it and turned it over. It was a postcard. On the front was a beach photo. *Hola! from Gran Canaria.*

She frowned. On the back were a few words:

Hi, Mum. Having a fab time. See you next week. Love, Zee.

"It's dated three days ago," Carrie said. "He's on holiday, in Gran Canaria. See! He can't have been in Dorset. You've got the wrong person."

Zoe looked at Lesley.

I'm not wrong, Lesley thought. She'd recognised Zee Watson's body. She'd shown photos to Zoe back at Harborne Police Station. It was him, alright.

She handed the card to Zoe. "Look at the postmark."

Zoe looked down at the postcard. "London."

"Yep." Lesley kept her voice low. "He got that card from someone, then sent it so his mum would think he was on holiday."

"When in reality he was involved in a prison break."

"Exactly."

Lesley turned the card towards their victim's mother, who had taken a step back and was breathing loudly. "I'm sorry, Mrs Watson. But we have video of your son taking part in a prison break on Friday. And I personally identified his body yesterday. This postcard was sent from London. I think he wanted you to think he was on holiday."

Carrie Watson had been standing in the doorway, her chest puffed out, her face red. Now she peered at the postcard and deflated, slumping into the doorframe.

Stanley appeared behind her. "No one else in the house, boss. But there's a laptop."

Mrs Watson turned to him. "Who are you? And what are you doing snooping around my house?"

Lesley looked at Stanley. "DC Brown. I want you to stay here with Mrs Watson. She needs someone to keep an eye on her."

Stanley wasn't trained as a FLO. But he'd seen her briefing them enough times. Hopefully he knew his real role: to make sure no evidence was removed while they got a warrant.

"Loud and clear, boss." He gave her a tight-lipped nod.

Good. "Thanks, DC Brown. Mrs Watson, I'm very sorry to be the bearer of such bad news. But we also believe your son was involved in the murder of another individual. And we will have to search this house."

"Have some respect."

"We do. To both victims. And we'll be careful. But anything we find here could help us identify your son's killer."

"That won't bring him back."

"No. I understand that. But why don't you let DC Brown here get you a cuppa while we get the search over with?"

CHAPTER FORTY-EIGHT

THE GATES to Boscombe Pier were closed, but the ice cream stall at the entrance was still open. Elsa bought herself a mint choc chip cone and walked along the promenade, attempting to inject some warmth into her body while she waited for the person she was meeting.

She passed a line of beach huts and was halfway through the ice cream before she turned to head back to the pier. A woman was at the ice cream stall, placing her own order.

Elsa picked up pace to join the woman just as a double cone was handed over: one scoop of vanilla and another of blueberry.

"Nice choice," Elsa said.

Sadie Dawes smiled, licking the blueberry ice cream on the top. "I saw you buying yours when I was walking down from the car park. And I never pass up an opportunity for ice cream."

"Even in March."

"Even in March. Shall we walk?"

Elsa turned and began walking, alongside the same beach

huts she'd already passed. This time, she didn't stop when she'd finished the rest of her scoop of ice cream. She bit into the cone, aware of Sadie slowly licking her own beside her.

"So," Sadie said between licks. "I have to admit I wasn't expecting this."

Elsa kept her stride even. The beach was quiet, but even so. Sadie was a famous face, locally. Elsa didn't want anyone spotting the two of them and wondering what they were discussing. Or even worse, listening in.

"I'm representing Dennis Frampton," Elsa replied. No harm in getting to the point.

Sadie slowed. "You are?"

"He's appearing before the magistrates tomorrow, which will be no more than a formality. Passing the case on to the Crown Court."

"It is murder."

"Indeed." All murder cases spent a few moments in the Magistrates Court before being referred upwards. Elsa often wondered why they even bothered with the first stage.

"In that case," Sadie told her, "I know why you're here."

"You do."

"Your new wife has told you that I've been poking around into Mackie's death for the last two years, and you're hoping I'll have information that can help you get DS Frampton acquitted."

"Strictly speaking, he's not DS Frampton right now. He's been suspended, which means—"

"I know how it works, Ms Short. Or are you Mrs Clarke now?"

Elsa smiled, thinking of the nicknames she and Lesley had for each other. "I'm not. But Elsa will do."

"Good. And if I give you information, what will you do with it?"

"You just said so yourself. I'll use it to help my client."

"I've been building this story for years. It'll be an exclusive. It'll—"

"It'll make your career, if you're right." Elsa swallowed the last of her cone, stopped walking, and turned to Sadie. "But what about Dennis? This isn't just his career on the line. It's his freedom. He didn't kill anyone."

"Oh, I know that."

"You do?"

A nod. Sadie carried on walking. "You know," she said, "last time I had a meeting like this it was with your wife's boss."

"Superintendent Carpenter."

"He's not a nice man. He threatened me. Told me that I'd regret it if I carried on digging where I wasn't wanted."

"You ignored him."

"Of course I did." A smile. "Best way to get me to dig further."

Elsa stopped walking, a thought suddenly hitting her. "Has it occurred to you that he knew that's what you'd do?"

"He's pretty stupid, if he did."

"No." Elsa put a hand on Sadie's arm. The journalist was wearing a black waterproof. Practical, both for keeping dry and for not getting herself noticed. It wasn't the yellow parka Elsa had seen her wearing onscreen.

"What I mean," Elsa continued, "is that Anthony Carpenter knows full well what you're like. He knows that warning you off is the best way to get you to do the exact opposite."

"That makes no sense." Sadie crumpled the paper her ice cream cone had come in and stuffed it into her pocket. Ahead of them, a flock of seagulls moved across the sand, feathers ruffling in the wind. "He's involved, I'm sure. He pulled Phipps off the official investigation, and he's tried to stop Lesley from investigating too. He wants us to leave well alone."

Elsa looked at her. "I think you could be wrong. I think Superintendent Carpenter wants us to find out who really killed Tim Mackie."

"Really?"

"It makes sense." Elsa put her hands in her pockets. She wasn't sure how this helped Dennis, but it felt important. She nodded. "Carpenter's a political animal. He knows how to manipulate people. I think there's a good chance that's what he's been doing with you."

Maybe Lesley too, she thought.

"OK," said Sadie, looking pensive. "Which means..."

Elsa nodded.

Sadie pushed the hood of her coat back and looked at Elsa. "Which means he knows who did it."

CHAPTER FORTY-NINE

"Sheila isn't in the office today," Zoe told Lesley as they drove away from Carrie Watson's house. "I spoke to her earlier, we're going to her house in Cradley Heath."

"That's fine," Lesley said. "No chance we can pick up some food on the way, is there?"

It was 1.30 pm and she hadn't eaten since a hurried slice of toast that morning.

"Ooh, yes please," added Stanley. He'd come with them, Zoe having called into Force CID and arranged for him to be relieved by a qualified FLO.

Zoe smiled. "Stanley, I'll have to introduce you to Rhodri. You've got a lot in common."

"Who's Rhodri?"

Lesley looked in the rearview mirror. "One of Zoe's team. He managed to get himself promoted yet?"

"He took the exam for the fourth time last week," Zoe said. "Still waiting on the results."

"Good on him. What about Connie?"

"She's got herself a transfer to local CID as a DS."

"Well done Connie. So there's just you and Rhodri left now?"

"Rhod'll move to another Force CID team if he gets promoted. Or if he doesn't. I'm transferring to another force."

Lesley glanced at Zoe. "You are?"

A nod. "Carl got himself a transfer to Cumbria. I'm in line for a posting up there. All we need to do is find somewhere to live and we'll be gone."

"I thought you'd never leave Birmingham."

They drove under the M5. Zoe pointed. "Keep going. There's a McDonalds drive-through in Halesowen. That do you, Stanley?"

"Perfect," replied Lesley and Stanley in unison. Zoe smiled. None of them were exactly healthy eaters. Lesley remembered that Zoe only ate home-cooked food when her son made it for her.

"How does your son feel about you moving?" Lesley asked. "He's at university now, yes?"

"Stirling. He sees Mo from time to time. I'll be closer to him, it'll be good."

Zoe didn't sound entirely convinced, but Lesley wasn't about to pry. If she'd been as closely involved as Zoe had been in the arrest of Trevor Hamm and the investigation into police corruption that had gone alongside it, she'd be thinking of moving away, too.

"Left at this roundabout, there it is," Zoe said.

They ordered their food and ate as they drove, Lesley balancing hers on her knee in between taking bites at traffic lights and roundabouts. She'd forgotten how stop-start the traffic here was, even on a Sunday.

"You'll find it odd, being in a rural team," she told Zoe. "I was like a fish out of water at first. I like it now."

Lesley turned left at a roundabout. Sheila's house was a couple of streets away.

"Don't remind me," Zoe told her. "I'm trying to focus on the positives."

"So why are you moving, if you're dreading it?"

Zoe shrugged. "Change of scene. I've got nothing to tie me to Brum anymore. My mum died, not that I ever saw her. Nicholas has gone off to uni. And you're gone, too."

Lesley turned to her. "You didn't stay here on my account?"

"Not entirely. But I liked working for you. Frank... not so much."

DCI Frank Dawson had been one of Lesley's DI's when she'd been up here. After her departure he'd been promoted into her role.

"I can imagine," Lesley said.

"Here we are," Zoe said.

Lesley found a parking spot and manoeuvred her car in.

They got out of the car and followed Zoe to a neat semi with a blue front door that needed a fresh coat of paint. Music pumped out of an upstairs window.

Zoe rapped on the door. "Bell's not working."

"And the music?" Lesley asked, gesturing upwards with her head.

"Dooley. Sheila's oldest."

"He likes Queen?"

"They. Dooley's NB. And yes. They bloody love Queen. If you spend any time in this house, you end up getting used to it." She smiled. Lesley didn't remember Zoe being particularly friendly with Sheila Griffin before, but it was nice to see her happy.

A short, dark-haired woman flung the door open. "Zoe!"

She pulled Zoe in for a hug, then spotted Lesley and stiffened. "Ma'am."

Lesley put a hand on Sheila's arm. "I'm not your senior officer any more. Lesley'll do. And this is Stanley, from Dorset."

"Right. Lesley it is. You're not on the force anymore?"

"Not *this* one."

"Ah, right. Anyway, come in. I gather you've been to see Carrie Watson this morning?"

"Yeah," Zoe said. "We told her about her son's death."

They entered a wide kitchen at the back of the house. It looked out over a garden that was in need of some weeding. A dog stirred in a basket near the back door.

"Don't mind Freddie, he's ancient and blind," Sheila said. "He won't bother you."

"Can I?" Stanley asked, making for the dog.

"Course you can. He'll love you forever."

Stanley bent to the dog and started rubbing between its ears. Zoe was at the sink, filling the kettle.

"Coffee for you, boss?" she asked.

Lesley raised an eyebrow at the *boss* but said nothing. "Please."

"Right-o."

Sheila was sitting at the formica-topped table. She looked up at Lesley. "So how did she take it?"

"Not well." Lesley took the seat opposite her. "She wasn't what I expected."

"I know. Crying shame how her boys turned out, given what she's like."

"What's their father like? Is he involved in the gang?"

A shake of the head. "We know nothing about him. No idea if he's ever been around."

Lesley shrugged. "Samuel and David are adults, I guess. It's not like they're juvenile delinquents."

Sheila took a cup of tea that Zoe offered her. "That's an old-fashioned phrase. And no. They were both good kids, from what I can determine. Went to school, got their GCSEs, went on to college and did apprenticeships."

"What kind of apprenticeships?"

"Plumbing, that kind of thing. Not sure of the details."

"So what went wrong?"

"We're not sure about that. But at some point we think Samuel – Zee – was introduced to Hamm."

Lesley shivered. "Hamm was a people trafficker. He sold kids to wealthy men."

Sheila shook her head. "I don't think it was that. Hamm's child victims don't tend to end up in organised crime themselves."

"You're sure?" Zoe asked. "Going through something like that..."

"Oh, I'm not saying they don't end up involved in crime. But the Watson brothers have overseen the rise of Brum Boys from a few lads selling drugs in Bartley Green to an organisation doing its level best to take over from Hamm. They've achieved a lot."

Lesley sniffed. "That's one way of looking at it." She sipped at the coffee Zoe had put in front of her.

"I say they're doing their level best," Sheila told her. "That doesn't mean they're there yet."

"And they're unlikely to get there, with Zee dead," Zoe added.

"Do you think Zee Watson might have got involved in Hamm's breakout as a way of precipitating his own gang's rise?" Lesley asked.

Sheila wrinkled her nose. "I don't see how Hamm being out of prison would do him any good. But I can see how Hamm being dead would."

"He was worried Hamm might still be running things from prison."

"It's happened before."

Lesley leaned back. "We saw Zee on CCTV. The accident they staged to get Hamm out."

"Any evidence of him being responsible for Hamm's death?" Sheila asked.

"Not yet."

"What about the other video, boss?" Stanley said. He was at the end of the table, listening. "The one from the lighthouse."

"They're all in balaclavas."

Lesley sighed. "They are." She downed the last of her coffee. "OK. Thanks, Sheila. This is helpful. But Stanley and I need to get back to Dorset."

"You're not staying up here?" Zoe asked. "It thought you had a house in Edgbaston."

"My ex bought me out. And I want to get home to my new wife."

"Congratulations on that," Sheila said. "I hear she's a lawyer."

Word gets around. "She is. A damn good one, too." Lesley hoped Elsa was finding a way to help Dennis. "Come on, Stanley."

Stanley nodded his goodbyes to Sheila just as the kitchen door opened and a young person wearing baggy jeans and a nose ring appeared.

"Mum. Who are these?"

"It's just my colleagues, Dooley love," Sheila replied. "They're going, we can make tea together."

"I'm going out."

"Oh."

The young person eyed Zoe. "How's Nick?"

"He's fine. Says hello."

Lesley looked from Zoe to Dooley. She wondered if Sharon had many friends, up in Birmingham. She hadn't brought any Bournemouth College friends home. But she must have made some.

Lesley had moved her daughter halfway across the country to be with her, but still she knew hardly anything about her. She needed to try harder.

At the door, she checked her phone. A missed call from Tina.

She frowned and hit voicemail. As she played the message, her mouth opened.

"What is it, boss?" Stanley asked. "You look like you've..."

Lesley put up a hand. "Sheila, are you aware of someone called Ewan Stephens?"

Sheila frowned. "He's a member of the Brum Boys. Why?"

"Because his sister works at Portland lighthouse. And my team believe she's the one who let them in to dump Trevor Hamm's body."

CHAPTER FIFTY

LESLEY GOT into the driver's seat of the car, Stanley beside her. It was getting dark. Lesley pulled her coat tighter and took out her phone.

"I think we're ready to arrest Dawn Stephens, don't you?" she said.

"I don't think you need my opinion, boss."

"I'd like it." Without Dennis, she had no one to bounce ideas off. No one to sense-check with before she made important calls. Zoe was still in Sheila's house and besides, she wasn't a member of the investigation team.

"OK," Stanley replied.

"Tina and Meera interviewed the woman this morning. They've spoken to her mum and already established that Dawn invented her alibi."

Two young men were walking towards the car. Lesley watched them approach in the rearview mirror and start to walk past. One of them put out a hand to touch the car then spotted her and withdrew it. She smiled.

"And," she added, "she's got a brother in the Brum Boys."

"Who Sheila knew about."

Lesley looked askance at him. "Sheila?"

Stanley reddened. "Sorry. DS Griffin."

Lesley laughed and gave him a playful tap on the arm. "If I remember right, they both told you not to be so formal."

"Ah. Sorry."

"Christ, Stanley. You need to lighten up."

"Sorry. Yes."

Leslie suppressed another laugh. Telling Stanley to lighten up had had the opposite effect.

"If you don't mind me saying, boss..."

"Go on," she told him.

"The sister of a gang member thing. It's circumstantial."

"It is."

"The real question is where was her brother, while all this was going on?"

Lesley looked at the DC. "You're right. Shit."

"What's up?" He looked at the steering wheel for what felt like the tenth time. He was anxious to get home, she realised.

"I'm sorry, Stanley. I've got bad news."

He frowned. "You have?"

"We're not going home yet." She sighed. "Elsa's going to be well pissed off."

"Why?" He tugged at his sleeve. "Why aren't we going home, I mean?"

"Because we need to talk to Ewan Stephens, before his sister does."

CHAPTER FIFTY-ONE

Tina threw herself into a chair. "God, I'm knackered." She leaned back, her body aching. She was used to sleepless nights, and long feeds sitting in uncomfortable positions, and being at the beck and call of a baby all day. She thought that was as exhausting as it got. She'd forgotten how much witness interviews took it out of her.

"You love it, though," Mike said. "I can see it in your eyes."

She smiled at him. "How are you getting on, here with Louis?"

A shrug. "It's boring, and tiring, and sometimes it feels like a day lasts a year. But I'm glad I've had the chance to do it."

"You don't think I'm a bad mum, abandoning him and going back to work?"

Mike slid off the sofa and onto the floor. He put a hand on her knee. "T, I went back to work when he was two weeks old. What kind of dad does that make me, by your logic?"

"It's different."

"Well, it shouldn't be. The DCI let us share the parental

leave, didn't she? That shows that she doesn't think we're any different, as parents. And she's right."

She placed a hand over his. "I know, love. But my mum gave up work when my big sister was born. I feel guilty for not wanting to do that."

"Your mum went back to work when you were three, though."

"I know." She yawned. "I'm sorry, Mike. I'm being illogical. Ignore me."

He picked up her hand and kissed it. "Never. So how was today?"

"We made a breakthrough."

"You did?"

"One of the lighthouse staff. She invented her alibi. Did a bloody shitty job of it, too. And she's related to a gang member in Birmingham."

"Wow."

"Yeah. It's almost like she wanted us to find her."

"Maybe she did. Maybe she was coerced."

Tina looked at her husband. "I hope not."

"Why?"

"Because then she'll use that in her defence. We might not get a conviction."

"She can't be your only suspect."

"She's not." She stifled another yawn. "What time is it?"

"Just gone five."

"Why am I so tired? I'd normally still be at work now."

"It's Sunday. And the boss said you only had to work till lunchtime."

"That's all the overtime they'd approved."

His face darkened. "You're not getting paid, for this afternoon?"

"Mike, we've both worked more than the hours we were paid for on murder cases. You know that's how it works."

His gaze went upwards, to where Louis was napping in their bedroom. "It's different now."

"It is. I'm sorry. Isn't it time we woke him, anyway? He'll never sleep tonight."

"It's hard to wake him up when the house is so quiet."

"I know."

Tina climbed the stairs. Her son was in his Moses basket, squeezed in beside their bed. Mike came up behind her and put his arms around her shoulders.

"We made that," he said.

"We did." She looked round. "Don't get any ideas."

"What? What kind of ideas?"

"You'll be after a little brother or sister next."

He squeezed her shoulder. "Even if I did want that, we couldn't afford it. Have you seen the price of nappies?"

Tina kissed him. "Good." She bent over to pick Louis up and kissed his forehead. He stirred, his arm pushing out against her chest.

"So do you have any other suspects?" Mike asked.

"Not yet. We need to piece together the events between the prison break and Hamm being taken to the lighthouse. And find out who was there. It looks like there was a whole bunch of them. If Zee Watson was involved, he wasn't alone."

"Zee Watson?"

"The second victim."

"Ah. You think one of the others might have killed him?"

"If they did, I've no idea why. Maybe one of Hamm's mates did it, revenge."

"From what I've heard, all Hamm's mates are dead or in prison."

"Yeah." Louis grabbed at her shirt. She sighed. "Looks like I'll be feeding him, then."

"You know you love it."

Mike was right. Sitting quietly in a chair, feeding her son, was just what she needed after the day's events.

"I'll give him his feed," she said, "then I want to call the boss. Find out if they've arrested anyone."

"I thought you didn't have any suspects."

"We do have one."

"OK. But don't overdo it, love."

"I won't."

CHAPTER FIFTY-TWO

LESLEY AND STANLEY were outside Ewan Stephens's flat, Stanley peering through the letterbox and Lesley checking the front window. Stephens lived in a fourth floor flat in a block where the staircase and landings were fully exposed to the elements. It was bloody freezing up here.

"He's not in, boss."

She sighed. "State the bleeding obvious."

Stanley let the letterbox flip shut and stood up. "Sorry."

Lesley's phone rang: Tina.

Not now.

"One moment, Stanley." She picked up.

"Tina. It's not the best time."

"I'm sorry, boss. I just wanted to share something with you about Dawn Stephens."

"Something helpful, I hope."

"It might be. I found a record of her applying for a police job, six years ago."

"Just applying."

"Yeah. She's never worked on the force."

"OK." Lesley considered. This didn't feel relevant, but it might turn out to be. "Everything alright back there?"

"Yeah." A pause. "Sorry. Louis's crying."

"You go, Tina. Stop thinking about work. It's Sunday evening."

"Sorry. Are you on your way back?"

"We're outside Dawn Stephens's brother's flat. He's not in."

"He could be at one of his mates' places."

"He could indeed. You let us worry about that, Tina. Spend some time with your husband and son. I'll see you tomorrow sometime."

"OK. Thanks, boss." Tina hung up.

Lesley headed along the open hallway towards the staircase. "We're not getting anywhere here."

"OK." Stanley followed her.

"Excuse me!"

Lesley was at the staircase. She turned back at the sound of the voice.

"Hello?" She couldn't see much in the darkness up here; half of the fluorescent lights above the flat doors were broken.

"You looking for that Ewan kid?" came the voice.

Lesley walked back towards the door they'd been knocking on. Another door was open, just past it. An elderly woman stood half hidden by it, a dog at her feet. She had it on a tight leash.

"We are. Have you seen him?"

"He went on holiday."

"Holiday?" Stanley asked. "Where?"

"Gran Canaria, he said. Asked me to look after this little bastard." She looked down at the dog.

"The dog belongs to him?"

"You think he'd have someone to look after it, wouldn't you? But no, he knocks on me door the morning before he buggers off to the sunshine and tells me the dog'll starve if he doesn't find someone to feed it. Well, I can hardly say no to that, can I?"

"Which day did he tell you he was going on holiday?"

"Wednesday. He knocked on my door at six. I remember cos *Pointless* was just finishing. He told me he'd be back next Wednesday."

Lesley exchanged glances with Stanley. She turned back to the woman. "I don't suppose he left you a key to his flat?"

"Why? You want to get in there?"

Lesley held up her ID. "We're police. A friend of Ewan's has been killed and we want to speak to him."

It wasn't necessarily accurate – fellow gang members weren't always friends – but it might be.

"He didn't give me a key, sorry."

Of course not.

"But Ethel, she lived in that flat before he did. And she *did* give me a key. Hang on a minute."

The woman disappeared into her flat, taking the dog with her. Lesley stamped her feet on the floor as she waited.

"Cold up here, boss," Stanley said.

"You're not joking."

"Here you are." The woman returned with a key held out. The dog had gone inside.

"Thanks," Lesley told her.

"You will give it back, when you're done. Won't you?"

"Of course."

"And you won't tell him?"

"Er, no."

"Cos he's a scary bastard. The truth is, I took his dog cos I thought he might kill the thing if he thought it was going to be a nuisance."

CHAPTER FIFTY-THREE

LESLEY KNOCKED on the door to the flat.

"We already did this," Stanley reminded her.

She nodded. "It's even more important now that we're breaking in. I don't want him in there waiting for us."

"We're not breaking in."

He was right. But they hadn't exactly got a warrant.

She opened the letterbox and bent to it. "Ewan? This is the police. Come to the door, or we're going to come in."

She straightened up and waited, her eyes on Stanley's face. He looked nervous.

"You're not used to this kind of thing, are you?" she asked him.

"What kind of thing?"

"Gangs. Concrete blocks in areas like this." She gestured with her arm.

"Dorset's not all cottages and meadows."

"And don't I know it. But Arthur Kelvin based himself out of a mansion in Sandbanks. Not a council flat in Weoley Castle."

"No."

"OK." Lesley rapped on the door one last time. "He's not in." She put the key in the lock and turned.

As she pushed the door open, she called out. "Ewan, this is the police. We're inside your flat. If you're here, show yourself."

Nothing.

The door opened directly onto a cramped living room. A sofa with stains she'd rather not think about dominated the space, along with a TV opposite it. Old takeaway wrappers littered the floor.

She wrinkled her nose. "Well it certainly smells like he hasn't been here recently."

"There's mould in those mugs." Stanley pointed to three mugs on the floor in front of the sofa.

"Yeah." Lesley scanned the room again. There was little in it apart from the TV, the sofa and the rubbish. Nothing that gave her any indication of what kind of person Ewan Stephens was, or whether he'd been involved in a murder plot.

"Next room," she said.

Stanley went out before her and opened the next door. A kitchen, the surfaces covered in dirty dishes, mouldering food and a bottle of milk that was more green than it was white.

"Ugh," Stanley said.

"He's not exactly house proud."

Stanley grimaced. "Who lives like this?"

Lesley smiled at him. "You're the tidy sort, are you?"

He shrugged. "Goes with being a copper. Tidy mind, tidy space."

Lesley wasn't so sure. The cottage she'd lived in in Wareham when she'd first transferred to Dorset had been a permanent mess. But then, that place seemed messy even when it was empty.

There was something about the low beams and wooden surfaces that screamed clutter. The flat she shared with Elsa was different – light, modern – but still Lesley managed to clutter it up.

"OK. Two more doors," she said.

"The bathroom's a state, but there's nothing useful."

"Let me look."

"You won't like it."

Lesley eyed the DC. "I'm sure I've seen worse."

She opened the door to the bathroom and wondered if maybe she was wrong. The walls were covered in black mould and the surfaces were layered in slime. There was a smell of damp mixed with decay. The tiles above the bath were grouted with more black mould and the bath – well, the bath didn't bear thinking about.

She closed the door, resisting the urge to gag. "Jeez."

"How does he live like this?"

"Maybe he doesn't. Maybe he never spends time here."

"There's no personal belongings."

"No. Maybe in the bedroom…"

She pushed the final door open.

"Wow."

This room was a stark contrast to the others. The bed was neatly made, the duvet threadbare but clean. A desk held notebooks and pens, all lined up. And on the wall were a series of maps.

"Portland Bill," Stanley said.

Lesley stepped closer. There was an Ordnance Survey map of the peninsula. A road map of the area around the prison. And what looked like a plan of the prison itself. Beside the maps were images of the lighthouse.

"Let's have a look at those notebooks," she said.

Stanley picked one of them up. "Lighthouse shifts," he said. "They're all in here." He handed it over.

"And he's circled his sister's shifts."

"So he knew when she'd be able to let them in."

"There are names in here, too. Zee Watson and Day Watson."

"Put the notebook down, Stanley. We need Forensics in here."

Stanley dropped the notebook back onto the desk. "He's part of the gang who broke Hamm out."

"And killed him."

CHAPTER FIFTY-FOUR

"LESLEY, it's Sunday evening. Surely this can wait until morning?"

"I'm sorry, Sir. But no, it can't."

Lesley was in her car, Stanley beside her, outside the block of flats where Ewan Stephens lived. After scanning that first notebook they'd put it down quickly and retreated from the flat. This was a place for a forensics team. Not for them.

She'd called Carpenter's mobile and it had taken three attempts before he'd picked up. There wasn't much point leaving a message, so she'd repeatedly dialled, knowing just how pissed off that would make him.

But she had to do her job, even on a Sunday evening.

She ran through what they'd discovered: Dawn Stephens from the lighthouse staff being caught on camera, Zee Watson being the second victim, Dawn's brother's flat and the maps and notes they'd found inside.

"The Watsons were working with Dawn Stephen's brother. He's suspected of being a gang member, like them. I believe we have enough evidence to arrest Dawn, Ewan and Day Watson too."

"Why the urgency?"

'It's a murder case, Sir. Suspects are starting to slip away. And one of them's already dead."

"West Midlands could make the arrest in the morning."

"With respect, Sir. We've still got to find Ewan and Day, and if Ewan's neighbour knows we're looking for him, someone might have contacted him. We need to bring Dawn Stephens in as soon as possible so she doesn't get a message to the others. And she's in Dorset. For now."

A pause.

"Sir?"

"Very well. You'll have your warrant. Make the arrest. Inform West Midlands and get them looking for David Watson and Ewan Stephens."

"Sir."

"And another thing."

Lesley had been about to hang up and start the ignition.

"Yes, Sir?"

"Is it true that you've got your girlfriend representing Dennis Frampton?"

"Wife, sir. We got married just over a week ago. And I haven't got her doing anything. She's a criminal lawyer. She takes on clients."

"It's a hell of a coincidence."

"She understands elements of his case that another lawyer might not."

"You mean she's got ties to organised crime."

Lesley clenched a fist. *What are you insinuating, Sir?*

"Just as long as you think it's wise, mixing work with your home life."

"It's not the first time Elsa has represented someone in a case I've been connected with."

"No. Well. I hope she's able to ensure justice is done."

"So do I, Sir. So do I."

She hung up, hesitating before starting the car.

Justice is done.

What the hell was that supposed to mean?

CHAPTER FIFTY-FIVE

LESLEY AND STANLEY had spent the night at Zoe's house. Lesley had been given Zoe's son's old room, while Stanley had slept on a pullout bed in the room Zoe used as an office. Lesley was intrigued to know how many case files Zoe had brought home and put in there, but she wasn't about to find out.

The room Lesley was sleeping in had a single bed and bookshelves which were mainly empty. On the other side of the room, under the window, was stacked a pile of boxes. She wondered if they were headed for Stirling, or for Cumbria.

She felt bad about leaving Elsa for the night, and at such short notice. They'd barely been married, and here she was back in Birmingham instead of at home.

It was seven am. Elsa would be up and about, if she was going to be at the Magistrates' Court with Dennis this morning.

"Hey, sweetie." Elsa's voice sounded thick with sleep.

"I didn't wake you, did I?"

"No. Hang on, let's switch to video."

Lesley held out her screen as the chat changed. Elsa was in their kitchen, dressed for court, a cup of coffee in front of her.

"You look ready for battle," Lesley said.

"*You* don't."

Lesley checked her own image in the corner of the screen. She was wearing an old T-shirt of Zoe's and her hair was rumpled. "I'm sleeping in a teenager's bedroom that's full of packing boxes. At least Zoe put us up."

"That's good of her. Will you be home tonight?"

"I hope so. I'm sorry, love."

"I wasn't saying that to make you feel bad. I miss you, is all."

"I miss you too." Lesley touched Elsa's image on the screen."

"You're obscuring the camera. I can't see you."

"Sorry." Lesley removed her hand. "Carpenter got an arrest warrant overnight. The team in Dorset are going to make one arrest this morning." She checked the time; they'd be there already. "But we can't find one of our suspects here. I need to stay up here till we do."

"You can't leave that to Zoe and her team?"

"Maybe. But it's my case."

"Sounds like it's theirs too, judging by who the victim was."

Lesley sighed. "You're right. I'll talk to Zoe, work something out. I'll need to get Carpenter to talk to her Super too."

"That's Dawson, right?"

"He's her DCI. Strictly speaking I should be working with him. But I trust Zoe. And she's got relationships in the Organised Crime team."

"Well, it sounds like you know what you're doing."

"How was Dennis, when you went to see him?"

"He was typical Dennis. Didn't give much away. But he hired me." Elsa gestured down at her suit. "As you can see."

"You've got court this morning."

"I have. And I spoke to Sadie Dawes. We're starting to change our thinking."

"Oh?"

"Your boss. Carpenter."

Lesley pulled the phone closer to her. "What about him?" she muttered.

'I don't think it's him that's involved in all this."

"Didn't Sadie tell you he threatened her?"

"She did. But think about it, love. You know what Sadie's like. Threatening her was always going to get the exact opposite response."

Lesley frowned. "You reckon he used reverse psychology on her?" She didn't think Carpenter was that subtle.

"I'm not sure. But there's someone else I'm looking into."

"Who?"

Elsa shook her head. "I can't tell you the details, sweetie. You're too close to it. Just trust me. Dennis will be fine."

"I hope so. I really do."

CHAPTER FIFTY-SIX

AT HARBORNE POLICE STATION, they went straight to Zoe's office. It felt strange to Lesley, being led like a guest through spaces that had once been so familiar. Stanley was behind her, his eyes roaming the corridors, no doubt imagining her working here. She half expected David Randle to walk out of a door and beckon her into his office, a thought that made her stiffen. He'd long since left Force CID.

Connie was in the outer office, HOLMES open on her screen.

"Hi, Connie," Lesley said before Zoe had a chance to intervene, "I hear congratulations are in order."

Connie glanced at Zoe, who nodded. She stood up, smoothing down her skirt. "Thanks, Ma'am. I'm looking forward to my new role."

Lesley laughed. "You don't need to be so formal with me, Connie. You working on a case?" She indicated the computer screen with a nod of the head.

"Er. The DI asked me to look into Ewan Stephens for you. We're trying to find out where he might be."

"Thanks, Connie. Any joy?" Zoe asked.

"We've got the addresses of a couple of the other gang members."

"He won't be there," Lesley said. "At least, not if he's got any sense." She looked at Zoe. "What are these guys like? How do they compare to Hamm?"

"Delusions of grandeur. Their operation is nowhere near as organised as his was. It revolves around drug supply."

"County lines," said Connie.

"How many pushers have they got?"

"We're still building up a picture, and it's changing all the time. But at various levels, a few dozen. Most of them are small beer. Junkies who've been brought in to push the stuff on to their mates."

"But it's growing?" Lesley suggested.

"It is."

"Where does Ewan fit in?"

"He's barely crossed our radar," Zoe said. "I guess he'll have higher status, now he's introduced them to his sister."

"What effect will Zee Watson's death have?"

"Connie's got a theory on that."

Connie straightened in her chair. "Zee and Day Watson are the ringleaders. I don't think there's anyone else with the capability to run the operation. So I'm expecting that once word gets out about Zee being dead, Day will make himself scarce, and someone from outside Birmingham will swoop in and take over."

"Take over the entire operation?"

"We aren't detecting much in the way of loyalty from their foot soldiers, even from the middle men. Some of them worked for Hamm, most of them didn't. Many of them have only come on board in the last couple of months. So whoever takes over, they'll inherit the entire organisation."

"Do your Organised Crime team have any idea who that might be?"

"Sheila's bosses are talking to the East Midlands force. West Mercia too. It'll come back to bite us in due course."

"OK," said Lesley. "So what you're saying is that we're not going to find Day Watson or Ewan Stephens in Birmingham."

"I reckon not."

"It's a fair assumption." Lesley looked at Stanley. "Which means we might as well get back to Dorset."

"You sure, boss?"

"Meera and Tina will be arresting Dawn Stephens. I want to find out what she's got to say about her accomplices."

"And about who killed Zee Watson," Zoe said. "Keep us in the loop on that one, yes?"

"Of course." Lesley shook Zoe's hand. "Sorry to dump this on you. It's been good working with you again."

CHAPTER FIFTY-SEVEN

"So, first order of business is to go to Dawn Stephens's house and make the arrest," Tina said. They were in the office, Tina pulling her stab vest from a drawer.

Meera looked at her. "You're not going in there until Uniform have checked it's safe."

"I do know that. I've spoken to them and there's a response unit on its way."

"With the kind of people she's involved with, we can't be too careful."

Tina bundled the vest under her arm and grabbed her coat. It had rained all night, and the window seals in her and Mike's house hadn't been up to the task. She'd woken to find a damp patch on the carpet next to her bed. She still felt like she'd never get warm again.

"You OK, Tina? You look drawn."

"Bad night. I'm fine."

"Baby awake all night?"

"That and the weather."

"Tell me about it. Suzi was scared of the rain on the roof.

Her bedroom's in the eaves. We had to bring her into our room."

"I dream of the day Louis sleeps in his own room."

"It'll come." Meera had her own coat on and was by the door. "We'll take my car."

"Works for me."

Tina's desk phone rang.

Shit.

"Sorry. Won't be a minute."

She went back to grab it. "DC Abbott."

"Tina, it's PS Lightfoot."

Tony Lightfoot was the duty sergeant at the front desk.

"Tony, I'm just on my way out to an arrest. Can it wait?"

"You've got a visitor."

Tina chewed her lip. "Give them my contact details, tell them I'll give them a call later today."

"She says it's urgent. I have to say, she looks pretty scared."

"This isn't a public police station. Can't you send her to Poole?"

"She says you interviewed her yesterday."

"Yesterday?"

Tina put a hand over her phone. "I think Dawn Stephens might be downstairs," she hissed to Meera. She removed her hand. "Tony, did you get a name?"

"She won't give it."

Tina sighed. It wasn't like her visitor could stay anonymous forever.

"OK," she said through gritted teeth. "I'll be right down."

She joined Meera at the door. "Sorry about that. But if it is her..."

"Then it'll save us a trip. Let's get down there before she changes her mind."

Tina nodded and followed the DS downstairs.

In the reception area, Dawn Stephens stood by a wall, shuffling from foot to foot. Tina and Meera approached her.

"Dawn?" Tina said. "Why have you come here?"

She was half expecting Meera to jump in and make the arrest. But both of them wanted to know what had brought Dawn to the station first.

Dawn turned. She glanced at Meera and her face darkened.

She stepped in, closer to Tina. She smelled of beer and sweat. Tina wondered if she'd been home since the interview.

"What is it, Dawn?"

Dawn's eyes roamed across Tina's face. They were red-rimmed and wild.

"Dawn. I can't help you if you don't tell me."

"It's Ewan."

"Ewan?"

"My brother."

"He's turned up?"

A shake of the head. "No. Yes."

Tina pushed down impatience. "Tell me what he's done."

"*He* hasn't done anything. Someone else has."

"He's been in a fight?" Meera asked.

"Has he been arrested?" Tina asked. She wondered what the DCI had discovered in Birmingham.

Another shake of the head. "No. None of that. He's dead. Someone killed him."

CHAPTER FIFTY-EIGHT

GINA O'TOOLE's front garden was neat and tidy, only one weed sullying the block-paved driveway. Zoe rubbed her hands together as she stood at the front door, waiting for someone to answer.

At last, the door opened.

"Zoe?" Gina asked. "What's happened?"

"Can I come in?"

"I hate it when you lot say that."

"Sorry." *Can I come in?* would have been the first question, on the night Gina had learned about her daughter's death. "I just wanted to update you on the investigation into Trevor Hamm's death."

"His murder."

"His murder."

"OK. As long as that's all. Come in."

Zoe followed Gina through the hallway and into the kitchen. It wasn't large, but there was just enough space for a table in the corner. Zoe took a seat while Gina went to the sink.

"Coffee, right?" Gina said. "I've got new pods."

"Sounds lovely, thanks. But I won't be long."

"You'll have newer cases to deal with." Gina turned towards Zoe, leaning against the kitchen counter. "Live ones."

"This one's live."

Gina shrugged.

"You know about Hamm's murder, of course," Zoe said. "But he's not the only one."

"Oh?"

"A man called Zee Watson was also killed very near the spot where we found Hamm. We believe he was involved in Hamm's death."

"So you think he was killed in revenge?"

"Possibly. Or the same person might have killed both of them. There's a bit of a turf war going on right now."

"Drug dealers." Gina turned away.

"Yes. But that's not your concern."

"Those people abused my Susie. Killed her. It is my concern. Everything they do is my concern."

"Sorry. Didn't mean to—"

"It's fine." Gina slammed a pod into the machine and closed the compartment.

Zoe sighed. She was doing this all wrong. Mo had spent months building up Gina's trust and now she'd only made the woman angry.

"I'm sorry, Gina. I know none of this is easy. I don't like being the one to bring back memories of—"

Gina's body went slack, still facing away from Zoe. "I don't need *you* to bring up memories." Her voice was rough. "They're here all the time. Why d'you think I bought this wretched coffee machine? Because I used to make instant. But whenever I get the jar out, all I can think of is how your FLO made it for me the day Susie died."

Zoe stood up. "Gina. You don't need to make me a drink."

Gina turned. "I want to." Her eyes were red.

"I'm sorry. Look, I came here because there's new information I need you to know about."

"Tell me. None of it makes any difference, not now."

Zoe stepped towards her. The coffee machine beeped. They both ignored it.

"The call you got from Trevor Hamm."

"The one from the prison."

"Yes. Except it wasn't from the prison. And it wasn't from Hamm."

Gina shook her head. "I'd know his voice."

"Would you? I don't mean to be rude, but you heard him speak briefly in court. That wasn't the best environment to—"

"It was him."

"We've spoken to the prison, and they have an approved list of numbers that inmates are allowed to call. They'd never include family of a victim. And there's no record of a call being made from the prison to your number."

"So someone got him a mobile. Smuggled it in. They do that all the time, don't they?"

Someone's been watching too much TV. "Not as often as you might think. We think it's more likely the call came from someone else. Someone pretending to be Hamm."

"Pretending?"

"Whoever killed him might have wanted to scare you."

Gina's gaze went past Zoe, towards the front door. "Scare me?"

Zoe put a hand on the woman's arm. "We can place a police watch outside your house. Or you might want to move to a family member's, until all this is sorted out."

"You've got two men dead and no suspect, unless there's

something you're not telling me. How long will it be before you get it *sorted out?*"

"I don't know. But Dorset police are working har—"

"It's not you?"

"Hamm was killed in Dorset. So was Zee Watson. It comes under their jurisdiction. And they've got a warrant to arrest two people involved in Hamm's death."

"You think one of them phoned me."

"I hope it was one of them."

Gina sniffed. She raised her gaze to meet Zoe's. "Arrest them, Zoe. Lock them up and throw away the key."

It doesn't work like that. But Zoe could understand why the other woman felt so desperate. "We'll keep you updated on progress. And if we work out where that call came from, you'll be the first to know."

CHAPTER FIFTY-NINE

Dennis's hands were clammy.

He'd told himself it would be fine. That he wouldn't be nervous. It wasn't as if he hadn't been in Dorchester Magistrates' Court plenty of times before.

But his body was betraying him.

He was accustomed to being in the public stands, observing. Or in the witness box, giving evidence about an arrest.

He'd never been in the position of the accused before.

It felt so public, so exposed. All those eyes on him. People taking about him like he wasn't there. His name being read out, his personal details discussed.

He gripped the railing in front of him as the magistrates' clerk addressed his barrister. A man he'd never met, someone Elsa Short had parachuted in at late notice. He wondered if she'd been ready all along, if she'd discussed his case with the barrister before he'd even agreed to hire her. It had been a Sunday, after all.

Sunday. Would he ever have a normal Sunday again?

Would he be able to go to church and hold his head high, without the fear that people were whispering about him?

Dennis Frampton, the killer.

Except they were wrong. Of course they were wrong.

"All rise."

A policeman to his left indicated for him to stand and walk along the row of seats, heading back for the cells. It was all over, and he'd barely heard a word of it.

Elsa was approaching, head down, steps determined. He looked across at her.

"Crown Court," she said. "Two months from now."

"Remand?" he whispered, his voice hoarse.

She shook her head. "Too high a risk, for you. You'll have a tag."

"Did they say that?"

"They did." She gave him a grim smile. She'd be used to clients not hearing a word of proceedings. He'd been determined to concentrate, to listen to every word. But instead it had all been a blur.

Was he losing his mind? Would he be fit to return to policing, if Elsa managed to get him acquitted?

Too soon to worry about that now. He had a date to focus on. Two months away.

"But I'll be talking to the CPS," she told him, as the policeman tugged on his arm. "Presenting evidence. It won't go that far."

"You have to leave now," the policeman said. Not someone Dennis recognised, thank goodness.

Dennis nodded thanks to Elsa as they guided him out of the room. He had to hope she'd fulfil her promise.

CHAPTER SIXTY

"You GO IN, Stanley. I just need to make a call."

"Oh. OK, boss." Stanley got out of Lesley's car and ran for the entrance to Winfrith police HQ. It had been welling it down for the last hour of the journey, making the A35 almost invisible.

Lesley parked away from the building. The windscreen became instantly obscured by rain within moments of the wipers stopping.

She was about to dial when she saw Tina running out of the building. Lesley wound down her window.

"Tina, get in out of the rain. I'll be in in a moment."

"I've been trying to call you, boss. It's about Ewan Stephens."

"Did you arrest Dawn?"

"She came here, boss."

"She gave herself up?"

"She wanted to report her brother's death. Ewan. They found him at his mum's this morning."

"Ewan?"

Tina nodded.

"OK. Has anyone gone over there yet?"

A shake of the head. "We were waiting till you got back."

"OK. Send Stanley back out. I'll take him with me. Where's Dawn now?"

"She's inside." Tina glanced back towards the building.

"Carry on with the interview. Don't arrest her, just caution her. We want her onside."

"No problem." Tina leaned into the car, her hair getting progressively wetter. She'd pulled her jacket up but it was doing nothing.

"Go on, then," Lesley said. Water was getting into the car. She should have told Tina to get in the passenger seat, but there wasn't time to spare.

"Oh. Sorry." Tina ran off.

Lesley took a breath. She'd take Stanley to Ewan and Dawn's mum's, then leave him to keep an eye on her. Just in case. But first she had a call to make.

She grabbed her phone and dialled.

"Lesley. I thought you'd delegated this to your wife."

"You've spoken to her, then."

"We met. I can see why you're attracted to her."

Lesley felt her forehead twitch. "What did you tell her, Sadie?"

"You really need me to go through this with you, too? She doesn't pass things on to you?"

"Client confidentiality."

"Maybe I'm bound by the same."

Lesley snorted. "You know as well as I do that you need me to provide you with information, and I need you to help get Dennis acquitted. Carpenter threatened you. I want to know if he—"

"Carpenter's got nothing to do with it."

"Really? I thought you had him pegged as corrupt."

"He's slimy as fuck, Lesley. But he's clean."

"What's made you decide that, all of a sudden?"

"First off, the fact that he tried to scare me off."

"Which he did because he knows more about Mackie's death than he should do," Lesley pointed out.

"No."

Lesley slumped into her seat. She'd driven the last hour and a half of the journey back from Birmingham and her back ached from so long in the driver's seat. She longed to go home and have a long hot bath, but it was 2 pm and there was a case to work on.

"Fine," she said. "Tell me what you know."

"OK. So Carpenter tried to scare me off. He and I have crossed each other's paths a few times, not surprising with him being the public face of high-profile CID cases. He must have known that doing that would be the best option if he wanted to spur me on to dig even deeper."

"A bit of reverse psychology isn't enough to prove that he's not involved."

Lesley glanced across the car park towards the building, suddenly worried that Carpenter might appear. How had she gone from feeling uneasy about Anthony Carpenter, to suggesting to a journalist that he might be bent?

"What else have you got, Sadie?"

"I spoke to DCI Phipps again."

"From Hampshire."

"That's the one. He finally admitted that the inquiry was dropped after pressure was put on his senior officers."

"By whom?"

"That's the thing. It was PSD. Apparently they told his

ACC that it was a matter for Dorset PSD to deal with, and that the investigation should be handed over to them. Given that there were police officers being investigated, including Dennis I assume, then the logic would have made sense."

"So they closed the investigation in order to open a new one," Lesley said.

"Yep. But then they didn't open the new one."

Lesley looked across at the building again. "Are you sure about this?"

"I need to spend some more time looking into a few senior PSD guys. I haven't got enough to go public yet."

Lesley felt a stab of panic. "You can't run this."

"I'm a journalist. You think I'm putting myself at risk like this just to help you and your beloved DS Frampton?"

Lesley bit her top lip. It was already bleeding.

How had that happened?

"Just promise you'll talk to me before you report on this," she said.

Silence.

"Sadie? Out of respect for Gwen Mackie. I know you've been talking to her."

"That was low," Sadie replied.

Lesley smiled. Low, yes. But it was working.

"OK," Sadie said at last. "I'll talk to you before I run the story. But you won't be able to stop me running it."

CHAPTER SIXTY-ONE

MEERA SMILED across the table at Dawn Stephens. The duty solicitor sat with her, hastily reading through a file. Tina was beside Meera, her hands shifting in her lap.

She and Tina had had a quick preparation session, standing in the corridor outside the interview room. It wasn't how Meera liked to conduct interviews. But the sooner they knew the circumstances of Ewan Stephens's death, and the extent to which his sister was involved, the better chance they had of avoiding more deaths.

"Dawn," she said. "I'm DS Vedra, this is DC Abbott." She raised her eyebrows at the solicitor.

"Rav Choudary," he said. "And my client, Dawn Stephens. Who is, I understand, not under arrest."

"No," Meera confirmed. "You are under caution though, Dawn. So anything you say here could be used in court."

Dawn was low in her chair, her skin grey. Meera wasn't sure how wise they'd been deciding not to arrest her, but the death of her brother had thrown everything up in the air.

"Dawn, can you confirm that you understand that," she said.

Dawn grunted.

"For the recording?" Tina asked. Her voice was soft.

Dawn shifted and leaned towards the recording machine. "I understand." She fell back into her chair.

"Thanks," said Meera. "You came to see DC Abbott this morning because you wanted to report the death of your brother."

A sniff. "Murder."

"Can you tell us more about why you think he was murdered?"

Dawn gave her a harsh look. "My mum found him in bed. Called 999. Paramedics said it was an overdose." She shook her head. "He doesn't do drugs."

Meera exchanged glances with Tina. "He doesn't?"

"I know what you think. But no. Ewan's clean." A pause, her voice dropping. "Was."

Tina swallowed. "So you think someone gave him the drugs."

"I do."

"He was at your mum's, is that right?"

"He turned up yesterday morning. He normally lives in Brum. If you're saying she gave him drugs—"

Tina leaned in. "We're not saying that, Dawn. But if he was given drugs and then took them at your mum's house, then I don't see why you think he was murdered."

"He was." Dawn looked from Tina to Meera. "He didn't do drugs. Someone must have spiked his drink."

"Did Ewan go out last night?" Meera asked. "Did he go somewhere that might have happened?"

A shrug. "Not sure. Mum'd know." Dawn's Brummie accent was coming out.

"We've sent officers to her house."

A nod.

Meera took a breath. "Dawn, before you arrived here, we were planning to come to you. We wanted to talk to you about last Friday. When you told us you were at your mum's, but we know you weren't."

"My brother's just died."

"I know that. And I'm sorry. But a man died on Friday and we believe you may have been involved."

The lawyer tapped the table top. "You haven't arrested my client. You can't—"

"We have cautioned her. She's here in a voluntary capacity, and we're trying to uncover information about an event that may have a bearing on her brother's death." Meera placed her hands on the table, looking at Dawn. "Dawn. If you think Ewan was murdered, then is that because he was involved in Trevor Hamm's death?"

Dawn shot a look at her solicitor. He shook his head.

"No comment," she said.

Meera sighed. Her two least favourite words in the English language.

"Dawn," Tina said, "Ewan's dead. If he was involved, then he can't be arrested. You can't hurt him. But you can protect yourself."

Dawn's eyes widened. "They wouldn't hurt me."

"They might," Tina said. "If Ewan was killed, as you believe, then you might be at risk."

Dawn's face had paled. Her solicitor flattened his hand on the table, touching her finger. She pulled her hand away.

"Can you protect me?" she asked.

"If you say something that leads us to arrest you," Meera told her, "then we can keep you here for up to six days."

"Forty-eight hours," the solicitor interrupted.

Meera looked at him. "We'll apply for an extension. In exceptional circumstances the magistrates will let us go up to six days." She turned back to Dawn. "Arresting you doesn't mean you'll be charged. If you weren't involved in Hamm's death, then that gives us time to find evidence that will make that apparent. You'll be safe. And it'll help us find the people who killed Hamm, and possibly your brother. There's another victim too, a friend of Ewan's, I believe."

"Who?"

"Samuel Watson."

"Zee?" Dawn's hand flew up to her mouth. "No."

"Did you know him?" Tina asked.

Dawn pursed her lips. "No comment."

"We don't have reason to believe you were involved in Samuel's death," Meera said. "But if you knew him, that will help us find out who did kill him. And Ewan."

Dawn blinked back at her. "I didn't want to do it. They threatened Ewan."

"Who did?"

"The Watsons. Nasty buggers, the both of them. Ewan... he'd done something, wouldn't give me the details." She looked from Meera to Tina and back again. The lawyer coughed; she ignored him. "Ewan can't be charged with anything, after his death?"

"He can't," Meera replied.

"Right. It was something to do with drug supply. Ewan stole from them. They told him if he did this job, they'd forgive him. They knew he had a sister, where I worked."

"And you let them into the lighthouse so they could leave Trevor Hamm's body there."

"I had nothing to do with killing him. Nor the prison break."

Conspiracy, Meera thought. It didn't matter that Dawn hadn't killed Hamm herself.

The lawyer put a hand on Dawn's arm. Squeezed tight. "You need to stop talking now." He looked at Meera. "I need time alone with my client."

"Are you going to arrest me, then?" Dawn asked.

Meera gave her a nod. She ran over the list of offences Dawn had committed in her mind. She didn't want to scare the woman off giving them more information.

"Dawn Stephens, I'm arresting you for assisting an offender. You do not have to say anything. But it may harm your defence if you do not mention when questioned something which you later rely on in court. Anything you do say may be given in evidence."

CHAPTER SIXTY-TWO

Two squad cars and a forensics van were already parked outside Maria Stephens's house. Lesley found a spot a few houses along and turned off the ignition.

Stanley's hand was on the door handle. "We going in, boss?"

She peered along their street, past the police vehicles and the cordon. It was a quiet street in Osmington, flowers growing in front gardens, the vague sound of the sea behind them. Not what she expected in a drugs death.

But drugs got everywhere. And Ewan Stephens hadn't moved down to Dorset with his mum and sister. He was a Brummie.

"I just want to get a feel for it, before we go in," she said.

"A feel?" Stanley looked perplexed.

"We don't yet know exactly how Ewan Stephens died. But there'll be people here who know things about him and his family that can help us get to the truth." She noticed movement in a window next to the car and turned to the DC. "Don't look, but there's a busybody in the house next to me."

"Where?" Stanley leaned around her.

She rolled her eyes. "What did I say to you, Stanley?" She sighed. She was tired from sleeping in that cramped single bed in Birmingham. She missed Elsa.

"Come on, then. Sooner we get in there, sooner we can be back at the office finding out what else we've missed."

She hauled herself out of the car and walked to the house. Gail was in the hallway, working with her colleague Gavin on the floor.

"What are you looking for?" Lesley asked, standing over her.

Gail looked up. "There's drugs residue here, at the bottom of the stairs."

"I thought he was given the drugs by someone else?"

Gail shrugged. "All I know is there's traces of it here."

"You'll tell me what, exactly. Yes?"

"Of course. We can have an answer on this in the next half an hour."

"Even better." Lesley patted Gail's arm. She knew there was a good reason why she preferred working in Dorset to Birmingham.

"Where's the body?" she asked.

"Gone."

"Gone?"

"Dr Bamford has examined it already, and it's gone to the morgue."

"But the SIO hasn't even got here yet."

"You were in Birmingham. Or that's what we thought. Couldn't leave him lying around for too long."

"Fair enough." But Lesley felt tension running through her. Whose call had it been, to remove the body without talking to her?

In the kitchen, Dr Gareth Bamford was packing up his bag.

"Lesley," he said. "I wasn't expecting to see you."

"It seems not."

"You're annoyed with me."

"I just wish someone had called me, before deciding to remove him. Where was he?"

Gareth pointed below the table. "Under there. Twisted badly, he looked like he'd tried to move around the kitchen, maybe get a glass of water."

"Is his mum around?"

A uniformed officer entered. "She's at Poole police station, Ma'am."

"And you are?"

"PC Simon Mullins, Ma'am. We've met before."

"Oh. Why is she at the police station? Do we believe she was involved?"

"She didn't want to stay here while we examined her son," Dr Bamford explained. "And there wasn't anywhere else for her to go."

Lesley glanced back towards the street. A sleepy village like this, and not a solitary neighbour would take the woman in for a few hours. What did that say about this family?

"Very well," she said. "What are your thoughts?"

"You're going to be disappointed," the pathologist replied.

"How so?"

"It was an overdose. We've found a blister pack of the drug, with his prints on. Nothing suspicious about it, unless you want to find the people who supplied him in the first place."

"You think he took it himself? What was it he took, anyway?"

"MDMA. He overdid it. Simple as that."

"You're sure?" Lesley thought back to Meera's voice on the

phone. Murder, she'd said. And Ewan Stephens had been a suspect in a double murder enquiry.

"I'm sure," Gareth replied.

"If he took the drugs himself, then maybe it's got nothing to do with the other cases," Stanley suggested.

"No shit," Lesley said. "Stanley, speak to the office. Find out if they've taken Dawn Stephens into custody yet."

"Why?"

"Because I'm not sure she needs protecting. And if she has been arrested, I want to know what for."

CHAPTER SIXTY-THREE

Meera was heading to Dawn Stephens's house, looking for potential evidence. Tina had stayed behind in the office; she'd been beyond the cordon at the lighthouse and it was best to avoid the risk of crime scene cross-contamination.

There was plenty to keep her busy. More CCTV had come in from the huts near the lighthouse, there was a post-mortem for Ewan Stephens to chase up, and she had Dawn Stephens's mobile in an evidence bag on her desk.

Tina sighed as she settled in her chair and looked at it, checking her watch. She couldn't start investigating Ewan Stephens's death on her own. When would the boss be back?

She wished Mike was here. Sure, the DCI talked her up, but he'd been a DC for years longer than she had, and he had more experience of procedure. He'd know how to kick things off, how to make sure they didn't miss anything.

She grabbed her phone. Mike picked up after five rings.

"Hey, love," he said. "Everything OK?"

She could hear crying in the background. "Sorry. You sound busy."

"It's OK. He's resisting a nap. He's started doing this."

"You sure he doesn't need something?"

"I'm getting to know him better, T. He cries for a minute or so, then he falls asleep like someone's knocked him over with a bat. It's quite impressive."

Tina smiled, then stopped herself. Her son's crying wasn't something to smile about. "If you're sure he's not in distress…"

"He's got a clean nappy, his tummy's full of the milk you pumped this morning, and he's had a lovely cuddle with his dad. He's fine. Did you call cos you were worried about him?"

"No."

"OK." Mike sounded surprised.

"We've had another death reported. The Portland Bill case."

"Right. Hang on." Tina heard Mike making shushing sounds. So he wasn't just leaving Louis to cry: good. "Sorry T, can this wait?"

"I'm on my own here and I'm not sure how to start."

"OK. What have you got?"

"A man who may or may not have been murdered, but probably just died of an overdose. The rest of the team out. And his sister's mobile, sitting on my desk."

"His sister's?"

"She's a suspect in the Hamm murder case."

"That's easy, then."

"It is?"

"Forget this new case. You've been working on material evidence from Hamm, haven't you?"

"Yeah."

"So can you access the phone, or do you need Forensics to work out the security?"

"She's given me the PIN."

"Even better. Open it up. See what calls she made in the days up to and around Hamm's death. Check messages."

Tina looked at the phone. "I feel like an idiot."

"Why?"

"Cos I should have known to do that."

"You're tired. You're just back at work after having Louis."

"Yeah, and my brain's mush."

"It's not mush, T. The boss asked you to come back cos you cracked the Blue Pool case, and let them think it was me."

"It wasn't quite like—"

"You know full well it was. Now turn on that phone. See what messages she sent."

"OK." Tina put on a pair of gloves and pulled the phone out of the evidence bag. She placed it back on top of the bag and clicked the power button.

"It's got twenty-five percent juice," she said.

"Good." The line was quiet, except for Mike's voice.

"Is he asleep?"

"Like the dead."

"Don't say that."

"Sorry. I need to get a shower. D'you need me?"

"Hang on." Tina went to the phone records. Various calls, mainly to Dawn's mum. "Wait."

"What?" Mike asked, his voice terse.

"There's a call on this that looks like... one moment."

Tina brought her computer to life and typed in the phone number from Dawn's phone screen.

"Shit," she said. "It's a Birmingham number."

"What have you found?"

"I thought you needed a shower."

"Not anymore, I don't. What have you found?"

"A call. In February."

"What sort of call?"

"To a Birmingham number."

"Her brother?"

"That's what I thought. But the boss said there was no sign of a landline at his flat."

"OK. So who did she call?"

Tina had typed the number into HOLMES. A name came up. "Gina O'Toole. That name sounds familiar. Who's Gina O'Toole?"

"Dunno," Mike replied. "One of the brother's mates, maybe? I'm gonna go get this shower now."

"OK. Love you."

Mike hung up and Tina clicked on Gina O'Toole's name.

A case number came up. The Canary investigation. From three years earlier.

She clicked through to the case files.

"Shit," she breathed. She leaned back in her chair, staring at her screen.

What was Dawn Stephens doing, phoning the mother of one of Trevor Hamm's victims?

CHAPTER SIXTY-FOUR

THE DOOR OPENED to reveal a grey-haired woman with a nervous smile on her face. Elsa took care to stand back, not wanting to appear threatening. She was in her best court suit and knew its sombreness could appear off-putting.

"Mrs Mackie?" she said. "I'm Elsa Short. We spoke on the phone."

"Ah yes." The smile lost its wariness. "Come in. I've just boiled the kettle."

"Perfect." Elsa followed DCI Mackie's widow through to a tidy kitchen overlooking a garden that was bright with daffodils and a sprinkling of snowdrops.

"You have a beautiful garden."

Gwen Mackie followed her gaze. "Thank you. Tim had big plans for it, after he retired. I knew he'd never have the patience for it, though."

"No?"

The woman shook her head. "He never liked gardening while he was in the force. Why he should suddenly become an archetypal pensioner overnight just because he'd retired, I've no idea."

"You miss him."

Gwen gave Elsa a sharp look. "Of course I do."

"Sorry. That was overly familiar."

Gwen bit her bottom lip, returning to the kettle. "Tea alright for you?"

"Yes please. Milk, no sugar." Elsa was a coffee drinker, especially since she and Lesley had invested in an expensive machine. But it looked like her directness had cost her the opportunity to choose.

"I'm sorry," she said. "I think I got off on the wrong foot. I'm grateful to you for letting me come here."

"You're not the first. I even had a DI from the West Midlands. And a man from Hampshire. Plenty of PSD too. Not that any of them got anywhere."

"I didn't know Professional Standards were interested in your husband's death." Elsa took the mug of tea that Gwen offered. The mug matched Gwen's: an illustration of the Isle of Wight.

Gwen gave her a look. "*Everyone* was interested. Especially after they decided it was suspicious."

"They reopened the investigation."

"Closed it again, almost immediately." Gwen gestured towards the kitchen door. "Why don't you come into the dining room? I've got some things ready for you in there."

"Oh. Thank you." It hadn't been more than half an hour since Elsa's phone call. Had Gwen been expecting a call, after Dennis's arrest?

Elsa followed her through to the dining room. It too looked over the garden and was dominated by a round table. On that was a pile of thin hardback books.

"Tim's books," Gwen said. "I was having a sort out, found them in the attic."

Elsa approached but didn't touch. "His police notebooks?"

"They go back to 1982, when he started at Bournemouth. They end the day before he died."

"But he'd retired."

"He carried on with them." Gwen picked up three books from the top of the pile. "These are different, you'll notice. Not police issue. But he liked them, carried on using the same sort of book."

"Did you know he was keeping these?"

A shake of the head. "I knew he used them, yes. But I assumed they were at a police station somewhere. Or destroyed. I guess they scan police notebooks, these days."

Elsa would have to check the procedure with Lesley. Either way, these might well be worth their weight in gold.

"So did Dorset Police return these to you, after the case was closed?"

Another shake. "I never gave them to them. I didn't even know he had them here. He'd retired, so it never came up."

So no one knows about them.

Elsa licked her lips. "Can I take a look?"

Gwen gestured towards the pile. "I don't know you, but Dennis Frampton called and told me to expect a visit from you."

"Dennis did?"

"He's been bailed. You'd know that, surely."

"I do. But I didn't know he was home yet."

Gwen shrugged. "I think he knew about the notebooks, knew that Tim kept them. If anyone knows whether there's anything useful in them, it's Dennis."

"I'll return them to you."

"I know you will. Don't let anyone in the police get their hands on them, will you?" Gwen's gaze lowered. "Not even DCI Clarke."

"Dennis trusts Lesl—"

"Not even her. I don't know who in the police I can trust, after all that's happened. Keep these between you and Dennis, please. I should have given them to him. But I hear he's got a tag."

"He has," Elsa replied. Which meant that if Dennis visited Gwen, the prison service would know.

Elsa picked up the top eight notebooks. They went back to 2020; four per year.

Would she need them all?

She didn't want to sit in Gwen's dining room sifting through them, working out which were relevant. That would take time.

She'd hired an office space, in Bournemouth. She'd take them there.

She'd buy a safe, on the way.

"Thank you, Mrs Mackie," she said. "I'll let you know if I find anything useful in these."

CHAPTER SIXTY-FIVE

LESLEY STOOD IN HER OFFICE, the blinds closed behind her. Low sunshine filtered through the gaps and into the eyes of anyone who looked towards the broad windows.

Tina and Meera stood near the board, to one side of the room. Stanley was in a chair, shifting his weight back and forth.

The team was depleted and Lesley didn't like it. They needed Dennis back.

Hopefully that would happen soon. She'd been greeted by Tony on the front desk when she'd arrived, who'd beckoned her in close and told her in a low voice that Dennis had been released with a tag. She'd smiled at him but said nothing.

"Right," she began. "We have three deaths to work on. Two suspicious, one probably not. But before we start, I need to update you."

Tina straightened. Meera looked puzzled.

"I'm sure you know that the DS had his appearance at the Magistrates' Court this morning. It was a formality, the case has been passed up to the Crown Court. But he's been allowed home with a tag."

Stanley opened his mouth to speak. Tina smiled and rapped her knuckles on the board next to her.

It was good to see such loyalty. But they couldn't be distracted. "None of you is to visit him," she said. "He's been told to avoid contact with colleagues past and present, as well as anyone involved in his case."

"He didn't do it," Stanley said.

"Unfortunately you won't be on the jury," Lesley told him.

"What will happen to him?" Tina asked.

"The normal procedure," Lesley said. "He has to wait two months for his case to come to Crown Court."

"I mean, after that. In prison. He's a police officer. He's... vulnerable."

Lesley pulled in a shaky breath. They all knew how badly Dennis would cope with prison. He might have been a police officer, but he wasn't your average police officer.

"I'm confident it won't come to that," she said. "He's got a good solicitor. My wife."

Meera coughed.

"You got a problem with that, Meera?"

"What? No. Sorry."

"Elsa's a good criminal lawyer. You've all seen her at work. She'll be working hard to find evidence that'll prove Dennis's innocence."

"You believe he's innocent, boss?" Stanley said.

Lesley turned to him, her eyes narrowed. "You don't?"

His cheeks reddened. "Of course not. You just heard me saying he didn't do it. I just... you've worked with him longer. You'll know more about the case."

"If you think I know more because my wife's his lawyer, you can think again. She doesn't share confidential client information with me. And she'll be even more wary than usual, with this case."

"I don't think Stanley was suggesting—" Tina began.

Lesley raised a hand. "I know. Look, everyone, I know we're worried about Dennis. I know we're short-staffed. I want him back just as much as you do."

She surveyed the team, remembering how Dennis had been before his arrest. Distracted, erratic. There'd been multiple days off.

Would that change, if he was acquitted?

She hoped so.

"But," she said, injecting breeziness into her voice, "we have two murder cases to solve. And we need to establish for sure that Ewan Stephens died of natural causes."

"I wouldn't call a drugs overdose all that natural," Meera said.

"No. And of course whoever supplied him with those drugs could be guilty of manslaughter. But you know what I mean."

"Yes, boss."

"Good. So, we've got the beginnings of a confession from Dawn Stephens. Her lawyer is sitting on her now, though. So we need to build a case. Let's start with Trevor Hamm. Take it step by step. What do we have on the prison breakout?"

"I've got something from before that," Tina said.

Lesley raised her eyebrows. "Yes?"

"Dawn Stephens's phone. There's a call on it from a month ago."

"To Hamm?"

Tina shook her head. "To a woman called Gina O'Toole. Mum of one of Hamm's victims."

Lesley clenched a fist. "Gina claimed to have got a call from the prison. From Hamm."

"The Canary case," Tina said. "Her daughter was Susie O'Toole. She died of a drugs overdose."

"There's a lot of that around," Stanley muttered.

"Susie was sixteen," Lesley said. "It's not funny."

"Sorry."

"Tina. You say there's a call from Dawn Stephens to Gina O'Toole. Do we know what was said? Are there any messages?"

"I looked at the file from West Midlands Police, boss. Your old colleague, DI Finch. She had a report from Gina O'Toole that she'd been called by Hamm from the prison. At around the same time."

"Are you thinking that it was Dawn Stephens who made that call?"

"We've already established that no numbers in Birmingham were on Hamm's approved list. So that could be what happened."

"OK. Cross-check times and dates. Ask Zoe what Gina said about the voice."

"Will do, boss."

"Anything else?"

"There's the stuff in Ewan Stephens's flat," Stanley said.

Lesley nodded. She brought up the photos from her phone and passed them round. "He was clearly involved in something on the Isle of Portland."

"There's plans of the prison here," said Meera. "How easy would those be to get hold of?"

"Can you do a search? See what's publicly available."

"Of course. I'll ask the prison, too."

"It's all circumstantial, though," Lesley said. "It doesn't directly relate to Hamm's killing." She drummed her fingers on the desk. "Everything we have is about the breakout. We need more on the poison Hamm was given. Where it came from, how it was administered. Did one of his accomplices simply pass him a bottle of Coke with it in? What else was in his stomach? And what were his movements from the moment they broke him out to the moment they dragged him into that lighthouse?"

"We've got more CCTV that might help with that," Tina said.

"From where?"

"The hotel at the top of the hill by the prison. Looks like they went that way after the breakout."

Lesley frowned. "They can't have headed back towards the prison."

"The van goes up New Road then off towards the west of the island. It looks like they were heading for the quarries."

"What quarries?"

"Portland's full of them," Stanley said. "They're more of a walkers' spot now. Used to be big business. St Pauls' Cathedral was built from Portland sto—"

"We don't need to know that."

Lesley felt overwhelmed. There was Dennis's bail, and the inevitable oblique conversation she'd have about it with Elsa later. Zoe's involvement. And three deaths with no idea how the first had taken place.

"Right," she said. "Stanley and Tina, I want you working on how Hamm died. Where he went after the breakout. Trawl social media. Find more CCTV. The hotel, and anything else you can get your hands on. I want to know where Hamm was between the breakout and the lighthouse. I want to know where Zee Watson went after dumping Hamm's body, and who he was with. We need to work out who had motive to kill him."

"It won't take me long to look at the prison plans," Meera said. "I can work on motive after that if you'd like."

"Do that," Lesley said. "I'll talk to the pathologist and to Gail's team. We reconvene at four pm."

"Boss." Everyone filed out, eager to find more evidence.

CHAPTER SIXTY-SIX

LESLEY LOWERED herself into her chair, watching as the team filtered back to their desks. She longed to go home and sleep. To slump onto the sofa with her new wife and do nothing for a few hours.

But if Trevor Hamm and Samuel Watson had been killed by a gang like the one Hamm had headed up, she knew what kind of people they would be. And how important it was to stop them.

She yawned and grabbed her bag. She wanted to go and speak to Gail, wherever she was. Find out if there were any more forensics. Getting out of the office and into a crime scene would keep her awake.

From inside her bag, her phone rang. She took it out. Probably Gail, saving her a trip.

It was Elsa.

"Hey, sweetie," she said. "I'm back from Birmingham, you'll be pleased to know."

"That's good. How was your trip?"

"Tiring. But fruitful. I think. How was Dennis's appearance with the magistrates?"

"It went without a hitch. He's home with a tag. You probably already know that."

"I've been reliably informed." Lesley leaned back in her chair. She could spare five minutes for a chat with Elsa. "I'll be home as early as I can tonight. I'm sorry I've not been around much since we got back from Scotland, I—"

"It's fine, love. I know what your job's like. If my business was going better, it would be me apologising."

"I hope you're making progress with Dennis's case."

"You're not going to ask me for details directly, though."

"Of course not." Lesley was too close to this case. She didn't want to do anything that might jeopardise it.

"Good. But I wanted to run something past you."

Lesley sat up, her elbows on the desk. "What kind of something?"

"I'm not telling you where I got this, but I've got a written source that refers to two police officers using codenames. At least, I think they're police officers."

"Nicknames?" Lesley knew what the police could be like for those.

"No. They're more oblique than that."

"Hit me."

"The first is Challenge. The other one's Beef."

"Beef?"

"That's what it looks like."

"You're sure these are people?"

A pause. "Yes."

"But you can't tell me why you're sure."

"Sorry, sweetie. Are those nicknames you've heard used?"

"You know me, love. Nicknames aren't something I've cottoned onto. Can't you ask Dennis?"

"I will. I just wanted to run them past you first."

"OK. Sorry I can't help."

"No. I shouldn't have asked. Sorry."

Lesley gripped the phone. "This written source you're referring to, does it include information that'll help Dennis?"

"I shouldn't have called you about this."

"Els? Tell me."

"It might do. I don't know yet."

"Good. He'll be glad."

Silence. Lesley could imagine how Dennis had been with Elsa: *glad* didn't really come into it.

"I'll see you later," Lesley said. "I'll cook."

"You're sure?"

"I am."

"Lovely. I look forward to it."

CHAPTER SIXTY-SEVEN

GAIL WAS JUST about ready to leave Maria Stephens's house. She'd taken samples of the MDMA that had killed Ewan, but found little else. Certainly nothing linking him to the other two deaths.

It was looking more and more like the man had died of a simple overdose. She wouldn't be surprised if whoever had supplied the drugs to him was mixed up in the other two deaths. But that was for Lesley to worry about.

Gavin was at the van, packing up the last of their kit.

"OK," Gail said. "Back to the lab."

"You're sure?" He gave her a plaintive look.

"What?" She laughed. "You're after an early finish?"

"By the time we get back to the lab it'll be almost four. We were both working on Sunday. I think we've earned some time off."

Gav was right. They'd take the van straight back to the Forensics lab in Dorchester, then finish for the day. They were using up too much overtime as it was.

"OK. But I'm sure Lesley'll have more for us in the morning."

"I'm sure she will." He smiled.

She climbed into the passenger seat, Gav at the wheel. As they drove away from Osmington, Gail's phone rang: Otto Novak at the DNA lab.

"Hey, Otto," she said. "What have you got for me?"

"Blood from the Portland crime scene."

"Which one?"

"The second one." Otto read out a reference number. It referred to the huts, the spot in which Samuel Watson had been found.

"OK," she said. "I'm assuming it's a match for the victim."

"Not just him."

Gail glanced at Gavin. "I'm putting you on speaker," she told Otto. "Blood from the Samuel Watson scene," she whispered to Gavin, who nodded.

"Have you got an ID?" she asked Otto. It would be another member of the gang. Possibly Ewan Stephens.

"Which officers were on the scene for that one?" Otto asked. "Was it the same as the lighthouse?"

"We were careful to use different people, as far as possible," Gail replied. Her skin bristled. "Why?"

"Because I've got DNA here, that's on the police database."

Gail turned off speaker and put the phone to her ear.

"It'll be a cock-up," she told Otto. "Tell me the name, so we can rule them out."

"DI Rowan Angus," Otto said. "Blandford Forum CID."

Gail didn't need to write the name down; it was one she was familiar with. She'd seen him at the lighthouse. But not at the huts. "Thanks," she said, before ending the call.

"What was that about?" Gavin asked. They'd stopped at a roundabout where the A352 and A353 met.

Gail's mouth was dry. "You know that shoe print we found?" she asked him. "At the lighthouse?"

"DI Angus. It was irrelevant, as he attended the scene."

Gail stared out of the window. "They found his DNA, at the huts."

Gavin turned to her.

"Look at the road," she snapped.

"Sorry. Did he attend that scene too?"

She shrugged. "Not that I know of."

"You think...?"

"I don't think anything," she told him. "But I'm going to have to call Lesley."

CHAPTER SIXTY-EIGHT

LESLEY GRABBED HER PHONE. Outside in the office, Tina picked up hers.

"Tina," Lesley said, "can you come in here a moment?"

Tina looked round, puzzled. Stanley, sitting next to her, followed her gaze.

Damn.

Lesley wrinkled her nose. "It won't take long."

"No problem, boss."

Tina and Stanley exchanged glances. Lesley rested her fist on the desk. She yawned.

Tina opened the door. "You need me to work on something else, boss?"

"No. Come in."

Tina frowned and closed the door behind her. Lesley leaned over the desk, her voice low.

"You know how the police like to use nicknames?" she said.

"Er... yes."

Lesley pushed her notepad across the desk. "Do either of these mean anything to you?"

Tina pulled the pad towards her. "Challenge beef."

"They're separate. Challenge and Beef. Do you know anyone with those nicknames?"

"Beef is DI Angus. Used to work in PSD."

"Used to?"

"He left about... three years ago, I think. Not sure why."

"I met him," Lesley said. "He was at the lighthouse. Told me he was from Blandford CID."

Tina nodded. "I've never met him. I try to avoid PSD if I can."

"OK. What about the other one?"

"Challenge." Tina shook her head. "Not heard of that one." She looked up. "Don't forget I've only been in CID eighteen months. Mike might know."

Lesley bit her bottom lip. "It's OK."

"You're sure? I can run it past him when I get home."

"Mike's on parental leave. I'd rather you didn't bother him."

"It's not exactly bothering him."

"It's fine."

"OK," Tina replied. "Is that everything?"

"Yes. Sorry. I know you're busy."

"Is this to do with Dennis?"

Lesley resisted a twitch. "What makes you think that?"

"I think Angus worked with the sarge at one point. They were in local CID together."

"When?"

Tina shook her head. "Sorry. I don't know."

"OK. Thanks, Tina. Don't talk to the rest of the team about this. We need to focus on the case."

A shrug. "Stan's new, and Meera's from the other side of the county. I don't think they'd know anyway."

"No. Thanks, Tina."

The door opened behind Tina: Meera. Lesley grabbed the notepad, drew it towards her.

"Boss? Sorry, I didn't want to disturb you."

"It's OK, Meera. Come in."

"I've had a call from Gail. They've found DNA at the second crime scene."

"The huts?"

Meera nodded and entered the room. Outside in the team room, Stanley stood up, looked at them for a moment, then sat down.

Meera handed over a printout: DNA profiles.

"Samuel Watson's DNA," Lesley said.

"No. They found someone else's blood."

Lesley looked at Meera. "Whose?"

"Gail told me to get you to call her. She wouldn't tell me."

Lesley picked up her phone. "Why not?"

"Don't know. She was insistent."

"OK. Thanks, both of you."

Lesley waited for the two DCs to leave the room then dialled Gail.

"Lesley. I was wondering when you'd get back to me."

"I didn't know you were looking for me."

"I tried your mobile a couple of times. But Meera clearly passed on the message."

"She did. Very cloak and dagger, too. What's happened?"

"We found DNA at the huts. Not Samuel Watson's. It belongs to someone who was also at the lighthouse."

Lesley felt her breath catch. "Who?"

"It might be nothing."

"Who?"

"DI Rowan Angus. He's from Blandford Forum CID."

"He must have been on the scene."

"That's what I thought. But I imagined you'd want to check."

"I will. Thanks. Have you told anyone else?"

"No. I thought..."

"Thanks. It could be helpful."

CHAPTER SIXTY-NINE

LESLEY PULLED up the police HR system on her computer.

If a member of Dorset Police was working with organised crime...

It made no sense. The gang was from Birmingham. If she'd discovered that a local officer was involved with Arthur Kelvin's gang, that would have been one thing. But killing Trevor Hamm?

She pulled in a deep breath and brought up Angus's personnel file. He'd been on the force for twelve years, with three years at Blandford Forum CID.

No incidents. No suspensions or investigations. She went back, all the way to his training.

2010, induction training at Chantmarle. He'd then gone on to work in Poole, followed by Lyme Regis, PSD at Winfrith and Blandford Forum. For six months in 2018 he'd been on the same team as Dennis.

There was nothing here to suggest a connection to Trevor Hamm, Samuel Watson, or the Stephens family.

Lesley leaned back, surveying the screen. She had a boot

print and DNA. The boot print had been ruled out, as he'd attended the scene.

She'd have to speak to Blandford Forum, to find out about Angus's shift patterns.

She pursed her lips. What could the connection be?

A Google search might help.

She fired up her browser, opened a private tab and typed in his name.

Two newspaper articles. One following a rescue in Weymouth bay. The other relating to a school event he had attended, advising kids on road safety. And a wedding notice.

She brought up the wedding notice.

She read it again. And fell back into her chair.

This explained it. Or at least some of it.

CHAPTER SEVENTY

Tina was in the ladies' toilets, leaning against the door of a cubicle. The team were getting used to her ducking out every now and then; first it had been the effects of pregnancy, now it was the pumping. A chair had been placed in the corner for her, but still it wasn't the nicest place to express milk for her son.

This time, she wasn't here because of Louis.

She dialled Mike.

"Hey, T, I'm mid nappy change. Can I call you back?"

"Sorry, love. It won't be a minute. I just wanted to run something past you."

He chuckled. "Glad to hear you still need me."

"Not as much as you think." She smiled.

"Tell me about it. Ow."

"What?"

"Sorry. I bent over to grab the wipes and Louis kicked me in the face."

"A four-month-old kicked you in the face, and you're complaining about the pain?"

"He's stronger than you think. He'll be the next Marcus Rashford."

"Or Beth Meade."

"True. So what is it you need to run past me? I'm going to be covered in a tidal wave of poo if we don't get this over with."

"Nicknames."

"Nicknames?"

"Of officers in Dorset force. Beef and Challenge."

"Beef's easy," Mike said.

"I know. DI Angus, from PSD. What about Challenge?"

"He's at Blandford Forum now," Mike corrected her. "But did you say Challenge?"

"Challenge."

Silence.

"Mike?" Tina asked.

"Sorry. No."

"No what?"

"No, I don't know. Never heard of it."

"You're sure?" she asked.

"Sorry."

"OK. Thanks, love. See you later."

"Yeah." The line went dead.

Tina held her phone in front of her. Mike's voice had sounded strained, when she told him the second nickname.

Was there something he wasn't telling her?

CHAPTER SEVENTY-ONE

LESLEY STEPPED out of her office to find Tina, Meera and Stanley focused on their screens.

"How's it going?" she asked them.

"We're running through social media and news reports," said Tina. "Trying to find anything relating to the prison break."

"Nothing yet," Stanley added.

"Meera?"

"I spoke to the prison, looked online. Plans for the building aren't publicly available. But apparently they used to be, a few years back. They were pulled down after someone shared them on twitter."

"So Ewan could have got hold of them."

"Feasibly."

"I've only just started working on motive," Meera added. "I'm trying to piece together the various players, work out what their goals were."

Lesley nodded. "I need you to check something. About Dawn Stephens."

Meera swivelled in her chair. "Of course."

"Is she still downstairs?"

"We arrested her two hours ago. She hasn't been charged yet, or released."

"OK. Can you find out if she's married?"

A frown. "You think there's an accomplice?"

"Just check for me."

"We can look in marriage records," Tina said.

"Can't we just ask her?" Lesley asked.

"It'll be quicker to check online."

"OK. Do that then."

Tina smiled. "I already have." She frowned at her screen. "What?"

"Who is it, Tina?" Lesley asked.

"It's... how did we not know this?"

"Tell me."

"Dawn Stephens married in 2004. She divorced in 2011."

"Who was she married to?" Lesley asked. She was pretty sure she knew the answer.

Tina glanced at Meera, then looked at Lesley. "Beef."

"Beef?" Meera asked.

Tina had paled. "Angus. Beef."

"What are you on about?" Meera asked.

Tina licked her lips. "The man she was married to. He's a police officer. DI Rowan Angus."

Lesley nodded. "We need to talk to him."

"Wasn't he at the first crime scene?" Stanley asked. "Why didn't he say anything?"

"That's a very good question, Stanley," Lesley told him.

She needed to talk to Carpenter.

"Carry on with what you're doing," she told the team. "Don't let this distract you."

Tina sniffed. She exchanged glances with Stanley, whose eyes were wide.

Lesley shook her head and returned to her office. Her phone was buzzing on the desk: a text.

She picked it up.

It was from Mike.

She frowned as she scanned it.

Nickname info. Can we meet?

CHAPTER SEVENTY-TWO

MIKE ENTERED the pub with his son under one arm, attempting to manhandle a buggy under the other.

Lesley stood up. "You OK there?"

"Fine. He just won't get in the damn thing. I thought they didn't start being contrary till they were toddlers."

"Surely you can just shove him in it."

"You want to hear how loud he screams if I do?"

"Fair enough. You need any help?"

"I'm fine. I've got this down to a fine art."

Lesley resisted a laugh. "It looks like it."

Mike gave her a hard look, then softened, clearly remembering she was his boss.

"I bought you a drink," she said. Two Cokes sat on the table she'd taken in the corner of the pub. It hadn't occurred to her that the advantage of this spot, its seclusion, meant that getting the pushchair and baby in would be particularly difficult.

"Oh. Thanks," he grunted. She remembered that Mike drank lager, but didn't imagine he'd want it when he was about to drive his son home.

He slurped at the drink, bouncing the baby on his knee. Louis reached out, a chubby hand brushing the glass.

"Oi," Mike muttered. "Not for you."

"What do you know?" Lesley asked him.

"You gave Tina two nicknames," he replied. He looked around the pub.

"I told her to keep it to herself," Lesley told him.

"She knew I'd been with the force for longer."

"Still."

"I can help you," he said. "If you want me to."

Lesley stared at him. "Of course I want you to."

He blushed. "Sorry, boss. I didn't mean to—"

"It's fine. Just tell me what it is you know."

"OK." He jiggled the baby, then reached into a vast shoulder bag and brought out a dummy. The boy grabbed it and plunged it into his mouth. "The two names you gave her. Challenge and Beef."

"I already know who Beef is."

A nod. "Tina told you."

"She did." Lesley was glad he hadn't used Angus's name. "What about Challenge?"

"It's literal," he said. "Challenge Wood."

"Challenge Wood?" she repeated. "What the hell does that mean?"

"I'm not saying it." He looked around the pub. A lone man sat at the bar and two women were at a table near the door. No one could hear them.

"Fair enough." Lesley brought out her phone and googled it.

Challenge wood. It was the meaning of the name Collingwood.

"The DI?" she said, looking at Mike.

He said nothing, but met her gaze.

Lesley leaned forward. "PSD?"

"I'm saying nothing."

"Shit."

DI Collingwood was a PSD officer. And whatever Elsa's source was, she was sure it wasn't saying he was a fine upstanding officer.

CHAPTER SEVENTY-THREE

LESLEY WAS SITTING on the sofa when Elsa arrived home.

"Hello, sweetie." Elsa bent to kiss the back of her neck. "I wasn't expecting you back yet."

"I wanted to talk to you."

"Can I get a glass of water first? I'm gasping."

"Of course."

Elsa went to the kitchen, filled a glass with water then returned to the living area. She sat next to Lesley on the sofa and put a hand on her knee. "I missed you."

"Sorry." Lesley turned to her. "I know it's not the best way to start married life."

Elsa gave her a peck on the cheek. "You've got the rest of our lives to make it up to me. It's fine. What's up?"

"Those two words you gave me. You said they were codewords."

Elsa's hand tensed on Lesley's thigh. "Yes."

"Where did you get them?"

"You know I can't tell you that."

"Was it from Dennis?"

"You're not going to get it out of me that way."

"OK." Lesley sighed. "I know what they mean."

"You do?"

"They're people."

"Mm-hmm." Elsa was trying to sound casual, but Lesley could detect the tension in her body.

"What's this about, Els?"

"I should never have asked you, love."

"You should have asked Dennis."

"I did. He didn't know."

"Really?"

"Either that or he wasn't telling me."

"That sounds like Dennis."

"Who are they, Lesley?" Elsa had her hand in her lap now.

Lesley cleared her throat. "OK. Two men. DI Rowan Angus, Blandford CID. He's Beef."

"Right." Elsa drilled her fingernail into her own thigh. "And Challenge?"

"DI Robert Collingwood. PSD."

"PSD?"

"PSD." Lesley hesitated. "What's this about, Els? Where did you get this?"

"I can't tell you. I'm sorry. But thanks."

"I just hope this information helps you get Dennis acquitted."

"So do I."

Lesley looked at her wife. "You don't know?"

Elsa leaned back. She closed her eyes. "I can't promise anything, sweetie. But now I'm more confident. And I appreciate your help."

Lesley grunted.

CHAPTER SEVENTY-FOUR

LESLEY ARRIVED at Winfrith at 8.30 am. She was tired; she'd cooked for Elsa last night, steak in béarnaise sauce, and they'd stayed up late talking about the wedding, looking at photos and enjoying thinking about something other than work.

She wanted to speak to Dawn Stephens, to find out if she was still in contact with her ex-husband. She'd need to set up a formal interview later in the day, give the woman an opportunity to involve her solicitor. But in the meantime, she wanted to check on Dawn's welfare. Dawn had committed a crime: possibly conspiracy to murder. But her brother had died, and she was here for her own protection. Lesley wanted to be sure she wasn't too uncomfortable.

Sergeant Jukes was on duty in the custody suite. "Morning, Ma'am," he said. "This is a surprise."

"Is it?" she asked.

"I didn't mean to be rude."

Lesley smiled. "I didn't think you were being rude. And I know that having a DCI turn up down here at this time of day isn't exactly regular. I just wanted to check on Dawn Stephens's welfare."

"Dawn Stephens?"

"We arrested her yesterday."

"I know who she is, Ma'am. But she's gone."

"Sorry?"

"She was released late last night, Ma'am. Orders of the Superintendent."

"Superintendent Carpenter?"

"Yes, Ma'am." Jukes looked uncomfortable. "I assumed you knew."

She gritted her teeth. "You're sure it was on his say-so?"

"That's what's on the paperwork. Is it not what you were expecting?"

Lesley sighed. "I've stopped expecting anything, with this case. But thanks."

"No problem, Ma'am."

She turned to walk up to the office, her senses on fire.

Why the hell had Carpenter had Dawn released?

CHAPTER SEVENTY-FIVE

ELSA DIDN'T WANT this search stored in her browser history. Even with a private browser window, she was concerned it might be too risky.

With her history of representing organised criminals, she'd learned to be wary. So instead of using her own laptop or mobile phone, she was in an internet cafe in Commercial Road.

It had taken a while to find this place; it seemed they were a dying breed. It was more like a shop than a cafe: shelves of food lined the walls. But it had what she needed.

She opened the browser window and typed in Angus's name. Two newspaper reports came up: a rescue in Weymouth bay and something in a school. And there was a mention of him marrying a woman called Dawn Stephens.

She googled the woman's name. She was on Facebook, lived in Osmington. Her privacy settings were light and Elsa was able to see much of her profile. She worked at the lighthouse on Portland Bill.

That was where Trevor Hamm's body had been found, the

escaped prisoner whose death Lesley was investigating. Was that crime related to the Mackie case?

It made no sense. Trevor Hamm was from Birmingham. He'd run a gang that, as far as Elsa knew, had no connections to Dorset police or to organised crime down here. And Elsa should know. She had – reluctantly – been Arthur Kelvin's lawyer, after all.

She shook her head. She'd have to speak to Dennis again, find out if he knew more than he was letting on. Asking Lesley about Dawn Stephens and the lighthouse case wasn't something that sat easy with her.

She had another name. DI Collingwood. She typed it into Google.

The police website was the first hit. She clicked on the link. Collingwood had been a PSD officer since 2008. That was all there was.

But there was a photo, too. Of a thin man with light brown hair and a faint birthmark on his chin.

Elsa zoomed in. She held her breath.

Oh, Jesus.

She'd seen him before.

She picked up her phone. No answer. She tapped her fingers on the table as she waited for voicemail to kick in.

The voice was one she'd heard many times before. Elsa held her breath as she listened to the outgoing message.

"I need to talk to you about a case I'm working on," she said. "I'll be at your office in twenty minutes."

She hung up.

CHAPTER SEVENTY-SIX

LESLEY PUSHED the door to the outer office open, her movements brusque. She'd resisted an urge to go straight to Carpenter's office. He probably wouldn't be in yet, and she needed to calm herself down before confronting him.

Meera was already at her desk.

"Meera," Lesley said. "You're early."

Meera nodded. She was on the phone. Her eyes were wide.

"What is it?" Lesley whispered. Meera shook her head.

Lesley waited as Meera spoke into the phone.

"That's definitely the correct address?" She wrote in her notebook.

Lesley looked at her. Something had happened. What?

She thought of Dennis. Was he OK?

Meera's throat shifted as she swallowed. "An IC1 woman, in her forties," she said, continuing to make notes in her pad. "Single stab wound."

Lesley felt her heart pick up pace. Another killing?

She grabbed the pad, turned it towards her. It had an address in Osmington.

"Shit." She gestured for Meera to hand the phone over, just as the DC put it down.

Meera stared at her. She was breathing heavily. "Why wasn't Dawn Stephens in custody?"

"Is she...?" Lesley pointed at the address on the pad.

Meera nodded. "She was found at her home this morning. By her mum. Someone broke in overnight and stabbed her."

CHAPTER SEVENTY-SEVEN

It felt strange, being back in this building. Elsa had left under a cloud; she'd never expected to walk through the doors again. And she'd fully anticipated that her next encounter with the woman she was waiting for would be in a courtroom.

The office she sat in was sleek and modern. The large desk held a neat laptop and not much else. It had been more cluttered when she'd last been here, more old-fashioned. She wondered what else had changed.

The fallout from Arthur Kelvin's death, for one. That would have changed this firm.

The door opened and Aurelia Cross entered. "Elsa." She rounded the desk and sat in her expensive chair, not offering her hand.

"Aurelia. Good to see you."

"You don't need to lie."

So we're playing it like that, are we?

"Thanks for seeing me at such short notice," Elsa said.

"From the tone of your message, I didn't imagine I had all that much choice."

Elsa shifted in her chair. *Relax.* "I'm representing a client in a case which may have some relevance to this firm."

"Well, we are the largest criminal law firm in eastern Dorset."

"There's someone I remember meeting. He's connected to it."

"I don't suppose you're going to tell me what this case is or who on earth you're referring to." Aurelia looked at her watch, making a show of the motion.

Elsa took out her phone. She'd taken a photo of the screen in the internet cafe, of the picture of DI Collingwood.

She slid the phone across the desk. "A year before I left the firm, I remember staying late one night and knocking on your door. This man was here. I never saw him again."

Aurelia sniffed. "If I remembered everyone who came into my office, I wouldn't need a secretary."

"He's a police officer. He works in their Professional Standards department."

"I don't remember him."

"It was gone seven pm when I saw him here. Your secretary had long since left for the night."

"What are you implying, Elsa?"

"I was just wondering if you could tell me if the firm represented him."

"You know I'm not going to breach client confidentiality."

"You don't have to breach confidentiality to tell me you represented him."

Aurelia looked across the table at Elsa. Her gaze was steely. "We did not represent him."

"No?"

"No."

"Was he an associate of somebody we did represent?"

"Now you're pushing it." Aurelia stood up. "Kindly leave."

"Was he involved with Arthur Kelvin?" Elsa asked.

"I asked you to leave. Do you need me to call security, have you thrown out?"

"No." Elsa stood up. She'd seen the look on Aurelia's face when she'd asked if Collingwood and Kelvin were linked.

Her former colleague was scared.

CHAPTER SEVENTY-EIGHT

LESLEY PULLED up outside Dawn Stephens's house. She sat for a moment, catching her breath.

She felt responsible, even though it hadn't been her idea to release the woman. What the hell had Carpenter been thinking?

She still hadn't spoken to him. She needed to approach this carefully. This might be a case of police neglect, even misconduct, and when the facts came out, there would be consequences. She'd need to read the transcript from Meera's interview with Dawn the previous day. If they'd explicitly said they were arresting her for her own safety...

She was brought back from her thoughts by a knock on the window: Brett, from Gail's team.

Lesley opened her door. "Brett. Gail not here?"

"She's still working on evidence from the Maria Stephens house."

Poor Maria. In less than twenty-four hours, she had lost both her children. How did you deal with a thing like that?

She shivered, thinking of Sharon. Her daughter was due

back in Bournemouth at the weekend. Lesley hadn't seen her since the wedding and she was looking forward to her return.

"OK," she said, climbing out of the car. "What have we got?"

"Evidence of a brief struggle."

"A struggle? Hang on." Lesley went to the boot of her car and brought out a forensic suit in a bag. She walked with Brett to the house then pulled it on. "Show me."

He nodded and walked into the house. Another tech was inside, taking photos. Lesley didn't recognise him, but then that wasn't surprising given the hooded forensic suit.

"In the kitchen," Brett said. Lesley followed him through.

Dawn was on the floor, curled around the edge of her kitchen cupboards. Her legs were twisted beneath her, her face turned upwards. Her eyes were open.

"Poor woman," Lesley said. She hung back, standing in the doorway. Blood pooled on the floor. A dark patch stained the t-shirt Dawn wore. Lesley tried to remember if it was the same outfit she'd been wearing when they'd arrested her.

God.

This was a fuckup of the highest order. Someone would lose their job over it. But more importantly, Dawn Stephens had lost her life.

"Send a FLO. The mum might be at risk. She might be targeted by whoever did this."

"That's not..."

Lesley looked at Brett. "Sorry." CSIs didn't have the authority to tell Uniform what to do. "I'll speak to someone." She looked at Dawn again. "Do we have a time of death?" She needed to establish when Dawn had been released, how she'd travelled home. Had the woman wanted to be released, or had she gone reluctantly?

"The pathologist isn't here yet," Brett replied. "He's on his way."

"Good. Tell me about the struggle."

Brett pointed at the wall beyond the body. "See the smear marks there?"

"Blood being dragged down the wall."

"It's consistent with her being pushed against the wall after the stabbing. I think she was probably alive for a minute or so afterwards. She tried to fight back. Look at her fingernails."

Lesley leaned in. One of the woman's fingernails had been ripped out. She winced. "We need to find that."

"We can't do a full search of the kitchen until Pathology have examined the body in situ and removed it. But don't worry. It's a priority."

"Yes." Lesley squinted, trying to imagine the events that had led to Dawn ending up dead on her kitchen floor. "Any sign of a break-in?"

"Nothing. We've examined the locks front and back and there's no sign of them being tampered with."

"A key that was kept in a flowerpot out front, maybe?"

"No flowerpots. But she does have a Ring doorbell."

Lesley turned to him. "So if she let her assailant in, there'd be footage."

"We'll need to access her account to find it. But yes."

"Excellent." Maybe they could finally get some answers. Was whoever killed Dawn the same person that had been behind the deaths of Hamm and Samuel? It was more than likely they'd killed Ewan, too, either supplied him with the drugs that had ended his life, or forced him to take them.

Again, she thought of Maria. She'd have to send a member of the team over there. She couldn't go herself: cross-contamination.

There was a knock on the front door behind them. "Hello?" A man's voice.

Lesley turned to see a man with thinning brown hair, wearing a shabby blue suit. She remembered him from the lighthouse.

"You carry on," she told Brett, and walked to the front door.

"DI Angus," she said.

"Ma'am."

"This is part of an ongoing MCIT investigation. We don't need local CID."

"I heard about the stabbing. I wasn't sure if we were needed."

Lesley noted that he said nothing about the fact he'd once been married to the victim.

"You're alone?" she asked.

"For now."

She cocked her head. Angus had one foot inside the front door, a hand on the doorframe. He wasn't wearing gloves.

You bastard. He was making sure that any evidence of his presence at this house would be masked.

"We don't need you," she told him. "Thanks for coming, but I'm sure your team's already very busy."

He looked her up and down. "Fair enough." He turned and went back to his car, a silver Nissan.

Lesley watched him retreat. He'd put up no argument when she'd told him to leave. She guessed he'd done what he came here for.

Bastard.

CHAPTER SEVENTY-NINE

"THANK YOU FOR COMING IN," DI Collingwood said as Dennis entered the interview room. "Sorry it's yet another office."

Dennis grunted. He was exhausted from the stress of the last few days and disgruntled at being sent to various police stations around the county for his interviews. But it made sense that they wouldn't want to bring him to Winfrith. The risk of him bumping into his colleagues was too high.

"It's fine," he replied, his voice thin.

"How are you getting on with the tag?"

Dennis pursed his lips. Were they going to spend the whole time making small talk?

"Fine," he lied. The truth was that wearing the thing was humiliating and uncomfortable. Sometimes downright painful. Pam had helped him work out how to take a bath while wearing it, a horrendously undignified affair involving lifting his foot onto the edge of the bath and having to fill it after getting in instead of beforehand.

Two months of this. He was almost beginning to think prison would have been better.

"We have some new evidence we wanted to run through with you," Collingwood said. His colleague was already in the room, the uncommunicative DC Dugdale.

"We'll need to wait for my lawyer," Dennis said.

"This is an informal chat."

An informal chat with a police officer awaiting trial for the murder of his former boss? The notion was insane.

"Let's wait," Dennis said. He wasn't about to remind Collingwood of his rights; the DI knew full well he couldn't interview a suspect who'd already been charged without a solicitor present. Even with Elsa Short representing him, Dennis wasn't about to waive that right.

The door opened and Elsa stopped just inside. "What's going on?" Her eyes were dark.

Collingwood stood up from his spot opposite Dennis. "Ms Short." He held out a hand, which she ignored. "Thank you for coming."

She shook her head. "What the hell are you doing, bringing my client into an interview room without giving him the chance to speak with me first?"

Collingwood looked from her to Dennis. "We've just entered. There's been no conversation."

"I'll believe that when I hear it. Dennis?"

"He asked me how I was getting on with the tag. I told him it was fine. Then I said we should wait for you." He felt like a naughty schoolboy. How old was Elsa Short? At least fifteen years younger than he was. But he supposed having a solicitor who made men feel like children had to be a good thing. As long as she was on your side.

"OK," she said. "Either the two of you leave us in here to

talk, or you find us a private room." She walked to the recording machine to check it was switched off. "And make sure the CCTV is off, too."

"We'll find you a room," DI Collingwood said. He gestured to DC Dugdale, who hurried out of the room.

Less than three minutes later, Dennis and Elsa were in a neighbouring room. This one had no camera and no recording device.

"Good," his solicitor said. "I don't trust them not to record us."

"What's going on?" Dennis asked. "They said they have new evidence they want to talk to me about."

She looked at him. "You weren't originally arrested by PSD, were you?"

"Organised Crime. But it's normal for PSD to take over when an officer is arrested."

She nodded. "Have you worked with Collingwood before?"

"Never had cause to."

"Did Tim Mackie work with him?"

"I'm not... yes. Yes, they were in CID together. Not sure how long for."

"Did Tim ever talk about Collingwood?"

He bristled. "*DCI Mackie* rarely referred to other officers."

"Was Collingwood around when Mackie retired? Afterwards, maybe?"

"What do you mean, around?"

"Did Collingwood have contact with Mackie?" Elsa asked. "Was he involved with the Kelvin investigation after Mackie retired?"

"I wouldn't know."

She sighed. "Dennis, you really need to start remembering things, if we're going to get you acquitted."

He met her gaze. "I'm not going to lie or exaggerate, if that's what you mean."

"That's not what I mean. Do you think I'm that kind of lawyer?"

He considered. "On balance, no."

"But you've thought about it."

"I didn't know you. I've had to observe you, try to work out what kind of person you are."

"Your DCI, who I gather you have a lot of respect for, chose to marry me. But that's not enough, it seems."

Dennis looked at her. Did he have a lot of respect for the DCI? He certainly hadn't when she'd started. Her brusqueness, city spikiness, and reluctance to listen to people who knew Dorset better than she did. Not to mention all the swearing.

He'd noticed that her wife swore too. He'd kept himself from mentioning it.

"I'm sorry. I do trust you."

"Good. Well in that case, I may have evidence that could point to other members of Dorset Police, and not yourself."

"What kind of evidence?"

She glanced at the door, then drew her chair closer to him. "Tim Mackie's notebooks. Did you know he kept them?"

"What do you mean, kept them?"

She pushed her hair out of her face. "Kept them, Dennis. In his attic. All the books going back through his entire police career."

"He didn't hand them back on retirement?"

"Are officers supposed to do that?"

"Yes. They're police property."

"So in that case, why didn't he hand them back? Was there information in them he didn't want colleagues seeing?"

"I never looked at his notebooks. I wouldn't know."

"Of course you wouldn't." She sighed. "OK. I've found two names in the diary. Mentioned repeatedly, using codewords. Collingwood and Angus."

"DI Rowan Angus."

"You know him?"

"Not for a long time."

"Why would either of them have been mentioned in Mackie's notes?" She held up a hand. "He continued keeping notebooks after his retirement. They're in those, too."

"How?"

"He bought notebooks like the police issue ones. Continued writing in them."

Dennis scanned her face. Mackie had never mentioned that he was gathering evidence. Certainly not that he was keeping records.

"I'm really sorry, Ms Short. But I can't provide any more detail on those two people."

"Fair enough. Let's get back into that interview room, then."

"You're going to ask about the notes?"

"I'm doing nothing of the sort. Never ask a question unless you know the answer. Surely you know that."

"It's one way of approaching suspect interviews."

"Well it's a damn good way of approaching them from the other side of the table. Don't bite, Dennis. Don't rise to him if he tries to present new evidence. Anything he says, I'll check. We can't trust him."

CHAPTER EIGHTY

As LESLEY PULLED up in the car park outside Dorset Police HQ, she spotted Superintendent Carpenter leaving the building.

She steeled herself. She'd been meaning to talk to him all morning. She guessed now was the time.

He saw her car, made a brief gesture of surprise, then strode towards her. She was still driving; did he want to get himself run over?

She swerved to avoid him then parked in a spot away from the building. There were few other cars here. If he was going to give her a bollocking, then she didn't want too many witnesses.

He yanked the passenger door open.

"Sir," she said. "I was about to come up and—"

He slammed the door shut behind him. "Were you, indeed?"

"Yes."

He turned to her, his face red. "What's going on, Lesley?"

She drew herself up. "I could ask the same of you."

"I beg your pardon?"

"I've just been at another crime scene. Dawn Stephens, a suspect in the Hamm investigation, was stabbed overnight. At her home."

"She was what?"

"She should have been here, Sir. We arrested her and took her into custody for her own safety after her brother died. I spoke to Sergeant Jukes this morning, and he told me she'd been released on your orders. Sir."

"My orders?"

"Yes." Jukes wouldn't have lied.

"They weren't exactly mine, Lesley."

"No?" She could feel her heart pounding in her chest. Was she about to get herself sacked?

Someone would lose their job over this. It shouldn't be her.

"Whose orders was Dawn Stephens released on then, Sir? Someone decided that she should go free."

"It's not your concern."

"Sir. My team arrested her. I was investigating her involvement in a double murder. It *is* my business."

"This isn't what I want to talk to you about."

"A woman is dead, Sir—"

He put a hand on her arm. She flinched, drawing back.

"Are you investigating senior PSD officers, DCI Clarke?"

"Sorry?" She shook off his grip.

"I've heard that you've been talking about a PSD officer. Insinuating that this person is somehow involved in DCI Mackie's death."

"That is certainly not the case, Sir."

"What is the case, then?"

"As you know, I don't believe Dennis had anything to do with DCI Mackie's death. I believe he was set up."

"By whom?"

"I'm working on that."

"By Collingwood?"

She inhaled. "Like I say, I'm working on it."

He eyed her. She stared back, her heart racing, her hands clammy.

Be calm, she told herself. *Don't let him rattle you.* She had a sudden flashback to Detective Superintendent David Randle.

Carpenter leaned towards her. She leaned back until her back was on the door of the car.

She glanced towards the building. Should she call someone?

No. Carpenter was her senior officer.

"Dennis didn't kill Mackie," Carpenter said.

"I'm sorry?"

"You heard me."

"Why was he arrested, then?"

"There was evidence. His son's bank account, mainly."

"That was coincidence," she said. "Jacob Frampton legitimately carried out work for the Kelvins, and was paid for it."

"I know."

"So..." Lesley blinked. "So if Dennis didn't kill Tim Mackie, who did?"

"That's what I expect you to find out."

"With respect, Sir. It isn't my case."

"No." He looked at her as if deciding something.

"Are you giving me the case, Sir?"

He continued looking at her, then shook his head. "I can't. You know that."

He put a hand on the door.

"Sir," she said. "If there's an enquiry into Dawn Stephens's death..."

"Which there no doubt will be. And should be."

At least he was acknowledging that.

He put up a hand to silence her. The car felt hot and claustrophobic.

"Keep digging, Lesley," he said. "You'll get to the truth, eventually."

CHAPTER EIGHTY-ONE

Elsa left the interview room in search of DI Collingwood. She wanted to get this over with. Whatever it was he wanted to discuss with Dennis, she hoped it would add to the information she had from Mackie's notebooks.

Her goal was to create doubt in the minds of the jury. If she could get them to believe that Mackie might have been killed by someone else, present reasonable evidence to indicate that, then they couldn't convict her client. She didn't need to prove that either of the two officers Lesley had told her about was the killer. All she needed to do was insert the firm idea in their heads that it might not have been Dennis.

On top of that, the CPS had to produce firm evidence pointing to Dennis's guilt. She'd already established that the payments to his son's account were irrelevant. His mental state was entirely circumstantial.

She knocked on the door of the room Dennis had been in when she had arrived. No answer. She opened the door.

The room was empty.

Maybe they'd gone to an office.

She walked along the corridor, back to the reception desk. She wasn't about to go barging into offices in the hope of finding them.

As she pushed open the door to the reception area, she heard a voice behind her.

"Ms Short."

She turned to find DI Collingwood standing in a doorway. He looked like he might explode with anger.

"Detective," she said. "I was looking for you."

He took a step forward. "You don't need to."

"Why not?"

"The case is being dropped."

She put out a hand to steady herself. "I beg your pardon?"

"I've had a call from the CPS. They're dropping all charges against your client."

"And you're not going to charge him with a lesser offence."

"It seems not."

She didn't want him to see her surprise. She'd been preparing her missive to the CPS, laying out the various ways in which the police evidence lacked credibility. She'd been hoping for exactly this.

But she hadn't got round to sending that email.

In which case, who had told the CPS that there was no viable evidence against Dennis?

"Have you presented new evidence to the CPS?" she asked him. "You were talking about new information."

He shook his head. "We certainly haven't given them anything that would make them drop the charges. And no, we haven't discussed the case with them since his appearance at the Magistrates' Court." He cocked his head. "It looks like you're going to miss your day in court."

She resisted a retort. "Thank you," she said, keeping her

voice steady. She walked past him and into the room where Dennis was waiting for her, pleased at what she was about to tell him.

CHAPTER EIGHTY-TWO

LESLEY SLUMPED ONTO THE SOFA, feeling like she would sleep for a week. Elsa was still out; helping Dennis, hopefully.

Her mind was racing. The case, and most of all, Carpenter's confusing behaviour.

First he'd warned her off, now he was telling her he wanted her to solve Mackie's murder. But he hadn't actually assigned an investigation to her.

She dialled Zoe. Could she risk involving her?

No. But she needed to find out if they'd tracked down Day Watson yet.

"Lesley," Zoe said.

"Well done. You remembered not to call me boss."

"I'm getting used to it."

"Just calling to see if you've arrested Day Watson yet."

"He's not at any of the addresses we've got for him. But we did get a warrant to search his flat."

"Tell me you found something helpful."

"Yes. His DNA is a match for samples your CSM sent through. Gail, is it?"

"Yes." *Good old Gail.* "Which samples?"

"From the pills Ewan took. They were able to extract faint traces of DNA from their surface."

Lesley clenched a fist. "That's brilliant. Thanks."

CHAPTER EIGHTY-THREE

LESLEY WAS WOKEN by the feel of Elsa's arms sliding around her.

She wriggled backwards and smiled, feeling Elsa's embrace tighten.

"Morning," she muttered. "What time is it?"

"Just before seven."

She tensed. "I need to be in work."

"You can spare five minutes."

"OK." Lesley yawned then turned to Elsa. "You been awake long?"

"Five minutes. I was debating whether I should wake you."

"My alarm will go off in—" Lesley was interrupted by the alarm on her phone, "—just about now." She yawned again. "He's back today."

"Who?"

"Dennis. He didn't want to waste any time."

"He was wearing a tag just yesterday."

"I know. But you know Dennis." Lesley stroked Elsa's cheek. "Thank you."

Elsa frowned. "I didn't do anything. The CPS decided they didn't have enough to pursue it."

"Still. You were gathering evidence. That must have helped."

"I don't see how they can have known what I'd found out. But don't worry. I intend to get to the bottom of what happened. Dennis deserves to know."

"By what happened, you mean...?"

"I can't investigate Mackie's death for you, if that's what you mean. You'll need to speak to Sadie Dawes for that."

Lesley smiled. "She's like a dog with a bone."

"She's *your* dog with a bone. Use her."

"She spoke to Carpenter."

Elsa brushed her hair back, as if considering what to say next. "He warned her off. She reckons he expected her to do the opposite."

Lesley felt her throat constrict. She'd talked to Tina, Mike and Carpenter about the potential PSD involvement. "Did you say anything to PSD? About your code names?"

"DI Collingwood wanted to interview Dennis, but he didn't get the chance. I barely spoke to the man."

"DI Collingwood was interviewing him?" Lesley asked.

A nod. "Didn't you know?"

"You know Dennis. He hasn't told me anything."

"He told me little enough. He's not the easiest client. You don't mind me saying that, I hope."

"He's not the easiest DS."

"But you're glad you're getting him back."

"I bloody am."

CHAPTER EIGHTY-FOUR

LESLEY SCANNED the car park as she walked towards the police HQ building: no sign of Dennis's Astra.

Inside, she climbed the stairs and opened the door to the team room. Meera was at her desk. She turned at the sound of the door, her face lit up.

"Boss. I've got good news."

"You have?"

"Forensics re-examined prints from all three murder scenes overnight."

"They found DNA on the MDMA pills, I know."

"Sorry, boss?"

Lesley looked at Meera. "Sorry. I got a call from Zoe Finch. They went into David Watson's flat. No sign of him but they got his DNA. The same DNA was found on Ewan Stephens's pills."

"Tell me there's a match."

"There is. I haven't got the ID yet, though."

Lesley approached Meera's desk. She had a feeling she

knew who the owner of these prints might be. "Send it to me. I'll check it."

Meera's brow furrowed. "I can do it, boss."

Lesley gave her a smile, trying to sound casual. "It's fine."

She went into the office and slung her jacket over the back of the chair. It missed, dropping to the floor. She'd pick it up shortly.

She opened her computer and picked up the email from Meera. The evidence would be on the system and probably in the team inbox too, but it was quicker this way.

There was one set of prints that had been found in all three murder locations. With Ewan Stephens's death being officially noted as a drugs overdose, that one wasn't being counted as a crime scene. Although Lesley wasn't so sure that was accurate.

The prints matched an individual whose details were on file. Not in HOLMES or in relation to this investigation, but because he was a police officer.

Lesley stared at the screen. She wasn't surprised. He'd been at Dawn's house yesterday, disguising his tracks. She'd seen him at the lighthouse, most likely doing the same thing. But he'd never been logged as attending the huts. Hopefully, with some more evidence gathering, she could make a strong enough case for him to be arrested and charged.

But first, she had to tell Carpenter.

She picked up the phone and dialled his mobile.

"Lesley. I'm driving to work. Can't this wait?"

"It's sensitive, Sir. Probably best not to discuss in the office."

"Over the phone will be fine." He sounded dismissive.

"We have matching prints from the three crime scenes in the Portland investigation."

"One of the Birmingham gang, I imagine."

"No. Quite different."

"OK. You've got an ID?"

"I have. It's a serving officer in Dorset CID. DI Rowan Angus."

There was an intake of breath at the other end of the line.

"Sir?" she asked.

"Why are things never straightforward with you, DCI Clarke?"

"It's evidence, Sir. I had nothing to do with it being there."

"You're sure this isn't just contamination?"

"He was present at the lighthouse and at Dawn Stephens's house. But very briefly. And the prints that have been found are in different locations. I was there, I saw where he stood."

"The man didn't use protective equipment?"

"He did not. And I believe he did that deliberately."

A sigh. "Very well. This is going to have to be dealt with at a more senior level. I don't suppose you have more conclusive evidence against him?"

"Not yet."

"You think you will?"

"I do." She hoped she was telling the truth.

"Leave it with me, for now. But keep it to yourself. At least until we have enough to arrest him."

"The man was involved in three murders, possibly four."

"The man was present at three murder scenes, Lesley. That's not the same thing. He won't be arrested. But he will be taken off his duties pending a more formal investigation."

"By whom, Sir?"

"By PSD, I imagine."

"Sir. I've already given you information about PSD." She wasn't about to say more, on the phone.

"It's not possible for me to bypass the system, Lesley. You'll have to put up with it."

Lesley shook her head. She was convinced that Angus and Collingwood were working together. Angus had been involved in Hamm's death, but she hadn't worked out why yet. And if Collingwood was working with him, did that mean Hamm's death was connected to Arthur Kelvin and his recruitment of bent police? And what was the link between Collingwood, Angus and the Watsons?

"Very well, Sir," she said. She would simply have to keep her nose to the ground.

"Thank you, DCI Clarke. And give DS Frampton my best wishes when he returns to work today." He hung up.

Lesley glanced out of the office. No sign of Dennis yet. She had a feeling there was only one person who could help her monitor what was about to happen.

She picked her phone back up and dialled.

CHAPTER EIGHTY-FIVE

Zoe waited, listening for the sound of footsteps inside the house. At last, the door opened.

"Gina," she said. "I'm hoping you've forgiven me."

Gina looked her up and down. "You were doing your job. What have you come for this time?"

"I've got news. On the Hamm murder."

Gina's eyes widened. "You'd better come in then."

"Thanks." Zoe followed Gina inside and closed the front door behind her.

Inside, the house was quiet. Gina took her into the cramped living room and gestured to a chair.

"Thanks for seeing me, Gina," she said.

"You've got news about Hamm." Gina tugged on a fingernail. Zoe noticed that all her nails had been chewed.

Zoe nodded. She leaned forward. "It's not entirely good. But you deserve to know what's been happening."

"OK." Gina didn't sound confident.

"We've established the identities of the men who broke him out of prison. Samuel and David Watson, known as Zee and

Day, and Ewan Stephens. They were all member of a drugs gang here in Birmingham. There was also a woman involved, called Dawn Stephens."

"You've arrested them, I hope."

"Dawn, Samuel and Ewan are dead."

"Dead?"

"Samuel's body was found at a spot not far from the lighthouse where Hamm was left. Dawn Stephens worked at the lighthouse, she let them in."

"She was married to... what did you say his name was?"

"Ewan. He was her brother."

"OK. He's dead too?"

"He and Dawn were each killed at their homes. We have strong forensic evidence linking the crimes to David Watson and to another man who we're not able to name."

"Why not?"

"He's subject to another investigation. I'm sorry."

"I don't get it. Why can't you name him?"

Zoe reached out, but Gina pulled her hand away and shoved it in her pocket.

"I don't get it," Gina said. "How am I supposed to be safe if you won't tell me who this man is? Is he a drugs dealer too?"

"He's not. We've never known him travel to Birmingham. And he has no reason to be concerned with you or your family. So you don't need to worry."

"I'll be the one to decide that. So have you arrested this Day person, or is he dead too?"

"West Midlands Police took him into custody this morning." Zoe knew that it was more likely he'd be convicted for drugs crimes than for being an accessory to murder, but she was working on that.

"That's something, I suppose."

"We've also discovered who it was who phoned you."

"Hamm."

Zoe shook her head. "The call came from Dawn Stephens. The woman who worked at the lighthouse."

"It was a man."

"She might have disguised her voice, or used a recording. But it came from her phone."

"OK." Gina had paled. "What else? Do I have to give evidence?"

"You don't, Gina." Zoe remembered Gina's evidence in the Canary trial. The woman had been shaking throughout her time in the witness box. "You really don't."

"That's something, I suppose."

"I'm sorry we can't tell you more." Zoe stood up.

"Why do you always say we, when it's bad news?"

Zoe felt her shoulders slump. Gina was right.

"You're right. I'm sorry I can't tell you any more."

"That's better. So you'll tell me when you're allowed to name this other bastard."

"We... I will. And I'm hoping that will be soon."

"It had better be. I can't live like this."

CHAPTER EIGHTY-SIX

LESLEY PUT DOWN HER PHONE. She knew it was risky bringing Sadie into all this, but she had little other choice. And the conversation with Carpenter made her feel like she'd been given permission, somehow.

She looked out to see that both Tina and Stanley had arrived in the office.

Carpenter was confusing her. He'd gone from shutting her down to actively encouraging her. And she still wasn't convinced of his motives in warning Sadie off.

The door opened. She held her breath. Dennis?

Tina hurried to the door and held it open. Lesley left her office and approached, to see Mike coming in with a baby carrier in his hand.

"Mike," she said, trying to mask her disappointment. "What brings you here?"

"Tina asked me to bring a cake."

She smiled. "For Dennis?"

"What did you get?" Tina asked. "Did you go to Nellie Crumb?"

"Cream sponge. And an eclair for Stanley."

"Thanks, mate," Stanley said. He stood up and approached Mike, bending over to look into the baby carrier. "He's cute."

"He is when he's asleep," Mike replied. "You wait till he wakes up."

A squawk came from the baby carrier.

"Mike," Tina said. "You spoke too soon."

"Sorry, T." Mike put the carrier down, scooped the baby up and handed him to Tina. She looked at Lesley. "He needs a feed."

"You want to use my office?"

Tina looked past her towards the glass-lined office. "No. thanks. I'll find somewhere."

"You don't have to hide away."

Tina gave her a look. "The sarge comes back into work after being released and the first thing he sees is me breastfeeding. I don't think so."

She had a point.

Lesley was about to tell Tina to use the meeting room along the corridor when the door opened again and Dennis appeared.

The team turned to him. "Sarge!" Tina cried.

"What's this?" He smiled at her, then at the baby. "A welcoming party?"

"Louis and me didn't want to miss out," Mike said.

"Thanks," Dennis replied. "I appreciate it." He clamped a hand on Mike's arm.

Louis started crying.

"Shit," Tina said. She looked at Dennis. "I'm sorry, Sarge. I need to give him a feed. Don't go anywhere."

"I don't plan to." Dennis looked tired. The skin of his

cheeks was grey, and he'd lost weight. "But please, try not to swear."

Lesley looked at him. It was good to have him back. She walked to the filing cabinet and opened the top drawer.

"Welcome back, Dennis," she said. "We'll have to fill you in on a tricky case we've been working on. There's still work to do, and some of it might be a bit traumatic for you."

"Don't mollycoddle me," he said. He lowered his voice. "I know I've been... off recently. It won't happen again."

She took an object out of the filing cabinet and placed it on the desk in front of him. "Don't pretend to be something you're not," she told him. "If you're unwell, you need to recover."

"Being back here will help me more than being stuck at home. I had enough of that with the tag."

"One moment," she told him. She retreated into her office and brought out her purse. She took out a pound coin.

Dennis was chatting to Stanley as she approached the desk. Tina had gone. Meera was standing to one side, looking uneasy. She'd met Dennis, but she didn't know him well.

The swear jar was on the desk, where she'd placed it. Dennis had hidden it in the filing cabinet after her arrival on the team.

She slid the pound coin into it. "This is for Tina."

Dennis looked round, breaking off from his conversation with Stanley. Mike noticed what Lesley had done and chuckled. "Nice one, boss."

"Welcome, Dennis," Lesley said. "It's good to have you back."

READ A FREE PREQUEL NOVELLA, THE BALLARD DOWN MURDER

How did DCI Mackie die?

DS Dennis Frampton is getting used to life without his old boss DCI Mackie, and managing to hide how much he hates being in charge of Dorset's Major Crimes Investigation Team. Above all, he must ensure no one knows he's still seeking Mackie's advice on cases.

But then Mackie doesn't show up to a meeting, and a body is found below the cliffs a few miles away.

When Dennis discovers the body is his old friend and mentor, his world is thrown upside down. Did Mackie kill himself, or was he pushed? Is Dennis's new boss trying to hush things up? And can Dennis and the CSIs trust the evidence?

Find out by reading *The Ballard Down Murder* for FREE at rachelmclean.com/ballard.

READ THE DORSET CRIME SERIES

Buy now in ebook, paperback or audiobook

ALSO BY RACHEL MCLEAN

The DI Zoe Finch Series - Buy in ebook, paperback and audiobook

Deadly Wishes, DI Zoe Finch Book 1

Deadly Choices, DI Zoe Finch Book 2

Deadly Desires, DI Zoe Finch Book 3

Deadly Terror, DI Zoe Finch Book 4

Deadly Reprisal, DI Zoe Finch Book 5

Deadly Fallout, DI Zoe Finch Book 6

Deadly Christmas, DI Zoe Finch Book 7

Deadly Origins, the FREE Zoe Finch prequel

The McBride & Tanner Series

Blood and Money, McBride & Tanner Book 1